Courtin' Murder
in West
Wheeling

Michael Allen
Dymmoch

DIVERSIONBOOKS

Also by Michael Allen Dymmoch

Death in West Wheeling
The Fall
M.I.A.
The Cymry Ring

Caleb & Thinnes Mysteries
The Man Who Understood Cats
The Death of Blue Mountain Cat
Incendiary Designs
The Feline Friendship
White Tiger

Diversion Books
A Division of Diversion Publishing Corp.
443 Park Avenue South, Suite 1008
New York, New York 10016
www.DiversionBooks.com

For more information, email info@diversionbooks.com

First Diversion Books edition May 2016.
Print ISBN: 978-1-68230-062-6
eBook ISBN: 978-1-68230-061-9

For
Ginny Grandt

a modest proposal

"Nina Ross, will you marry me?"

Nina's the woman I been sweet on since she was jail bait.

Me.

Homer Deters.

Sheriff of Boone County.

She looked surprised; I don't know why. I'd been courtin' her since spring an' had her grandad's permission.

We was stretched out in the sun, next to the Glass Mountain Reservoir, the first weekend in October. Injun summer. The grass was still green and sweet. The trees was startin' to turn. An' we'd had a killin' frost a week earlier, so there was nothin' left to bug us. I was on my back with my feet propped on a rock. Nina was lying cross-ways to me, with her head resting just north of my belt buckle. We'd polished off a fair-sized picnic lunch an' washed it down with moonshine. God was in heaven an'—far as I knew—all was right with Boone County. Not that it was my concern. It was my day off.

B'fore I could get a answer, my radio started squawkin'.

"Sheriff!" Festus Reagan—Deputy Reagan—sounded like he'd got his tail in a ringer. Damn all!

I'd a ignored him, but Nina said, "Homer, ain't you gonna answer?"

"I axed you—"

"No! Answer Festus?"

"Yeah. But why'd he have to call now? It ain't like I been all that busy the last two hours."

"Sheriff?" This time Festus sounded like he'd lost his best dog.

I got up an' keyed my radio. "This is Sheriff Deters. What do you want, Festus?"

He said, "Thank God! Sheriff, we got a 10-50-an'-a-half over on County C, just off the interstate."

"What'n hell's a 10-50-an'-a-half?" I axed.

"Sump'n you tole me never to announce over the radio."

I 'membered that. I also 'membered—finally—what 10-50-an'-a-half meant.

"Do tell. You jus' hang tight till I get there." I turned back to Nina, but the magic had leaked outta the moment. She was gatherin' up the leavin's of our picnic, an' shakin' out the blanket we'd been lyin' on.

"Stop by for dessert if it ain't too late," she said matter-of-factly. Her tone reminded me of the doc tellin' me to be sure to get my tetanus booster.

"Aw, Nina, I'm sorry."

She shrugged. "Guess I'll have to get used to it." She handed me the blanket. "By the way, what's a 10-50-an'-a half?"

"That's West Wheelin' police lingo for a corpse."

gaper's block

I burned up the highway gettin' to the scene, but it seemed like half a Boone County was way ahead a me. Festus had his cruiser angled across the road, blockin' the scene on one side, but that left the other end open. Assorted pickup trucks an' a big ol' white Lincoln Continental lined up on the shoulder behind Handy Taylor's dredgin' rig.

Handy's the contractor the county hired to dig the sand—what the highway department dumps on the roads in winter—outta the ditches so there's room for next winter's dump. It's a pretty good deal 'cause Handy's contract don't specify what he's s'posed to do with the dredgin's. Usually he picks up a couple bucks sellin' it to people who need sand an' a bundle sellin' the rest back to the county. Anyway, he'd left the motor runnin' an' the amber safety lights flashin', an' he was standin' just outside the *po*lice line, chewin' the fat with half a dozen locals, includin' the mayor; Nate Williams, the barber; an' councilmen Cramer an' Andrews.

They was all behind the line, but I could see by the

tracks every one of 'em had been down in the ditch to see the body. So much for *securin'* the scene. I didn't see no percentage in makin' a federal case of it at that point, so I just said, "Afternoon, Mayor. Boys."

There was a chorus of, "Afternoon, Sheriff." I just nodded and said, "You-all had your look. Now clear out." Then I tole Festus, "When I get back from viewin' the body, we're gonna run in anyone standin' 'round who don't have evidence to give."

Most of 'em muttered about unfriendly peace officers an' started driftin' towards their wheels.

Festus looked at the mayor an' swallowed hard. Festus is young an' he's been crippled all his life by his ma namin' him after a *Gunsmoke* character. Personally, I allus thought Festus Hagen was a straight shooter. An' Deputy Reagan is eager an' honest. As Nina's pointed out, at least he wasn't named for no dead president.

The mayor's small an' feisty as a banty rooster. "I expect a report first thing, Sheriff," he said.

I could see he'd started puffin' hisself up for a jurisdictional dispute. I just said, "Yessir."

He couldn't tell was I bein' smart or not, but we'd locked horns on previous occasions an' he knew I won't back down. When I fixed him with my best State Trooper stare, he started headin' fer his car. I went to look at the remains.

That was a good description. Remains. Weren't no question they was human, but they was nothin' left 'cept disjointed bones, heaped in a pile like pick-up sticks. They was lyin' in the ditch, half buried in the sandy bottom, with grass an' the weeds that'd took hold since spring growin' up between 'em. There weren't no sign a clothes or personal effects that might help identify 'em. The grass was trampled in a circle all 'round, an' the same tracks I'd seen up by the road—gaper's tracks—was showin' in the sandy patches. Whoever'd dumped the body was long gone—mebbe since spring.

I got down on all fours for a closer look. The bones was dry an' yellow as old dirt. Far as I could see, none of 'em was showin' any breaks, scrapes, saw marks, or bullet holes. There wasn't no sign they'd been gnawed by critters. The skull was face up, grinnin' at the blue October sky. It had teeth wore down like a old dog's, but no cavities or fillin's.

Festus come up an' said, "This what they call a 'John Doe,' Sheriff?"

I stood up and dusted off my hands. "Yeah, 'less it's a Jane."

Handy was still waitin' up by his rig. "Where's your truck an' driver, Handy?" I asked, meanin' the truck he hauled the dredgin's with. "Al Holland, right?"

"Al didn't feel too good about hangin' round no dead body, Sheriff. An' he about had a load anyway, so I sent him to call you, then finish up an' go home."

Which meant by now he'd told his story to everyone in Boone County who'd listen. And he'd prob'ly embroidered it considerable.

I nodded. "How 'bout you tell me what went down?"

Handy kept shootin' quick looks at the ditch. "Was he murdered, Sheriff?"

"Can't say, Handy. What happened?"

"Well, we'd worked our way down this side'a the road, when I had to take a leak. While I was standin' there, gettin' my business done, I happened to look down an' spot somethin' funny in the ditch. Naturally, I climbed down for a better look. That's when I seen it. I yelled for Al to come look. An' he near-to passed out. I figured it'd be best to send him to call you. I's about ready to think no one was comin' when Festus showed."

"You got any idea who this might be?"

He shook his head.

"Much obliged, Handy."

"I kin go?"

"Shore. Jus' come by my office tomorrow an' fill out a statement."

Soon as he was outta sight, I give Doc Howard a call on my cell phone. Doc's the Boone County coroner. He used to just be the local pathologist—when Nate Williams was coroner. But when Nate got back on a deadbeat customer by declarin' him dead, it riled Doc up enough to run against him in the next election. By that time, the story'd got out. An' there was so many folks scared they'd be dead before their time, Doc won by a landslide.

When Doc come on the line, I explained the situation. He told me to take lots a good pi'tures an' bring the bones on in.

"Ain't you gonna come take charge a the body?" I asked.

"Doesn't sound to me as if there *is* a body. I trust your judgement, Homer. Pictures'll be good enough."

So I sent Festus off to scare up a box, an' I got out my camera. First a roll of just the bones from every angle, then a second roll with a ruler next to the skull, and everything that looked like it might be evidence marked with numbered cards. Time I was done, it was nearly dark, an' Festus was back with the carton a satellite TV dish come in. We collected up John Doe, an' I headed fer the morgue.

• • •

"I don't guess I need to hang around for the autopsy," I remarked as I handed Doc the box of J. Doe's mortal bits.

Doc just said, "Humph. I stayed up for this?"

I shrugged.

"You could've left these in the trunk overnight, Homer, and brought them in tomorrow with the photos."

"'Gainst procedure, Doc."

"Has that ever stopped you before?"

I couldn't answer that one honest, so I shut up an' cleared out.

the truck stop

After I got my pictures developed at the One-Hour photo, I locked 'em in the trunk of my cruiser an' stopped in at Hardsetter's—a.k.a. the Truck Stop—for a bite to eat an' a nightcap. Rye Willis was settin' at the counter contemplatin' a old-fashioned glass half full a West Wheelin' White Lightnin'. Rye makes it hisself, so he could drink it at home a whole lot cheaper. But half the pleasure of savorin' good likker is drinkin' it in company. I set down next to him an' said howdy to the waitress, Charity Nonesuch, an' let my glance linger in appreciation of her generous endowments. That woman is *blest*.

"What can I get you, Homer?" she asked.

"I'll have one a them," I said, pointin' to Rye's glass. "An' the Special."

Hardsetter's Special was chicken fried steak'n mashed potatoes with sides of greens, black-eyed peas, an' corn. Coffee an' apple pie was optional but not extra.

Rye finally took notice of me an' said, "Hi, Homer." He

sounded blue. "I heard you found a body."

"Handy Taylor did, actually."

"Anyone I know?"

"John Doe."

Charity'd pulled a jug a shine from under the counter an' was fillin' another glass. I could almost see her ears prick up.

"Humph," Rye said.

When I didn't add no details, Charity seemed to lose interest. She set the glass in front a me, an' put the jug back, then moseyed off.

"Rye," I said. "You feelin' all right?"

"Middlin'. Why'd you ask?"

"Seems like your natural curiosity's down a quart."

"Aw, Homer..." I waited. "It's Awful Lonesome."

Awful hated Rye's guts. "What about 'im?"

"He told me he was siccin' the ATF on me. Then he come back later an' told me ATF wouldn't bother with me. Said I'm too *in-sig-ni-fi-cant* for ATF to give a damn about."

"I thought you was tryna think a ways to get ATF off yer back."

"It ain't just that." Rye reached down the counter, an' grabbed a newspaper somebody'd left. He pounded it with his pointin' finger. "Lookit that, Homer." '*That*' was a full page ad for Kellerman's Cheap-Ass Likkers. "How kin I compete with that?"

I looked. Kellerman was sellin' Budweiser for $5.99 a case, an' Jack Daniels for $6.99 a fifth. It didn't seem as though a independent contractor like Rye could stay in business with the competition low-ballin' 'im like that. I looked over the other ads. Coors was average, Sam Adams highly overpriced. Imports, like Bass, an' Heinekens, was outrageous.

"Seems to me you're goin' at this ass-backwards, Rye. 'Stead a tryin' to compete against these booze factories, you outta cut your production an' double what you're askin'. Put a fancy label on it, an' it'll be like that Evian stuff. Yuppies'll trample each other beatin' a path to your still."

"You think?"

"Worth a try."

"Yeah, but what'll I do with all the time that'll free up? The Devil shore 'nough finds work for idle hands. 'Specially Willis hands."

"Well, Festus's been complainin' he don't get enough time off to spend with his girl. You could be a deputy sheriff part time."

Mary Lincoln

Ever since becomin' a daddy—a little over six months ago—I been makin' a point to set a good example by havin' breakfast every day. Neither me nor my boy, Skip—Skip Jackson Deters—cooks so we usually eat at the truck stop or the café. The mornin' after Handy Taylor'd come across John Doe's remains, me an' Skip stopped at Hardsetter's fer a bite to eat an' a bit a local gossip.

As luck would have it, Rye had the same idea. We was sittin' at the counter when he come along. He said, "Mornin', Homer, Skip," an' sat down on the stool next to mine. "I'm ready when you are, Homer."

"Fer what?"

"Deputy trainin'."

Skip leaned over the counter to look at Rye—tryin' to figure was he kiddin', I guess. "Ain't that like settin' a fox to guard the chickens?"

I give him *the eye*. "Some'd say takin' a Jackson under my roof was a risky proposition."

Skip hung his head. He don't like to be reminded he come from West Wheelin's crime family.

I clapped him on the back an' said, "Everybody oughtta have a chance to prove hisself."

I told Rye to stop by the office later an' fill out a application.

• • •

Time I dropped Skip at school, it was too late to catch Nina at home and too early fer her to be to work yet. So I went on in to my office to start catchin' up on my paperwork.

I begun by callin' Doc Howard, who told me he needed a few more days 'fore he could gimme the autopsy report.

"The victim's just a box a bones, Doc," I said. "You don't need more'n a couple hours for a Cracker Jack job on a real corpse. What gives?"

"I'd like to do a few more tests."

"You mean pass my victim 'round the Med school like a cold germ." He didn't say nothin' to that. Couldn't. I'd hit the nail hard'n true. "Least you could tell me was it a John Doe or a Jane."

"The remains are those of an adult male," Doc said.

"Don't s'pose you wanna guess what killed him or when?"

"No. I wouldn't."

"Well, then, jus' be sure you get that chain of custody sheet signed."

'Fore he hung up on me Doc said, "Teach your grandmother to suck eggs."

Doc's a old friend, so I didn't take offense, but I wondered who'd put what burr under his saddle.

. . .

When I come into the Post Office half a hour later, Nina was sortin' envelopes into the little cubby holes she has for General Delivery. She knew I was there, but she didn't look up 'til she was done. Then she said, "You lose your cell phone, Homer? Or broke your dialin' finger?"

"Didn't seem to be much sense in wakin' you up to tell you I wasn't comin' over."

"Do tell. Real anxious to get the answer to that question you put to me, weren't ya?"

"Aw, Nina."

"You even get me a ring?"

"Yes, ma'am." I held my hands up to make a hold-everythin' signal. "You wait right here."

I come near to settin' a land speed record gettin' out to my cruiser. I'd been carryin' the ring around with me ever since our first date. Now I had the chance, I made the Flash look like Aesop's tortoise gettin' it inside the P.O.

Nina was standin' behind the counter with her arms crossed, lookin' like Judgement. I set the ring box on the counter facin' towards her, an' flipped it open.

It was like magic—watchin' it turn a statue into a goddess. Nina's eyes widened, an' her face lit up like a kid at Christmas. "Homer, is this real?"

"If it ain't, there's a jeweler's gonna be doin' some serious time fer fraud."

She got down to stare the ring in the eye.

"Which reminds me." I took off my hat an' dropped down on one knee. "Nina Ross, will you marry me?"

She was so speechless, she didn't think to answer—just

stared at the ring.

I got up, an' she took the ring outta the box an' put it on her finger, holdin' her hand out so she could admire it.

It fit, too, thanks to Martha Rooney. She'd took Nina window shoppin', once, to scout out what kinda ring I oughtta get.

Nina swung her legs over the counter an' jumped down right in front of me. She grabbed me by the shirt pockets an' pulled me to her, startled the wits outta Handy Taylor, who was just comin' through the door.

Outta the corner of my eye, I could see his jaw drop—like to unhinge it—just before Nina kissed me full on the mouth.

I could feel Handy's eyes drillin' into me, but I couldn't help myself—I kissed Nina back.

When we finally come up fer air, Handy stammered, "I'll jest wait outside."

I felt myself get all hot; Handy backed out the door.

Nina laughed. "Bound to get out sometime." She shrugged an' walked back around her counter, still admirin' her new ring.

I put on my hat and said, "Best I get back to work."

"Stop by fer dinner later. Bring Skip."

"I'd love to, but I'm on duty tonight. Probably be pretty late 'fore I can get a break."

"Well, then, stop by *pretty late* fer dessert."

• • •

Handy followed me back to the office, an' I took his statement regarding John Doe. Right after he left, Rye come in. His timin' was so good, I figured he musta been waitin' outside fer Handy to leave.

Rye took off his hat an' sat down in my visitor chair. "What do I gotta do, Homer?"

I fished out a pen an' a job application, an' told to him fill it out. Which he did.

"You gotta have a physical an' a background check—"

"Background check! You already know more about me than God does!"

"You got a point there. Not to mention a checkered background. Guess we can skip that step. But you *will* have to let Doc look you over, and you'll need to take the State Cops' Gun Safety Course."

"Pshaw! I could teach that!"

"No doubt." I reached him down a couple books from the shelf over my desk. "You gotta read these, too."

Rye looked like he used to on the first day of school, when teacher passed out the text books. "I gotta learn all that?"

"Naw, just the parts underlined."

When I took Festus on, I knew he'd never get through all the how-some-evers and where-ases in the State Criminal and Traffic Codes, so I went through the books an' underlined all the parts I figured pertained to West Wheelin' or Boone County.

In most of the books *Rye* ever come up against, the parts underlined was the sally-a-shus parts. He'd never had trouble 'memberin' *them*. Now he flipped through the books, noddin'. "I guess I can do that."

"Come back when you got it down. Meantime, I'll call Doc, and Sergeant Underhill over at the state cop shop, an' set you up."

Rye put his hat back on an' tucked the books under his arm. "Be seein' you."

I was just reachin' fer the phone when Martha Rooney come on the radio. "Homer, you still ten-eight?"

Martha's been sheriff's dispatcher since her kids went off to school. She keeps the radio an' phone number books in a big old roll top desk in her kitchen.

"Yes, ma'am."

"Wilma Netherton just called. She's hysterical. I couldn't understand a word she said. Could you swing by an' see what's up?"

"Ten-four, Miz Rooney."

• • •

"Rats!" Wilma said. "You got to do somethin', Sheriff. The place is crawlin' with rats!"

I looked around. Half a dozen cats'n three dogs was lyin' on the porch. The yard was so tidy, you'd never know it was a farm. I said, "Where, ma'am?"

Wilma pointed out at the road. "Cross the road. That woman's harboring rats!"

It took me a while to get her to settle down an' start over. Seemed a stranger had moved in across the road an' started collectin' trash, storin' it in the yard. Rats had taken up residence an' were spillin' over into Wilma's yard. So far, the cats an' dogs had kept on top of the problem, but Wilma was sure it was just a matter of time 'fore she had rats comin' in her kitchen.

I allowed as I could mebbe look into it. An' I moseyed across the road to do just that.

• • •

The name on the mailbox was "M. Lincoln," an' the post was sunk into a tub of yellow flowers. I pulled up to the front steps of the house, right next to a old, orange Ford pickup. The truck had runnin' boards and a winch in the back for slingin' heavy stuff into the bed.

I got outta my cruiser an' put on my hat, takin' my time so I could have a look around.

Since the SOLD sign had been removed from the property, there'd been considerable changes. I didn't see no rats, but there was a lot of places they could be hidin'. Like the piles of stuff—old glass bottles, neatly sorted by color; a small mountain of old tires; assorted car parts; firewood an' scrap lumber; bricks, an' bikes, an' old TVs. An' lots of other junk. All of it was neatly stacked an' fairly clean.

Pretty soon a tall, handsome woman strolled out the front door. She was wearin' a man's blue work shirt, with flowers stitched on the collar an' pockets; a pink flowered apron over her overalls; an' steel-toed boots. She wiped her hands on the apron an' held out her hand to shake. "Good morning, Sheriff. I'm Mary Lincoln."

I shook her hand. "Mornin' Miz Lincoln."

"Call me Mary, Sheriff. What can I do for you?"

"You startin' a junk yard here, ma'am?"

"Good Lord, no!" I waited. "I just can't throw away anything useful. And this is all good for something."

"Yes, ma'am. You bring it all with you?"

I meant, when she moved in. When the place was sold, it was empty as a politician's promises.

She understood. "Oh, no. I picked it all up along the

highway. Could I offer you a cup of coffee, Sheriff? Or some tea?"

West Wheelin' don't take quick to newcomers, an' somethin' in her voice made me think she must be lonely. So I said, "Coffee'd be nice, if it ain't no trouble."

"None whatever." She waved at the rockin' chair on the porch. "Have a seat. I'll be right back."

While I waited, I sorta took a inventory of the junk. There musta been three 5-yard loads of stuff—more'n the County Highway Department crew would pick up in a year.

When Miz Lincoln come out of the house, she had a TV tray with coffee an' fixins, an' a plate of chocolate-chip oatmeal cookies. I stood up an' settled the tray fer her while she went inside fer another chair.

The coffee was good'n strong, an' the cookies was quite tasty. After I'd had three, I asked her where she'd moved here from.

"Chicago, Illinois, Sheriff."

"Call me Homer, ma'am. Everybody does."

"Okay, Homer. I used to be a trauma nurse at Cook County Hospital. County is where they bring all the gunshot and burn victims. It's unbelievably busy. One day I just had too much. I'd put in enough time to retire, so I did. I came here because I thought it would be peaceful."

I nodded. "Is it?"

"Oh, wonderfully."

I pointed to her piles of trash. "How'd you come to pick up all this stuff?"

"In Chicago, I used to run to keep fit. You have to run in Chicago—to stay ahead of the panhandlers and muggers.

"Here, I walk. But when you slow down, you notice

things more. In my case, litter. I've made picking up litter part of my exercise routine. When I find something too heavy to carry, I come back for it in my truck. The trash, I dump. But all of this—" She waved, takin' in the whole yard. "Is a waste of landfill space."

I couldn't disagree. Miz Lincoln 'peared to be quite a asset to our community. Still, there was the problem of them piles of junk makin' a perfect breedin' ground fer rats. Somethin' would have to be done about that.

Some folks swears by traps or poison, but for my money, nothin' beats a good rat dog fer keepin' vermin under control.

"You got any dogs, Miz Lincoln?"

"Why, no, Sheriff. Homer. I had one years ago, but it was such a wrench when he died, I couldn't bring myself to get another."

Which was a good sign. All I'd have to do would be to get her close enough to a dog to get attached to it, an' the rat problem'd be solved.

But that raised another problem. Where was I gonna get a good rat dog?

Martha interrupted my wonderin' when she called me again. "Homer, get over to the Truck Stop, pronto! Charity Nonesuch just called to say all Hell's broke loose out in the parkin' lot!"

wild horses

When I got to Hardsetter's there was a ruckus goin' on out back where the semis park. A couple locals had the driveways blocked off but they let me through right off. Once I got past 'em I seen why. A big ol' stock truck was center stage in the lot with its doors open an' ramp down. Mebbe two dozen skinny horses, paints an' bays an' duns, was millin' around, tryna find a way out. Hardsetter has a woven-wire fence around the lot to discourage local used vehicle parts entrepreneurs from preyin' on his customers. That fence an' the driveway patrol was all that was standin' between the herd an' freedom.

Charity Nonesuch was standin' out behind the restaurant with her hands on her ample hips. When she spotted me, she bustled over to fill me in.

"Good thing you're here, Homer. I was sure we were gonna see murder done." She pointed to where a truck driver—big as your average pro defensive lineman—was faced off against a small, feisty female.

The lady was wearin' a Grateful Dead T-shirt under a pair'a bib overalls, an' pint-sized work boots. If her hair'd been red instead'a light brown, you coulda took her for Little Orphan Annie—she weren't much bigger'n a ten-year-old kid.

The two of 'em spotted me about then, an' come rushin' over, both talkin' at once. I held up my hands an' yelled, "Whoa!" over the racket.

They shut up.

"S'posin' you start, ma'am," I tol' the woman.

'Fore she could get a word out, the truck driver yelled, "This bitch turned my stock loose!"

I gave him my best State-Trooper stare, an' he shut up.

I turned to the woman. "That right, ma'am?"

"I've been following him all the way from Nebraska. Those poor horses haven't had any food or water since he left there!"

I wondered was she one of those animal rights nuts, though she didn't seem daft. 'Sides, we got laws about interstate livestock transfers. I turned back to the driver. "You got your shippin' papers?"

"In the truck."

I followed him over to it. The trailer was knee deep in muck an' smelled ferocious. There was two horses down in the back; one looked dead. And way up front, near the cab, I could just make out the outline of a pony-sized critter with ears like a mule.

I went round to the cab, an' the driver gimme his papers. After studyin' 'em a while, I said, "Says here you're headin' for Grover. Seems like you mebbe missed your turn-off."

He got all red an' started puffin' up like a hedge-hog

fixin' to make a stand. I raised a eyebrow. He musta thought better of startin' somethin', cause he backed off, lookin' sheepish. "Guess I'm not much on geography."

"Yeah," I said. "You mind if I look in your truck?"

"What for?"

"I dunno. You got somethin' to hide?"

"No, but I know my rights."

I held my hands up like 'I surrender.' "I'm real sure you do." Then I closed the truck door an' fished my han'cuffs outta their case. "Put your hands on the truck."

"What?" He held his hands out to the side like he didn't know what to do with 'em.

"What I said. Put your hands on the truck."

He did, but all the time I could see him lookin' fer a way out. "What'd I do?"

I put the cuffs on him. While I patted him down, I told him, "Since you know your rights, you know you got the right to remain silent."

"WHAT'D I DO?"

"Ain't what you did. It's what you ain't did. You ain't give them critters any water lately. They's laws against that."

"The hell, you say! I watered them this morning."

"That musta been some trick. You ain't got a bucket in the truck, or nothin' else big enough to water one horse, much less a herd."

"I want a lawyer!"

"In due time."

"I got a right to a phone call!"

"Just hold yer horses."

He 'bout gagged on that, an' I took the opportunity to finish *re*citin' Miranda. I put him in the back seat of my squad an' buckled the seat belt 'round him. Then I deputized one'a the driveway patrol, to keep a eye on him.

"What're you gonna be doin', Sheriff, while I'm watchin' your priz'ner?"

"Well, I got to make arrangements fer these horses, an' get some infermation from the witnesses."

While I was tellin' him that, Charity'd hauled out half a dozen milk crates an' lined 'em with plastic garbage bags. She was fillin' 'em with water from the hose they use to wash down the back, an' them horses was linin' up eager as pigs at a trough to empty 'em.

One of the fellers standin' 'round, bein' entertained by all this, was Mars Boone, biggest farmer in Boone County. "Don't give 'em too much water at once, Miss Charity," he said. "They might founder."

Charity reached the hose in his direction an' batted her eyes at 'im. "Maybe *you* should do it, Mars honey. I don't wanna hurt the poor beasties."

Pure moonshine. Sweet Charity.

Mars wasn't much of a tippler, though. He fell for it like he was pole-axed. He blushed all the way up to the roots of his red hair an' damn-near tripped hisself runnin' over to take the hose.

I caught Charity's eye'n said, "Call Doc Clydesdale, will you, ma'am? See if he can't do somethin' for them horses in the truck."

Emmet Clausen piped up, "That there little one ain't a horse, Sheriff."

Everyone laughed, thinkin' mebbe I don't know a horse from a jackass.

"That's right, Emmet," I said. "Ain't in need'a no

health care, neither."

Emmet changed the subject by pointin' at the truck. "Speak a the devil—"

We all looked. The small jackass Emmet was talkin' 'bout had got up the nerve to squeeze past the sick horses an' was standin' at the top of the ramp. He threw up his nose an' opened his mouth to sing. "Hee haw haw haw. Hee hawwww," trailin' off like a bag-piper that's run outta air.

Most of the two-legged by-standers started laughin' fit to bust. The horses flat-out panicked. They took off runnin' 'round the lot, bouncin' off cars an' each other, scatterin' the people like bowlin' pins on a good night.

Havin' cleared hisself a place at the trough, the jackass skittered down the ramp an' bellied up to the water bar.

jackass

I hung around an' dickered with Mars Boone over how much he'd charge the county to round up all them critters and park 'em 'til I got the situation worked out. Mars'n me settled on four bucks a head per day fer storage. That pretty much meant Mars'd drop 'em off in a back pasture somewhere an' keep a eye out fer horse thieves. From the looks of 'em, I didn't think that'd be much of a job neither. They'd be hard to steal 'cause they was skittish as ruttin' squirrels, an' not worth the effort 'cause they was mustangs. Roy Peterman piped up in the middle of our negotiations, offerin' to store the horses fer three dollars a head, but I said no. Fer four bucks, Mars'd feed 'em.

The main witness in the case was the lady in the overalls. After the jackass got done stirrin' things up, I cornered her an' got her statement. She didn't want to give her name at first, but eventually she did—Alice Bowne.

After I let *Ms*. Bowne go, I took the prisoner over to the State *Po*lice lock-up, bein' as West Wheelin's too small to have much of a jail. They took his prints an' pi'ture, an' ran his name through their computer fer any wants 'n' warrants. After they give him his phone call an' showed him to a room, I headed back to the truck stop to see how the round-up was proceedin'.

Mars an' his hands had backed a truck into the exit drive. An' them mustangs—'fer all they was wild animals—musta been used to bein' run into chutes an' herded onto trucks, cause they was all in Mars' big stock truck, starin' out through the slats like so many carnival-ride ponies.

The jackass, on the other hand, was givin' them good ol' boys a run fer their money. Every time they got him near the ramp, he'd stampede on past, or he'd wait til they was right up on him, then dodge 'n' feint, or turn around an' start kickin'. Mars was red as a sailor's sunrise an' sweatin' like a Derby winner. When he come up to me, I could see he was mad enough to shoot the damn critter. "Deal's off, Sheriff," he told me. "I quit!"

"Aw, Mars. Cool off. Jus' take the horses. I'll figure out somethin' else to do with the jackass."

Mars took a deep breath an' clamped his jaws shut. He nodded. Then he an' the boys closed up the truck an' took off.

Which left me to deal with the donkey—me an' five other jackasses that had nothin' better to do. We chased 'im round the parkin' lot another twenty minutes, then decided to give up. Soon's everybody stopped chasin' him, the jackass wandered over to the perimeter fence an' started prunin' the grass along the base of it. He didn't pay no more attention 'less folks got within kickin' range—which they mostly didn't after one feller got too close an' had the legs knocked out from under 'im.

'Bout that time, Rye Willis showed up to make a delivery, somethin' he don't like to do in front of a audience. He figured out quick what was goin' down an' had a good laugh at my expense.

"Bet you don't have no better luck," I told him.

He thought about that an' said, "Think I ain't read *Tom Sawyer*?"

I didn't answer. I know he hadn't, but I'd told him the story one time.

Rye added, "How much is it worth to you to get that critter outta here?"

"Alive?" I said.

He shrugged an' nodded.

"Twenty bucks is all I got on me."

"Fair 'nough."

Rye went inside Hardsetter's an' come out with a beer keg an' a tapper. He tapped the keg, commandeered a bucket, an' proceeded to fill it. Then he carried it over to just outside kickin' range from the jack. He looked around at his audience an' said, "I outta be chargin' admission."

"My money's on the jackass," one of the boys said.

"How much?"

"I got twenty bucks says that critter'll make a jackass outta you."

"You're on," Rye told 'im.

At that point, Charity come out to see what was up an' Rye asked her to hold the bets. Charity's got a great head fer figures, so she kept track of the action when Rye offered to cover everybody.

"How 'bout you, Homer? You want a piece of this?"

I'd noticed, while they was dickerin', that the critter'd

sidled over to the bucket an' was givin' the beer a try. Seemed like he was formin' a favorable opinion, 'cause he started puttin' it away pretty fast. So I told Rye I was a repersenative of the Law, and they was laws against gamblin'.

He just said, "Ah-hunh."

Pretty soon the jackass started shakin' his head an' staggerin'. He took about ten steps, then stood with his legs splayed out an' his head down. He didn't even move when Rye walked over an' slapped him on the neck. "Somebody get me a rope," Rye said.

Charity put Rye's winnin's in her pocket an' fetched one. Rye twisted it into a halter that he tied on the donkey's head. He said, "Sweet Charity, you got any old gunny sacks around?"

She reckoned she could find a old table cloth. While she was huntin' it up, Rye called Truck Towing on his cell phone an' told 'em to bring the big winch an' a small truck. "The one you use fer haulin' parts'll do just fine."

Time the tow truck arrived, Rye had the jackass blindfolded with the table cloth so it couldn't see the truck.

The rest of the project went down smooth as West Wheelin' White Lightning. Dwayne "D.W." Truck—who'd come hisself to see what all the fuss was about—backed the tow truck up to the jackass, an' him an' Rye eased the canvas sling underneath it. 'Fore the poor critter knew what was happenin' they had him hung from the tow-hook, all four legs danglin'. Then Patrick Truck, D.W.'s baby brother, backed the parts truck up under the critter an' Dwayne eased him down into the back. They cross tied him, so he couldn't climb out or kick down the tailgate, an' Rye asked, "Homer, where'd you want him delivered?"

Which is how I ended up with a jackass fer a lawnmower.

car wrecks

'Bout 4:15 p.m., my cell phone rang, an' when I answered, it was Skip. Musta *just* got home from school.

"Homer, there's a super-sized rabbit tied to our front tree, eatin' the roses!"

"Dammit! Shorten the rope, would you, so he can't reach the flowers. An' give him a pail of water."

"Who's he belong to?"

"If I knew that he wouldn't be there."

"What's his name?"

"Far's I know, he ain't got one."

"So I can name him."

"Hell, no! We ain't keepin' him."

• • •

It was nearly suppertime 'fore I picked Skip up at home an', dropped him at my sister's house fer supper. After which, I drove back to the state cop shop to interview my prisoner.

When I asked fer him at the lock-up, the guy in charge said, "He's gone, Sheriff."

"How kin that be? He ain't even been arraigned."

The trooper shrugged. "About a half an hour after he made his phone call, some guy showed up who said he was Ames's lawyer. He had an order to show probable cause why his client was arrested in the first place. He tried to get the judge to drop all the charges because you weren't here to testify, but Sergeant Underhill convinced the judge to postpone the hearing. Sarge told the judge you were dealing with the disaster Ames created, so the judge continued the case until tomorrow an' let Ames out on bail."

"Well, we still have his truck and license," I said. "Guess he'll have to come back."

I asked where could I find Sergeant Underhill, an' the trooper steered me to the 24-Hour Café across the highway.

* * *

Underhill was sittin' in a back booth, tuckin' away a order of steak an' eggs. When he seen me, he waved me over an' pointed to the empty bench across from him. "Take a load off."

I set my hat on the bench an' sat down next to it.

The waitress hurried to bring me a mug of fresh coffee.

Underhill waited 'til she'd took my order 'fore he fished somethin' outta his shirt pocket and laid it on the table. Ames's CDL. He pointed at it an' said, "What's wrong with this picture?"

I'd looked at it when I took it off Ames, an' I hadn't found nothin' wrong. So I knew I'd have to study it close if

I was gonna find anything amiss. "The pi'ture looks just like him," I said. "That's unusual."

Underhill gimme his gotcha grin, so I studied the license some more. Somethin' was off about the feel an' the weight of it. "It's counterfeit."

Underhill pointed at me an' nodded.

"It's a damn good one," I added. He agreed. "So who is Ames really?"

Underhill said, "I ran his prints through N.C.I.C. They came back to a Samuel Loomis. He lost his own license for DUI."

"Is there a real Henry Ames?"

"Yeah. But according to his daughter, he's blind, deaf, and senile. Currently resides in a nursing home in Atlanta."

"Well, we still got the truck."

Underhill shook his head. "He won't come back for it. Probably belongs to some bank. I've got an APB out, but we'll be really lucky if we ever see *him* again."

We pondered that while we finished our steaks. At least the steaks was good.

• • •

I was really glad I was already on duty that night, cause I would'a got called back in if I wasn't. I'd just tucked Skip in for the night at my sister's, stopped by the house to see was the jackass okay, an' made my early rounds—checkin' that doors was locked an' such—when D.W. Truck rung me on my cell phone.

"Homer, that truck you impounded's just been hijacked."

I didn't ax was he sure. D.W. would know. S.O.P. fer

vehicle impoundment is when the fine's been paid or the judge finds the owner not guilty, the feller gets a paper to take to the Impound Officer. That's Dwayne. He gives the guy a release form to fill out—says his vehicle ain't been bruised or burglarized. Once he signs it, he gets his keys back and he's on his way.

"What happened, Dwayne?"

"The truck was fine when I locked up fer the night— 'bout ten minutes ago. Then the dogs started in. When I went out to see what was up, the truck was gone. Sommabitch took my gate right off the hinges and drove over it."

I told him to keep everybody away from the scene, an' I'd be along directly.

Happens, I was wrong. I was halfway out to Truck's when Martha called me.

"Homer, you'd best get out to Car Wrecks. There's been an accident…."

• • •

The two-mile stretch of county highway runnin' along our local river is called Car Wrecks. Ten or fifteen streams feed it down steep ravines an' gullies. The road zigzags across half of 'em on bridges built or rebuilt over a span of years. 'Tween the zigzags an' the mismatched bridges, there's plenty of curves an' places a car can go off the road in spite of the guard rails the county keeps replacin'.

Time I got there, I didn't have to look long or hard to find the crash site—seemed like the whole of West Wheelin's fire department was turned out, linin' up to make a human guard rail in the gap where somethin' big had took out the standard-issue railin'.

There was a dozen cars an' pick-ups parked along where the road curved 'fore goin' over a old Roman-style stone bridge. The Fire Department's pumper truck was parked near the gap, in the middle of a mare's nest of hoses. The scene was lit by the car headlights an' the floodlights on the fire truck. Outside the circle of light, the trees was black on black—you couldn't see the river or anything past the far side of the bridge.

Boone County's only got four full time firefighters—firemen. They was all there. Along with—looked like—most of the volunteers. We'd recently got a squad of new-comers, includin' Angie Devon an' Jesus Lopez, an'—I wasn't too surprised to see—Miz Mary Lincoln. All the old-comers was there, too—Nina an' Rye, Merlin Willis, Junior Jackson, an' the Jefferson twins. Rumor had it Tom an' Jeff was descended from a dead former president. Probably more'n a rumor. Tom had a way with words an' always had a pen stuck into his afro; Jeff had really good penmanship.

I shouldered my way into the line-up an' leaned over the space where the guard-rail used to be. The ravine below was dark as a gateway to Hell. A fire burned cheerfully in what I judged to be the center of it. Smelled like a barbecue where the cook used diesel fuel instead'a lighter fluid.

"You guys on strike?" I asked the Chief, who was one of the full-time guys.

"Nope. Outta water."

Which explained why the hoses was lyin' around like road-killed rattlers.

"Don't worry, Sheriff. That little brush fire we had last August cleaned out all the combustible material. There's nothing left to burn."

"'Cept my evidence."

The Chief sighed an' gave the order, an' all the firefighters fell to an' got back to work. Took about a hour 'fore the chief pronounced the fire out an' sent everybody home but the on-duty man.

By that time, I'd called the state cops an' they sent out their crime scene van, evidence techs, an' more lights. It was close to sun-up by the time they was done.

I waited 'til it was light enough to get good pictures of the scene without a flash. When I'd run a couple rolls off, I woke up Doc Howard, an' asked him to send a couple interns an' a ambulance to pick up the crispy critter that'd been the truck driver.

I never did get by Nina's fer dessert.

The Grassy-ass Cafe

By the time I collected Skip from my sister's, it was 8:30 a.m. We went home so I could change clothes an' feed the jackass. On the way, I called the school an' told 'em Skip'd be late, then I called Nina an' offered to buy her breakfast if she'd meet us at the café.

When Skip an' I got to the house, we found that the critter had chewed everything he could reach—pretty much the whole front yard—down to the roots. He musta figured out I could help him get more, 'cause soon as I got outta the cruiser, he let me hear why jackasses is called mountain canaries. His "hee-haw-haw-haw" echoed off all the neighbors' houses an' brought at least two residents out to see what was up.

Folks around here mostly don't comment on other folks' business, least not to their faces. But Mrs. Shaklee, next door, stuck her head out the kitchen window an' yelled, "Couldn't you have just gotten a rooster, Sheriff?"

Skip just said, "Wow!"

I untied the critter from the tree he was attached to an' tried to lead him behind the house where there was more grass. He planted his feet an' wouldn't budge.

I pulled harder; jackass started backin' up. Skip nearly busted a gut laughin'.

"Knock it off!" I said, "An' gimme a hand."

Even with both of us pullin', we couldn't get the critter to go forward.

Finally, Skip said, "We might just as well swing him around an' back him up where we want him to go."

So we tried that. It took about twenty minutes, but we finally got him 'round behind the house, tied to the only tree there was. I had Skip fill a wash tub with water for him while I got a shovel an' rake to pick up the free fertilizer he'd produced the day before.

Then I got cleaned up, an' we went to eat.

• • •

The little restaurant Maria Lopez'd opened across the street from City Hall was officially called the Gracias A Dios Café. Only nobody but Maria an' her husband could pronounce that. So folks mostly call it the Grassy-ass. It was usually pretty crowded mealtimes 'cause Maria's a damn good cook, an' not just Tex-Mex. She can cook anything you can describe.

When we pulled up there was a beat-up old GMC pickup parked out front. It had runnin' boards—which ain't unusual on trucks hereabouts—and the slickest paint job I ever seen—a wide baby blue an' white plaid with a red pin stripe runnin' through it. The sign on the door said *Donatello*

Firenzi Masonry & Whimsy. There was a mason's level in the gun rack, an' a big brown Maine Coon cat curled up on the passenger's seat. I made a note of the license plate 'fore we went inside.

The place was pretty crowded. I made the plaid truck's driver right off—the only stranger in the place. He was sittin' at the lunch counter, tuckin' away a plate a ham an' eggs. A male white, mid-40s, dressed in a denim jacket over a blue work shirt, Levis, an' work boots. He had a Chicago Cubs gimme hat hangin' out of a back pocket.

Me an' Skip took the only table left, an' Maria brought us coffee an' took our orders. We was almost done eatin' when Nina finally showed. She wasn't wearin' her ring.

"Lost it already?" I asked.

She looked hurt. "It's safe enough." She pulled out the chain she wore 'round her neck to hold the gold cross her daddy give her. An' sure enough, there was her ring. She let it drop back inside her shirt, settlin' it between her assets. I sure did envy that ring.

I looked at Skip an' could see his mind was movin' along the same track. "Keep your eyes to yourself," I told him.

He dropped his head, but he didn't try to hide his smirk. When I pointed out that Nina was gonna be his stepmom sometime soon, he got redder'n strawberry soda.

"If you're done," I told him, "you can be excused."

"I'll wait in the cruiser."

I tossed him my keys an' turned back to Nina. "Why you hidin' your ring?"

"We can't set a date yet."

Some guys would'a got mad, but I grew up with three sisters so I know women got their own kinda logic. You can understand it fine if you're patient, an' listen, an' fill in the steps they skip getting from A to Z. I just said, "Why not?" an' waited.

"Rye's been courtin' me just as long as you. If we tell him we're tyin' the knot without he's even got a girl, he'll be heart-broke."

"Long's he thinks he's got a chance with you, he ain't even lookin'."

"So we gotta find him one."

"He's a grown man. He kin find his own."

"I know, but he'll find one a whole lot faster if we help."

I knew that was one place Rye wouldn't want no help, but there was no point in pointin' that out. "What did you have in mind?"

"We could start with a list of eligibles."

I signaled Maria fer the check, an' tole Nina, "You start. I got a crime to investigate an' a autopsy to attend."

Maria handed me a check.

I handed her a ten an' a twenty. "I got Nina's, too. Keep the change."

I give Nina a peck on the check an' beat feet 'fore she could think a anything else.

post mortem

Doc Howard was waitin' when I finally made it to the morgue.

"I finished the post on your John Doe, Sheriff."

"Good."

"Are you sure you got all the bones?"

"I ain't sure of nothin' but death an' taxes. But you're welcome to go out there an' look for yourself."

"I'll take your word for it."

"What killed him?"

"I can't say."

"That's helpful. How'm I gonna arrest—"

"I cannot manufacture evidence." He shook his head. "Come with me."

He led me to a empty classroom—acoustical panels an' fluorescent lights on the ceilin'; tall windows lookin' out on the campus; green an' white linoleum tile floors; an' rows of tables with chairs facin' a chalkboard at the back of the room.

Doc had John Doe's bones laid out in order on the table

closest to the chalk board. Least it looked like the bones I'd brung him. Skull an' back bones, ribs, and arm an' leg bones was all about where they'd be if the feller had just laid down on Doc's table an' died. The dead give-away was that Doc looked happy as a pig in slop. Or like he'd just finished one of them 1000-piece giant-jigsaw puzzles.

"At least this time you brought me something to work with, Sheriff." Musta been referrin' to the guy the bear ate some time back.

I ignored the dig. "This how you maintain a chain of custody?"

Doc looked insulted. "This isn't John Doe. This is Mortimer Oliver, the best anatomy assistant who ever lived, assisting even after death."

I rolled my eyes.

"It was his last wish," Doc said. "He willed his body to the Anatomy Department."

"What's that got to do with—"

Doc held up his hands. "There were no signs of perimortem violence on your remains, no projectile wounds or knife marks. Of course, he may have been suffocated or strangled—the hyoid bone was missing—but I'm inclined to go with natural causes—disease or infection. He was old, arthritic, and had bad teeth."

"How old?"

"About 500 years."

"No shit!"

"Even if I could make a case for homicide, the killer has escaped your clutches."

I shook my head. "That makes it easier fer me, but it's still against the law to dump human remains in ditches."

"Not to mention disturbing Indian burials."

"How'm I gonna catch the S.O.B. that done it 'fore he dumps again?"

"An interesting problem."

"An' you still haven't told me what's your point with your assistant here." I hitched my thumb at what was left of Oliver.

"Let's suppose for a moment that he *is* your John Doe."

I nodded.

Doc handed me a cardboard box. "Pick him up and put him in the box."

I did.

"Now," Doc said. "Dump the box out on the table."

I did that, too.

Doc pointed to the pile of bones on the table. "Look familiar?" Looked like a pile of giant pick-up sticks. It also looked just like—

"How John Doe looked in the ditch!"

"Bingo."

"Well, it ain't no surprise he was dumped. He sure didn't climb in the ditch by hisself."

"Humphf." Doc looked annoyed.

"What did all your experts find out?"

"It's all in the report." Seemed like Doc was a tad bent outta shape.

"Which is where?"

"In the box with the remains. In my evidence locker."

• • •

I locked John Doe in the trunk of my cruiser an' went back inside to watch Doc examine what was left of the truck thief. The heat had kinda curled him up around the steerin' wheel, an' he still had it in a death grip. When they'd finally got the fire struck, D.W. an' me had just took the wheel off the steerin' column. Doc's interns worked the body bag around the corpse an' loaded the whole mess in the meat wagon fer Doc to sort out.

"Lucky he was wearing his seat belt," Doc said as his assistant unzipped the body bag.

We was all wearin' safety glasses, blue plastic gowns, an' purple nitrile gloves.

"How's that, Doc?" I asked. "'Pears to me a hard-headed feller like this might a survived goin' head-first through the windshield."

"That's debatable. As it is, since the truck ended upside down and fire burns upward, he's not as badly damaged as he could be."

"Small comfort."

Doc just snorted and started separatin' Mr. Truck Thief from his consolation prize. Most of the skin come off his hands an' stayed with the steerin' wheel.

"You can take this to the state crime lab," Doc told me as he handed it to me. "Maybe they can get fingerprints."

I put it in a plastic bag an' set it aside fer later.

Then I watched while Doc finished up the slice'n' dice an' set me up with a cooler full of samples to take with me.

Later, as I was drivin' away, I felt like I just come from a bad pig roast, with the main course burnt on the outside an' undercooked inside. Sure made me want to arrest the chef.

a likker heist

Doc said he'd fax me the autopsy report soon as he had the toxicology results. "Preliminary cause of death is blunt force trauma from the crash...."

After droppin' the steerin' wheel and other *evidence* at the crime lab, I headed back to town to try'n find out who our truck thief was. 'Fore I got half a mile my cell phone rang.

I turned it on, an' D.W.'s voice asked, "Homer, could you mebbe swing by here? Sump'in you oughta see."

I sighed an' said, "Ten-four."

• • •

I found him on a creeper, under a truck, where he was disconnectin' a differential. He scooted out an' got up, wipin' his hands on a shop rag. He musta been on a tight schedule 'cause he didn't offer me coffee. He led the way to where he'd stowed the burnt-out remains of the semi tractor in a padlocked chain-link cage. D.W. fished out a ring of keys and opened the lock.

"Han' me that trouble light," he said, pointin'. "An' get us a couple creepers."

The light, with its cord neatly coiled, was hung on the wall next to the cage. I took it down an' plugged it in, then handed the business end to D.W. I set the creepers on the floor next to the wreck. We got down on 'em an' rolled under the cab. D.W. shined the light at the underneath side of the chassis. The paint an' undercoating had burned off, an' the frame an' ferrous metal parts had already started rustin'.

"What're we lookin' at?" I asked.

"See if you kin find it."

When I did, I whistled. "Somebody cut the brake line."

• • •

Martha radioed 'fore I got a mile down the road.

"Homer, Wilma called again. Wants to know what you're doin' about the rats. What rats?"

I told her about Wilma an' Mary Lincoln. "Martha, you know anybody's got rat-dog pups fer sale?"

"You tried Owen?"

"Good idea. If Wilma calls back, tell her she's on my list."

• • •

I got a Quarter Pounder an' coffee at McDonald's drive-through an' had lunch at my desk. After lockin' John Doe's remains in the closet that doubles fer a evidence locker, I spread out all the stuff I had on the truck, truck driver, an' truck thief. It didn't come to much. I figgered the next question—after who our truck thief was—was who'd want to kill him. Cuttin' the brake line mighta been some new anti-theft strategy, but it'd have to've been cooked up by a idiot. So mebbe the truck thief had a accomplice who wanted to do him in.

All my useless speculatin' was brought to a halt by a call from Sergeant Underhill. "Got a report on the fingerprints you brought in this morning," he told me.

"That was quick."

"Our lab rats love you, Deters. They get bored with the usual DUIs and shootings. You always give them a challenge."

"That's nice. I guess. What'd they find?"

"Your crispy critter was Samuel Loomis, a.k.a. Henry Ames. Guess you won't be going to court this afternoon."

"Don't s'pose they figgered out who done him in."

"Car Wrecks."

"Wish it was that simple—I could close both his cases—but somebody cut his brake line."

"Do tell. Glad he's your problem."

Underhill hung up an' I went back to work. I was outta leads an' about outta ideas when Sergeant Underhill called back.

"We got a situation just east of Okra," he said. "We need you to be on the lookout for a dirty white International tractor with Kentucky plates and a plain white trailer. Got hijacked at the oasis. Two suspects wearing ski masks, armed with sawed-off shotguns. No other description." He gave me the license number of the semi and hung up.

Hopin' to head the hijackers off, I put on my body armor an' hat and headed for the highway.

Just before I got to the on/off ramps by the truck stop, I come across a dirty white tractor—no trailer—nosed into a access road to one of Mars Boone's hay fields. The tractor had a Florida plate an' a flat tire on the front but otherwise it fit the description of the missing rig.

I pulled onto the shoulder an' put on my safety lights. I was careful not to screw up any evidence, as I checked the truck to make sure there weren't anybody or any bodies inside. Then I called the state boys and told 'em I'd found their missin' vehicle.

I didn't have much time to think on how the truck come to be there 'fore Dan Underhill arrived with three state troopers an' a evidence van. One of the troopers—the greenest one—pointed to the Florida plate an' said, "That's not the one we're looking for."

Underhill come up behind him an' cuffed him on the head. "Son, you leave the thinkin' to the suits. And while you're doin' that, call up and see if that plate's been reported stolen yet. If it has, find out where and when."

The troopers set up a perimeter like they was processin' a murder scene. An' Underhill paced like a caged wolf while the evidence team swarmed over the tractor.

"What's got *your* tail in a ringer?" I asked him. "You gotta get a couple hijackings a week."

"Yeah. But these're different."

"How's that?"

"Most of the hijackings we get are crimes of opportunity—some jackass leaves his truck runnin' while he goes in to take a leak and comes back to find it gone. These guys're so slick they could sneak sunrise past a rooster. They only go after the good stuff—mostly liquor and cigarettes.

They plan ahead—pick their ambush where there's no witnesses, and hit the driver fast and hard. With big guns, so there's no argument. Then they make the rigs they steal disappear. This is the first one that's ever turned up."

"Sure it's the same crew?"

"Yeah. After the first dozen heists, some of the distributors started shipping their goods in unmarked trailers and varying their routes. Doesn't seem to have helped much. It's like these hijackers have radar."

"Or a inside man."

"Naw. At least nine companies've been hit. Delivering to fifty or so locations. They'd have to have a gang of inside men."

"Why ain't I been appraised of this situation?"

Underhill give me a look. "You've been a bit distracted lately. If you spent as much time reading our bulletins as you do the wanted posters over at the post office, you'd probably have this solved already."

I could feel myself gettin' hot. Guess me an' Nina bein' a item wasn't a secret no more. "Point taken."

"How'd you know to look here?" Underhill axed.

"Just a hunch. If I'd'a stole a vehicle worth more'n a house, I'd wanna get it off the highway 'til I could change the plates an' mebbe slap on a new coat of paint or a couple distractin' decals. An' this ain't too far from where the hijack occurred."

"That reminds me," Underhill said. "I got a little more on your crispy critter." I waited. Underhill went on. "He was arrested once for driving a stolen vehicle, a truck that'd been hijacked a month earlier—same MO as these."

"When was this?"

"Good five years back. Charges were dropped because Loomis had a passable bill of sale and registration. But it's quite a coincidence."

"I don't believe in coincidence. Mebbe I should take another look at the truck he wrecked. Might be he didn't have any trouble financin' it 'cause he didn't."

Underhill nodded. "It's a theory."

"Think I could get copies of your reports on these hijackin's?"

Underhill shrugged. "Another pair of eyes can't hurt."

"If it wouldn't be breakin' no State *Police* code of silence."

"Who's gonna tell?"

BLM

First thing next mornin'—after I fed an' watered the jackass an' dropped Skip at school—I went by the state cop shop and collected their reports on Sam Loomis, a.k.a. Henry Ames, an' the likker truck hijackin's. I took 'em back to my office an' spread 'em out on my desk, read through everythin' twice. It didn't give me no better idea who was behind any of the crimes.

I still had the shippin' papers fer the horses—which was eatin' their heads off over at Mars Boone's.

The U.S. Bureau of Land Management was shippin' 'em from Nebraska to Grover, just over our state line. So I called the contact number on the bill of lading an' asked to talk to the local BLM man in charge. The guy who finally come on the line—after three transfers an' twenty minutes of canned messages—said his name was William Smith.

"You any relation to that actor in *Men in Black*?"

"Certainly not!"

Made me wonder was he a bigot or just full of hisself. I

said, "Well, no matter."

He axed who was he talkin' to.

"Sheriff Homer Deters, Boone County."

"What can I do for you, Sheriff?"

"Well, fer openers, you can tell me about the feller you hired to deliver them mustangs I got in protective custody."

"I don't know—"

"Sam Loomis?"

"Never heard of him."

"You prob'ly knew him as Henry Ames."

"Isn't he the one who died in the accident?"

"That's him. How'd you hear about it?"

"Someone must've called me."

"Who?"

"I don't recall."

"Male or female?"

"Male."

I waited to see if he'd volunteer any more. He didn't. I said, "You know Ames well?"

"To the best of my knowledge, I never met him."

"How'd you come to hire him?"

"The office in Nebraska would've hired him. I don't know anything about it." I waited. Finally, he said, "Will there be anything else, Sheriff?" He sounded annoyed.

"When're you gonna come pick up your horses?"

"What horses?"

"The mustangs Loomis/Ames was haulin'."

"I was informed they were destroyed in the crash."

"Who's been lyin' to you?"

"The State Police reported that the truck was totaled."

"Yeah, but the horses wasn't in it."

"I have a preliminary report from the insurance adjuster. He was out at the site, and he assured me he saw carcasses. As far as we're concerned that's the end of it."

I sighed. It'd be easier to unload the horses myself than to try'n argue with a man who'd made up his mind. Facts wasn't gonna confuse him. I said, "You wanna send me a official letter to that effect. So's I can legally dispose of these horses I got that ain't yours?"

"Will a fax do?"

"Guess it'll hafta." I give him the City Hall fax number an' told him to send it to the attention of Sheriff Deters. I hung up wonderin' who I could sucker into takin' them nags, and who was gonna pay fer their upkeep in the meantime.

· · ·

Usually, in a murder investigation, I would interview everybody the victim knowed, payin' special attention to his enemies an' rivals. Problem was, I didn't know who Loomis knowed—didn't even know who he really was 'cause his latest ID was phony, an' his previous license was suspended. Still, I done the minimum in that department—called the PD that was local to his old address an' axed would they make some inquiries. They would. I left it with them and went on to the next thing.

Besides the BLM shippin' papers, I had Loomis's log, phony driver's license, an' insurance card—probably phony, too. He'd also been carryin' four credit cards, $38.76 in cash, an' a Illinois lottery ticket.

After I'd checked out the idiot insurance adjuster, I could follow up on some of Loomis's credit card purchases.

I called the first credit card company on the phone and explained the situation. A nice lady give me Loomis's real address—a P.O. box in southern Indiana—an' promised to fax me a record of his purchases. Two of the other three card companies promised to do likewise.

What with all the goin's-on lately, I was startin' to have trouble keepin' things straight. So I wrote down each item on a Post-it, an stuck 'em all on my filin' cabinet, with the Loomis/Ames case at the top. It didn't help much with solvin' any of 'em, but at least I wasn't likely to forget one. An' it made my office a little more colorful.

I was on my way to pick up my faxes an' a copy of the fingerprint report, when I got one more phone call—from my landlady.

"Homer," she said, "that mountain canary you adopted has been singin' like a choir member the last hour an' a half."

Dammit! I'd completely fergot the jackass.

insurance adjuster

West Wheelin' ain't all that big, an' everybody knows everybody's business, so it wasn't hard to locate the insurance man Mr. Smith'd mentioned. He was stayin' at Motel 6.

The manager pointed out which room he was in, an' I went an' knocked on the door.

The man who opened it was a nervous, Don Knotts kinda guy. He looked at my badge and turned a shade white.

"You always this nervous?" I asked. "Or did you just rob a bank?"

He pulled hisself together an' said, "I haven't done anything illegal." The guy was so nervous I couldn't tell was he lyin' or not.

In general though, folks lie to the police. So I said, "Then you won't mind if I come in an' look around."

He almost fell for it. I could see his mouth formin' the word, "no," 'fore he realized what he was sayin'. Then he stood hisself up taller in the doorway an' changed his "no" to a "Yes. *Hell, yes!* I *would* mind. You want to come in, get a warrant."

I had to admire that, but I had a crime—a couple crimes—to investigate. I said, "Fair enough. But we gotta talk. Guess you'll have to come back to town with me."

That set him back a bit. He hemmed an' hawed but finally stepped back from the door an' waved me inside.

I took a quick look around an' set down on the only chair.

The insurance feller started to take offense. "What's this—"

"You tell the Bureau of Land Management their horses burnt up?"

"Why do you ask?"

"It's my job."

"Well, investigating insurance claims is *my* job. The truck those horses were in was totaled. What's the problem?"

"Them horses ain't dead."

"Of course they're dead. I saw the burned carcasses."

"Where?"

"In the ravine. At the crash site."

"Let's go have a look."

• • •

There was two burned carcasses in the ravine, all right. Cows. One of 'em had a bullet-hole between the eyes, the other looked like road kill. It appeared a local farmer was tryin' to save a few bucks on the disposal fee, or mebbe work a scam on some fool claim-adjuster by settin' it up to look like his stock was killed in the truck crash. Wouldn't work on anybody local, but the fact that this guy was here was proof somebody'd fall fer it.

When I pointed out the horns, the insurance man turned bright red. "If the horses weren't in the truck, where *are* they?"

"In protective custody, over at Mars Boone's. 'Cept for the jackass. He's at my place." I gave him my address an' told him he was free to take the jackass any time. "An' you can get your horses soon's you pay their board."

"That's not my job," he said. "I'll amend my report. BLM can worry about the horses."

a truck stop an' a prison

From the truck stops Loomis had patronized an' the dates
he'd patronized 'em, it seemed like he spent a lotta time goin'
to Nashville an' Grover. I figgered the state cops'd know
those towns an' the truck stops between 'em, so I called
Trooper Yates an' asked for some info.

"Besides The Grand Ole Opry," Yates told me,
"Nashville's got lots a health care companies, a Nissan
plant, an' some church headquarters—mainly Baptists an'
Methodists. Grover has a state prison an' a distillery. This
about your barbecued trucker?"

"Yup."

Yates gimme a sketch of all the truck stops on Loomis's
credit card receipts. And, since Grover was a lot closer'n
Nashville, I decided to start my canvass in that direction.

I stopped at the Best Buy on my way to the Interstate
an' axed their techno-genius, Merlin Willis, to use his demo
machines to turn Loomis/Ames's DMV photo into a couple
dozen "Do-you-know-this feller?" posters an' some four-by-

six snapshots. I figgered I'd get more calls if folks' curiosity got stirred up, so Merlin added "Call Homer Deters" an' my cell phone number, with no mention of the Sheriff's office.

"That desktop the town's buyin' you come in, Sheriff," Merlin said when he was finished. "You want me to deliver it to your office?"

"I'd be obliged."

"Sure thing."

"An' even more obliged if you set it up an' show me how to use it."

He nodded. "I'll install it this afternoon, an' you can let me know when you got time fer a lesson."

• • •

The rest of the day, I drove around an' handed the posters to every local waitress, hooker, an' fillin' station attendant I thought Loomis might have run into.

I hit pay dirt just outside Grover.

The Trucker's Inn 'N' Out was one of them super-sized truck stops with room fer fifty semis to park an' enough pumps to service half a Texas. It had a Down Home Cookin' restaurant, a mini-mart, an' the Taj Mahal of comfort stations, with plastic seat covers that changed when you waved your hand in front of a 'lectric sensor. After I'd checked the plumbing, I went into the restaurant to sample the *cui*sine.

The waitress put a menu in front of me and said, "Coffee, hon?" Her name tag said Penny. She had a voice like Sharon Stone, but she was built like a brick shithouse. Made me think of phone sex.

I said, "Much obliged."

She set a big coffee mug in front of me an' filled it to the brim. Good coffee. The food was pretty good, too.

When I was done, an' Penny'd refilled my coffee mug, I showed her my improvised poster an' asked had she ever seen this guy.

"Bad tipper," she said.

"Anything else?"

"You some kinda law?"

"That be a problem for you?"

She shook her head. "He comes in here once every two weeks or so. Treats waitresses like shit." She pulled a wipe rag outta her pocket an' started polishin' the table top. "He do something bad?"

"Got hisself killed."

She shook her head again. "He was a jerk, but I can't see anybody killin' him for that. Hell, half the truckers that come in here are jerks."

"He ever come in with anyone?"

"Not that I saw. I heard him tell somebody to go to hell once, over his cell phone."

"Recently?"

"Last time he was in. Can't remember what day that was. Sorry."

I could find out the date from Loomis's log an' credit card records. I said, "You been a great help."

Which is why I left her a generous tip.

• • •

One of the places Sam Loomis delivered stuff to was a new minimum security state prison where they was s'posed to teach young felons to be farmers. The Hiram Walker Agricultural Arts Facility looked pretty much like any small farm 'cept for the 12-foot fence with razor wire toppin' it, an' the big ugly square lockup between the front gate an' the farm buildings. I pulled up to the gate an' showed my badge to the guard.

"What can we do for you, Sheriff?"

"Guess I need to talk to the warden. He in today?"

"He's in every day."

The guard opened the gate an' said, "Drive up to the front entrance and park in a visitor's space. I'll let 'em know you're coming. You'll have to check your piece."

I did what he said.

• • •

The guy who let me in and locked up my sidearm looked more like a recruitin' ad for the Be-All-You-Can-Be Army than a standard issue prison guard. An' inside, the place looked like a new high school, with wide hallways and high ceilings. Everything was clean as a ad for Spic and Span.

The warden's office had a picture window out onto the prison yard, which looked like a garden project from one of them ladies' magazines. The warden was a wonder, too—fit as a marathon runner. An' he couldn't of been more than twenty-five. He stood up behind his desk an' offered me his hand, then a seat.

I took both. "Nice place you got here, sir." I handed him one of my "wanted" posters an' asked had he seen the feller.

He studied the picture, then shook his head. "Too old to be one of ours."

"Well, far's I know, he wasn't never in prison. But he was a truck driver. He may'a made deliveries here."

"I could let you talk to Mr. Ridley, our farm manager. He might remember him."

"I'd be obliged. Also, if you could tell me what he delivered."

"What company did he work for?"

"He was a independent. Last time out, he was haulin' for the Bureau of Land Management."

The warden looked surprised. "That'd be our horses."

"He was s'posed to bring 'em here?"

"Supposed to?"

"I got your horses."

"Not *our* horses. They were delivered this morning—three days late, but they're here."

"Mebbe they're not yours, but I got *your* shippin' papers. An' *somebody's* horses. "What do *you* do with horses?"

"Our inmates gentle them, get them used to being handled and ridden, then we auction them off to the public. It's a great program. The inmates learn useful skills and get a certain emotional benefit from working with animals. BLM gets rid of surplus mustangs without inciting horse-lovers. And the horses usually end up with good homes.

"We also have beef cattle, milk cows, sheep, chickens, and pigs. We teach farming techniques and equipment repair. Mr. Ridley will give you a tour if you like."

• • •

I did like. Ridley turned out to be younger than the warden. *And* he made a point to say *he* was a graduate of the program. He'd done his time an' learned a trade—gentlin' human mustangs.

The place was run better'n any farm I've seen possibly exceptin' Mars Boone's. I asked Ridley could they take on a bunch more horses.

"We just got a shipment. Maybe in a month or two."

By which time the county'd be in hock to Mars Boone for at least a couple grand.

Ridley remembered Loomis—who'd delivered horses on two occasions—as a real jerk. "He didn't give them enough food or water en route. And he refused to help us off-load them, then wanted us to clean out his truck."

"Did you?"

"Hell, no."

Lower Fork Distillery

Long as I was down that way, I decided to check out another of the concerns Ames/Loomis had delivered stuff to—Lower Fork Distillery. I done a tour of the Jim Beam Distillery, in Kentucky, when I was in the service. Big place. Big buildin's. Steam comin' out the stacks. Lots a truck traffic. Plenty of cars in the parkin' lots. People comin' an' goin' like ants at a picnic.

From my side of the front gate—one of them motorized, slidin' affairs—the Lower Fork Distillery looked just about deserted. The perimeter fence was taller an' nastier than the one at the prison farm an' decorated with large NO TRESPASSING signs set every hundred feet or so. There wasn't any sign of life behind the fence, much less signs offerin' tours. There was a couple large buildings that looked like down-at-the-heels warehouses an' a smaller building—off to the side—that coulda been a office. Just one semi was parked out front. There wasn't any way I could see to contact whoever was inside—no phone at the gate or sign with phone numbers.

I got back in my squad an' made a note to call the county records clerk, when I got back to the office, 'bout who the property belonged to.

I pulled out Loomis's phone record sheet an' studied the numbers. There was one he'd called, an' got calls from, that had the same area code as the prison. So just for the hell of it, I pulled out my cell phone an' punched in the number.

After four rings, a man's voice said, "Yeah?"

"This the Lower Fork Distillery?"

"Yeah."

"This is Sheriff Homer Deters."

"Yeah?"

I wasn't sure was he questionin' my identity or askin' what I wanted so I said, "I'm callin' about a Henry Ames."

"Yeah?"

"You know 'im?"

"No."

Least the fella could say somethin' besides 'Yeah?'. I said, "Well, that's strange 'cause I got your number from his phone record. An' it shows he had a couple calls from you."

"I don't know nothin' about that. And I don't know you."

He disconnected, so I called him back.

"Yeah?"

"This is Sheriff Deters. I didn't get your name."

"Jones."

"Mr. Jones, I really need to know what Henry Ames'd be callin' you about."

"Why'n't ya ask him."

"I would if I could."

"How'd I know you're a sheriff?"

"If you come to the front gate, I'll show you my badge."

He was quiet a while, then said, "What'd Ames do?"

"Got hisself killed."

"How?"

"Truck crash."

"When?"

"How 'bout I ask the questions?"

There was another long quiet spell during which I watched a man come out of the smaller building and get in the semi.

Jones come out of his thinkin' spell an' said, "What'd you want to know?"

"What's your connection to Ames?"

"He made deliveries and hauled stuff out of here."

"What kind of stuff?"

"This is a distillery. What do you think?"

"You know him well?"

"Couldn't pick him out of a line-up."

"You have any problems with him?"

"If I did, I'd remember him."

"Is that a 'no'?"

"Yeah, that's a no. Listen, I gotta go. I got work to do." He disconnected again.

I noticed the semi was fired up an' headin' for the gate. I thought about drivin' in when the gate opened to let the truck out, but decided against it—I didn't have a search warrant or any probable cause or exigent circumstances. An' I wasn't keen on gettin' myself arrested for trespassin'.

What I *could* do, an' what I *did* do, was wait for the semi to pull out, then pull the driver over. I was out of my jurisdiction, but I was a peace officer investigatin' a homicide.

So I didn't think usin' my Mars lights to get the trucker's attention would be a chargeable offense.

When he realized I wasn't after him, the driver was pretty cooperative. He'd never met Henry Ames or Sam Loomis, or anybody else except Wilcox who worked for the distillery. Wilcox was the office manager.

"Was he talkin' to someone on the phone just now? When you pulled out?"

"Ah hunh."

"What's his full name?"

"Harry Wilcox is all I know him by."

"You see any other vehicles while you was in there?"

"Just Harry's truck."

"Where was that?"

"Back behind the office where you can't see it from the road."

"Make an' model?"

"Ford F-250."

"Color?"

"Black."

"Didn't happen to notice the license number?"

"No. Sorry."

I thanked the man an' let him get on his way. Then I went back to the distillery an' took a few snapshots of it with my crime scene camera. I debated whether it'd be worth it to wait outside the gate until quittin' time. Probably not, but I sure didn't wanna come back.

Harry "Jones" Wilcox saved me the trouble by keepin' banker's hours. A little after three, a black Ford F-250 pulled out from behind the little building an' up to the gate. The driver, a white male, pulled through it an' waited for the gate to close 'fore he drove off, givin' me plenty of time to get his license plate number. An' to call an' ask Trooper Yates to run it for me.

I gave Wilcox a half-mile lead an' followed. I was kinda surprised when he pulled up to a Cheap-Ass Likkers store an' went inside. While I was waitin' for him to come out, Yates called me back.

"That number's registered to a black Ford F-250. Belongs to Harry R. Wilcox." Yates give me Wilcox's address an' hung up.

When Wilcox come out of the liquor store, he was carrying a paper sack—why they call it package goods, I guess. He got in his truck an' drove to the address Yates just give me. The place was a two story brick colonial on at least a acre lot. There was a black Escalade an' a Mercedes S 500 parked out front. All pretty pricey for a liquor company dispatcher.

After Wilcox went inside, I parked in front an' took down the plate numbers of the yuppie-mobiles. Then I dialed the number I'd got "Jones" at earlier, the one from Loomis's phone record.

Musta been a cell phone, 'cause Wilcox come on the line. "Yeah?"

"It ain't smart to lie to the *po*lice."

• • •

I was just pullin' into the parkin' lot behind my office when Martha Rooney called.

"Homer," she said, "Mayor asked me to remind you to be on time for the town council meeting tonight. They're having that zoning hearing on the Peterman property, for that project Silas Hanson's so set against. Mayor thinks he might need some crowd control."

I said, "Ten-four," like I was on top of everything, but truth is, I'd completely forgot.

I had to interview Hanson anyway 'cause the dead Injun was found on his property. I figgered it was probably just his bad luck the remains ended up in his ditch. But it wouldn't cost nothin' to find out fer sure.

town meetin'

West Wheelin' town council meetin's is held the first Wednesday of every month—that bein' a night that don't interfere with any bowlin' leagues. Sheriff's office is required to maintain order an' provide crowd control as needed. Usually ain't much needed unless there's some pet project in the works or a zonin' matter's got the neighbors riled up.

The council generally rubber-stamps Mayor's resolutions an' appropriations—drawn up by the mayor's secretary, who really runs the town. Then they take up old business, then give members of the public a chance to air their grievances—called 'Business from the Public.' They save new business an' stuff they'd as soon not have too many people know about fer the end, by which time most everybody's got tired of all the hot air an' went home.

I was startin' to nod off when Mayor finally said, "'Fore we get to the main event, we got any business from the public?"

"We need a street light at Fool's End," Councilman

Cramer said.

Fool's End is a T-intersection along a stretch of Car Wrecks. Fools who don't stop fer the sign end up in the bottom of the ravine, an' sometimes in the cemetery.

"Sure your concern ain't mainly 'cause you sell street lights?" Mayor asked.

"We had another accident there just last week. Ask Homer."

Mayor said, "Well, Sheriff?"

"That crash had more to do with Lenny bein' under the influence than 'cause there ain't no street light."

Councilman Andrews jumped up an' said, "That's a slanderous accusation, Sheriff! How dare you accuse my client of being drunk?"

"Didn't actually say he was drunk. I said he was under the influence—mainly 'cause he blew a 0.29 on the breathalyzer."

"Allegedly blew a 0.29."

"Ain't no alleged about it, Mr. Andrews. I personally administered the test. I kin swear to it."

Andrews looked like he was fixin' to bust, so I was glad when the mayor banged his gavel an' said, "Lenny's guilt or innocence is somethin' to be determined by the courts. Meantime, this sounds like a matter for the Traffic Commission."

Sendin' somethin' to the Traffic Commission is kinda like sendin' it into the Twilight Zone. Anytime anyone makes a fuss about a traffic matter, Mayor appoints him to the commission—must be 50 or 60 members by now. Nothin' ever gets settled 'cause gettin' a quorum together is like winnin' the lottery. Anybody really wants a new traffic sign or street light just calls up the County Highway

Department. They send a engineer out to take a look, an' if he recommends somethin' they send out a crew to put it up.

Mayor looked real hard at Councilman Pappy Jackson, who piped up with, "I move we send this to the Traffic Commission."

Mayor looked around fer a second an' got it.

"All in favor?"

Six of the nine councilmen raised their hands.

"Any opposed?"

Two hands went up. Andrews's an' Cramer's.

Mayor banged his gavel and said, "Motion carried."

Cramer opened his mouth, an' Mayor pointed at him with the gavel. "I'm appointin' *you* to the Traffic Commission. You kin bring up your fool idea at the next meetin'."

Cramer looked fit to kill but he shut his mouth. Mayor glared at Andrews, who kept quiet.

Then Mayor banged his gavel as if that settled everythin'. "Moving right along, I understand we got some new business."

That was Roy Peterman's cue. He jumped up an' said, "Yes, Your Honor."

"This ain't a court a law," Mayor said. "Just Mayor'll do."

"Yes, sir. I got a proposal that'll bring life to the town an' revenue to the county. I propose annexing my farm to the town, an' changin' the zoning from agriculture to business."

"Fer what?" Pappy Jackson demanded.

"Fer a shoppin' mall. I got a anchor store all lined up."

"What'd that be?" Pappy asked.

"Cheap-Ass Likkers."

Silas Hanson

Silas Hanson was one of them thin-as-a-post fellas that could work sunup to sundown, then put away a six pack at the local choke 'n' puke 'fore goin' home to sleep. On Sundays, he favored the Baptist church. He had a wife he never talked about, an' two grown sons. Nobody'd ever seen him drunk, or heard him say a mean or angry word. Until Roy Peterman asked for that zoning change. Peterman's farm was right next to Hanson's.

Silas was one of the loudest opponents of the rezonin' plan, goin' on about how it'd ruin the best farmland in the county, promote the evils of drink, an' attract flocks a yuppies. For twenty minutes, everybody just listened gap-jawed—in his whole life Silas had never spoke so many words all at once. When he started repeatin' hisself, Mayor cut him off.

"We ain't takin' no action on this matter tonight, Silas." Mayor looked at Pappy Jackson. "I'm lookin' for a motion to table this project 'til next month. By which time Silas an'

Roy will've had plenty a chances to buttonhole the council members an' make their positions known."

Pappy Jackson sat up straight in his chair and said, "So moved."

Mars Boone, who was knowed to be a early riser, yawned an' said, "Amen." When Mayor glared at him, Mars blushed an' said, "Seconded."

"In favor?" Mayor said, an' there was a chorus of ayes. "Opposed?"

Councilman Cramer said, "I am."

"You're outnumbered, Cramer," Mayor said. "Motion carried. Let's get the hell outta here."

Silas Hanson sat lookin' like he'd been pole-axed while everybody else stampeded out. I took the opportunity to amble over an' interview him.

"'Fore you take off, Silas, I need to know what you kin tell me 'bout the skeleton turned up in your ditch."

Silas shook his head—sorrowfully it seemed to me. I waited, figurin' he was just getting' over his first town council meetin'.

Finally, he said, "Nothin' Homer. I can't be expected to keep track of every litterbug that drives past my place."

"You have any disagreements with anybody lately?"

"Just Roy Peterman."

I couldn't think why Peterman'd dump a skeleton in Silas's ditch, so I asked, "Your opposition to this zonin' request wouldn't be 'cause you got two sons who're farmers an' only one farm to leave 'em?"

"Well, of course. Peterman's place is one of the best farms in the county. Why'd anyone with two wits to rub together wanna cover it with asphalt?"

I could think of a few reasons. But I didn't want to get Silas more riled up so I kept 'em to myself.

"An' once it starts, it's all downhill," Silas added. "Next it'll be go-cart tracks, an' X-rated en'ertainment, an' ultralight airports."

"Ah hunh. Anybody you know fond of practical jokes?"

He shook his head. "Dumpin' a body in a ditch ain't a practical way to get rid of it. An' it ain't especially funny."

dead ends

Next mornin', after droppin' Skip at school, I went back to my office to catch up on my paperwork. First thing I noticed when I walked in was the new computer on my desk. Second thing was all the Post-it notes I'd had stuck up on my filin' cabinet was missin'. I turned on the computer an' a white box come on the screen askin' for my name an' password. I grabbed the phone.

"Merlin," I said when he come on the line, "how'm I s'posed to get into this thing. An' what'd you do with my Post-its?"

"Take it easy, Sheriff. Type 'Sheriff' an' 'Deters' on the password screen an' it'll let you in. If you get stuck from there, call me back an' we'll set you up with a lesson. Oh, an' I transferred your notes onto your desktop an' put the Post-its in your top desk drawer."

I hung up the phone. I fished the Post-its outta the desk drawer an' stuck 'em back up on the filin' cabinet. Then I turned off the computer an' got down to work.

Most cops hate fillin' out forms an' writin' reports. If I ain't bein' rushed, I don't mind much—gives me a chance to put the facts in order an' check was I overlookin' somethin'.

Facts was, I had two bodies—two different cases, I was pretty sure; a truck load of wild horses; an' a jackass. Not to mention Wilma Netherton's rat complaint; a peculiar distillery; an' a on-usual stranger in a plaid truck. As far as solid information goes, I had a shovelfull a chicken tracks.

Loomis's murder was the most serious problem, an' the rule in dealin' with homicides is if you don't nail the killer in the first two days, chances are you never will—the forty-eight hour rule. We was already well past forty-eight hours, so I stacked up my files on the other cases and spread out the photos I'd took at Car Wrecks and at D.W. Truck's.

'Fore I was done writin' up my report, the fax machine spit out the autopsy report. I read it over—mostly it backed up what Doc'd told me already about the cause of death. Loomis died from a head injury 'fore the fire could do him in. Small comfort. I added the report to the file.

I didn't have enough facts to know who'd cut Loomis's brake line. Best bet was someone he'd hurt or *coulda* hurt—a former friend or lover, a business associate or boss. Not likely anyone from BLM, but maybe someone else. A jilted wife or girlfriend mighta shot or stabbed or poisoned him. Probably wouldn't cut his brake line, though. That was more of a guy thing to do, 'specially in the short time between when he got locked up an' when he stole his truck back. Which left former friends an' business associates.

I rang up Sergeant Underhill an' asked him who Loomis had made his phone call to when I brung him in.

"Dunno," he said. "We tried it on the reverse directory—

it's an unlisted number—probably a cell phone."

"Who bailed him out?"

"Bail bondsman."

"You talk to the bondsman?"

"Your prisoner," Underhill said. "Your job."

"You got this bondsman's name?"

"Billy Bonds."

"You're kiddin'!"

"Deters, you ever know me to kid?"

I rung off an' started a "To Do" list: Do pick up Loomis's personal effects an' look 'em over. Do interview this Billy Bonds. An' find out the name of the lawyer that got Loomis released 'fore I had a chance to interview him. *Do* find out if Loomis really lived where his fake license said when he wasn't on the road. And who he lived *with*. Whether anybody'd seen any suspicious person hangin' 'round Truck Towing between the time D.W. towed the truck an' it was stolen from his yard. An' whether anybody seen Loomis in the vicinity of Truck Towing the night he stole back his semi an' crashed it.

That was about all I could get from what I had so far, so I shuffled all the reports an' pictures into the Loomis file and started on the John Doe file.

Nothin' jumped out at me right off. Accordin' to Doc, the killer—if there was one—had long since passed away. An' illegally dumpin' a body didn't seem like much of a 'mediate threat to the community. So I added Doc's "autopsy" report to that file an' set it aside, too.

One of the notes I'd made earlier was to check out Donatello Firenzi, so I asked our State Police dispatcher to run his plates. Then I called the Illinois State Police to see if he had any wants or warrants. Hit pay dirt there. Firenzi was wanted in Highwood, Illinois. For attempted murder. I put in a call to the Highwood Police to see how bad they wanted him.

Not very, as it turned out. After spinnin' a yarn about the most half-assed attempt to knock somebody off I'd ever heard, the Highwood detective asked me if I had Firenzi in custody.

"Hell, no. He ain't broke no laws here."

"What made you call about him?"

"Jus' checkin' up. I thought maybe he was crazy, the way he painted his truck."

"If you see him again, arrest him. We'll get an extradition order."

"I'm kinda short on time an' manpower just now. But you're welcome to come arrest 'im yourself." I hung up 'fore he could tell me what he thought a that.

Next item on my agenda was the horses an' the jackass. The feller from the BLM hadn't wasted any time sending me the fax sayin' his truckload of horses had been killed when the truck burned up in Car Wrecks. I wasn't all that sure a faxed letter was gonna cover my behind if I got rid of the horses an' the BLM decided they wanted 'em back, so I took Mr. William Smith's fax an' meandered down the hall to the County Attorney's office, where I laid out the problem to get his professional take.

He read the fax an' said, "Well, Homer, this makes it pretty clear your horses don't belong to the U.S. government. I'd say they were unclaimed property. All you have to do is put an ad in the paper three weeks running, asking the owner to come forward and claim his property. If no one does, you can auction 'em off just like anything else you've got in your lost and found."

"What if someone does claim 'em?"

"Then you present him with a bill for storage."

• • •

When I got back to my office, Rye was sittin' at my desk with the Loomis file open an' spread out all over the desk top.

"Mornin', Homer," he said.

"Rye."

Rye's of the opinion that if somethin' ain't forbidden, it's allowed. So I didn't lay into him for messin' with the file, just dropped the BLM's fax on top of the page Rye was studyin'. He looked over the fax, then held it up and waved it at me. "How'n Hell did they come up with this?"

"The *in*surance adjuster seen cow bones down in the creek bottom. 'Member when Mars Boone's prize heifer got herself stuck down there an' starved to death before he found her?" The cow'd been dead a week an' the meat was spoiled, so Mars just left the carcass to rot. That'd been a year ago. The cow was just a skeleton, now. "An' there's been a couple a road kills dumped down there recent."

"I 'member those," Rye said. "Don't see how even a city fella could mistake cow bones fer a truckload of horses."

"What about huntin' season?" Lots a cows got blown away in the fall, even ones that had COW painted on their sides in big red letters.

"Oh, yeah. Right. But them hunters is usually drunk."

I just shrugged. "Most likely the BLM don't want them horses to be alive for some reason."

Rye put the fax down, an' I axed him if anything else in

the file had jumped out at him.

"Just this." He held up my picture of the Lower Fork Distillery. "This looks more like a warehouse to me. If it's a distillery, they're makin' their likker with a replicator."

"What's a replicator?"

Rye looked at me like I was feeble-minded. "One of them gadgets on Star Trek—looks like a microwave. You put in your order an'—*vwal-la*—you got likker. Or steak an' fries, or whatever."

"Gotcha."

I shooed Rye outta my chair an' put in a call to the County Clerk to ask how I could find out about county records in another jurisdictions.

Three phone calls later, I had the name of the Lower Fork's parent company, an' a promise that they'd fax me a copy of the company's incorporation papers. ASAP. Which I took to mean sometime in the next month or so.

I called the State Police back and had 'em run the plates on Wilcox's yuppie cars—found they was registered to his wife.

I was just fixin' to take Rye out fer a policin' lesson when Martha called to say she'd located some rat dog pups— Owen Rhuddlan oughta have a couple left—an' if I hurried I could get one.

Then Nina called to ask me to drop by the post office an' take a crime report when I had a minute.

Time I got off the phone, Rye was squirmin' like he'd sat on a ant hill. "I thought you was gonna show me how to do *po*lice work."

I scooped up all the pictures an' put the Loomis file back together. "What do you think I been doin' all mornin'?"

'Fore he could answer, the lady who'd turned the horses loose stepped through the doorway.

I said, "Mornin', ma'am. May I present my new deputy, Rye Willis. Rye, this is Ms. Alice Bowne."

I could see right off she made a impression. While he was stammerin' his how-de-dos, I locked my open cases in my safe. Then I said, "What can I do for you this mornin', Ms. Bowne?"

"I'm thinking of settling in West Wheeling, Sheriff. Before I make up my mind, I'd like to look at your crime statistics."

"Sorry, ma'am. We don't have any."

"Crime?"

"Statistics."

"How can you run a police department like that? How can you budget?"

"Well, the county just budgets fer me an' the dispatcher and two part-time deputies. An' we get new vehicles every ten years or so."

"What about equipment?"

"We supply our own firearms. City Hall pays fer ammo along with paper clips an' forms. The radios is paid for. They don't wear out real often."

"How do you outrun criminals in such old cars?"

"We don't outrun 'em, we outsmart 'em."

She just shook her head.

Me an' Rye made a run for the door 'fore she could think of somethin' else to ask.

bribe

Rye was getting' antsy with all the callin' an' follow-up aspects of police work, an' I needed someone patrolin' the streets while I was out chasin' leads, so 'fore I headed for the state cop shop, I run him through the basics. Didn't have to go into too much detail 'cause he's had plenty experience with traffic stops, but I took a little more time to show him the finer points of workin' radar. We'd just set up on County C, when this silver-colored Beemer come dustin' on by. I put on the Mars lights an' pulled it over, all the while fillin' Rye in on what we was doin'.

All of which took so long, the driver got out of the car an' sauntered towards our cruiser. The guy looked kinda like Kojak—big an' bald, with a pricey pin-striped suit.

I got out an' put my hat on, an' pointed to his car. "Get back in your vehicle, sir."

"Could I just have a word with you, Sheriff?" He glanced at Rye. "In private?"

"Let's just go back to your car."

'Fore followin' the driver, I told Rye to run the plates.

I give the Beemer a look-over. Didn't see nothin' suspicious, so I asked the driver could I see his license, registration, an' proof of *in*surance. He told me the registration was over the sun visor, help myself.

That seemed a mite peculiar, so I watched him close while I checked. Didn't find the registration, though a twenty dollar bill dropped down on the seat. At that point I reached in an' took the keys outta the ignition.

"I don't see no registration."

He come over an' looked, acted like he was really surprised.

"An' you better put your money up 'fore it blows away."

Then he offered me his driver's license wrapped in a fifty dollar bill.

I told him, "Just the license, sir."

He said, "Oh, sorry," an' put the money 'n' license back in his wallet. Then he took the license out again folded up in a hundred dollar bill.

I said, "'Scuse me, sir," an' I signaled Rye to come on over.

Rye rabbited out of the cruiser. "What's up, Homer?"

"I need someone else to see this, Rye. Otherwise won't nobody believe it." I turned back to the driver an' said—real slow an' clear 'cause I figured he must be feeble-minded, "I need to see your license, registration, an' proof of *in*surance. Sir."

This time when he handed me his license, it had two hundred dollar bills wrapped around it. I took it an' offered him the money back.

He wouldn't take it. "There has to be some way we can

work this out, Sheriff."

I just shook my head an' handed the money to Rye. "Hold on to this for me."

He said, "We get to keep it, Homer?"

I give him a stern look.

Rye said, "Sorry. Sheriff. Just kiddin'."

I sighed an' shook my head. Then I looked over the license an' got out my note book. I ripped out a blank sheet an' wrote *Received from Mr. Austin Glenlake $200 confiscated for evidence.*

I gave the receipt to Glenlake an' he about shit a brick. "What's this?"

"What it says," I told him. "A receipt for yer two hundred dollars. There ain't no law against bein' a fool, so I'm chargin' you with tryin' a bribe a peace officer.

"An' I *still* need to see your registration an' proof of *in*surance."

Austin Glenlake

Austin Glenlake's driver's license seemed genuine enough. The registration also seemd to be the real deal—said the Beemer was his own. The insurance card, from a reputable company, told me he was covered for the next three months. So Glenlake offerin' me a bribe to overlook a speedin' ticket seemed kinda crazy. Made me wonder what he was wanted for.

The state police station was closer'n my office, an' they got a fingerprint set-up lets 'em run prints through N.C.I.C. in under a hour. So me an' Rye hauled Glenlake over to the state cop shop fer processin'. Trooper Yates managed to keep a straight face while he took Glenlake's pi'ture and run his prints. Watchin' the show, Rye got to shakin' so hard—tryin' not to laugh—that I had to send him out to wait in the car.

I wrote Glenlake a ticket fer speedin' an' did the paperwork fer the bribery arrest. All the while he was blowin' up like a toad. When I was done, he posted the whole $1050 bond hisself—outta his wallet.

Sergeant Underhill come in as Glenlake was drivin' outta the parkin' lot.

"Deters, you get anything from Loomis's lawyer?"

"Loomis's lawyer?" I pointed towards the road. "That guy?"

"Yeah."

"Why'n't somebody tell me?"

"Nobody can tell you anything, Deters."

I set a record gettin' out to the cruiser. Rye had it runnin'—he was amusin' hisself listenin' to the state police calls on the radio—so I just climbed in the passenger seat an' told him, "Follow that car."

"He excape, Homer?"

"More like failed to tell the whole truth an' nothin' but."

With Rye drivin', it didn't take long to run Glenlake down again.

"This is harassment," he snarled when I come up to his car.

"No, this is a murder investigation, an' you got information I need to solve it."

"You're crazy! I haven't killed anyone."

"Never said you did. But you represent Sam Loomis."

"Never heard of him."

"A.k.a. Henry Ames."

Glenlake looked like he thought I'd lost my mind, so I added, "Truck driver you got out on bail a couple days back?"

"Oh, him. What about him?"

"How long you represent him?"

"About twenty minutes."

"How's that?"

"He called me at my office. Said he'd been arrested on a

trumped-up charge and asked me to help him out. I arranged to have him charged and released on bond. That was it."

"How'd he come to call *you*?"

"Got my name from the phone directory? I don't know."

I give Glenlake my best State Trooper stare.

"He told me he was a victim of police harassment. And I can certainly see what he was talking about. If you're not going to arrest me again, I'm leaving. I'll see you in court."

Billy Bonds

I figured there was no use wastin' more time on Glenlake—he'd just claim attorney privileges. But bail bondsmen don't have 'em, so I'd get more outta the guy that bailed Loomis out.

Rye's got a arrest record nearly as long as US-41, but to the best of my knowledge, he's never spent a night in jail. I could see where he might know a bit more'n me about local bondsmen. Soon's I was back in the car I axed him, "You familiar with a feller named Billy Bonds?"

Rye's ears got two shades redder. "Why'd you ask?"

"He bailed Loomis out."

"She."

"She who?"

"Billie Bonds is a she."

"You know where we can find her?"

Rye just turned on the flashers and stepped on the gas.

• • •

He pulled over into a little strip mall that'd sprung up next to one of the exits from the interstate. It'd started out as a Shell station with a sign high enough to be spotted from the highway. Somebody'd opened a convenient store, then a cell phone shop and a bait an' ammo emporium. They was all doin' so well, some entrepreneur added four more little storefronts, three of which was still vacant. The fourth had burglar gates over the windows an' door, an' a sign that said, "Bail Bonds."

Rye stopped the car an' cut the engine. "I'll just wait out here an' keep a eye on things."

I undid my seat belt an' said, "Might as well come clean."

Rye didn't look at me. "We got history."

I waited.

Rye kept lookin' straight ahead, at Billie Bonds's front door. "Used to do occasional business with her old man— meaner'n a skunk he was—back when I was young an' inexperienced." He stole a sideways look—I guess to see how was I takin' his yarn—then he looked ahead again. "After he passed, Billie took over—she's a hard woman. I only done business with her once. Didn't turn out good."

I waited some more. But that was all he was willin' to part with.

"Guess I'll have to get the story from her, then."

Rye grinned an' undid his seat belt. "I'd like to see that."

We got outta the car an' went inside.

• • •

The woman behind the desk was a looker—hair black as anthracite, big doe eyes, pert nose, an' lips like Angelina

Jolie. What I could see of the rest of her—behind the desk an' under her Levis jacket an' boot-cut jeans—was likewise easy on the eyes.

When we come through the door, she took her scuffed cowgirl boots off the desk an' sat up straight.

"What can I do for you, officers?" Then she musta noticed one a the *officers* was Rye, 'cause her eyes got big as saucers.

"There's a first," Rye said. "Billie Bonds speechless."

She proceeded to make a liar outta him by lettin' out a string a cuss words that'd make a Jackson blush. Then she reached in her desk drawer for a Dirty Harry pistol.

I stepped sideways to her an' grabbed the barrel of the gun, twistin' it back at her, 'fore she had time to think. The pressure on her wrist made her let go.

I broke open the .44 Magnum an' emptied the chambers. I put the gun on her desk an' the cartridges in my pocket.

"Any reason I shouldn't run you in fer threatenin' a peace officer?"

"Him?" She pointed at Rye, then looked at me. "Who're you?"

"Sheriff Deters."

I could see by her expression she knew she'd made a mistake.

"I didn't mean—"

"Why'n't we just let bygones be bygones?" Rye interrupted. "I'm sure if the sheriff knew the whole story he'd understand."

She looked from Rye to me, an' her look changed to mad, then scared. She said, "Ah—"

"But we ain't got time fer ancient histr'y," Rye said.

"We're on a case an' we need yer help."

"If I can." She seemed about as happy as a cat facin' off against a big dog.

"Good," Rye said. "What is it we need to know, Homer? Sheriff."

I said, "Who bailed Sam Loomis out?"

She gimme a blank look. "Who?"

"A.k.a. Henry Ames."

She thought for a minute. "Truck driver?"

"Yeah."

"Arrested in Boone County for animal abuse?"

"That's him."

"Got no clue."

"You just put up his bail 'cause he asked you nice?"

She gimme a *don't-be-stupid* look. "Not for my own mother."

We waited.

"Somebody called and said he needed bail and I'd get my fee directly, then I should go bail him out."

"Who?"

"I don't know. Long as I get the money, I don't need to."

"What if Loomis don't show up for court?"

"He's gonna wish he was dead."

At that, Rye broke out laughin'—like to bust a gut.

I said, "Much obliged, Miz Bonds," an' hustled Rye out 'fore he got her riled up enough to kill him.

rat dog pups

On the way back to town, Rye wasn't no more forthcomin' 'bout his dealin's with Miz Bonds. I didn't push it. I dropped him at the Grassy-ass to get some lunch while I went on my own to take care of other county business.

Owen Rhuddlan was a good old boy farmer, knowed fer breedin' the best rat-dogs in the state. When I pulled up, he was settin' on his porch, scarfin' down lunch.

I got outta the car an' put on my hat to give 'im time to stow anything I wasn't s'posed to see.

Owen put down his dinner pail an' said, "What brings you to these parts, Sheriff?"

"Martha told me you might have a pup you'd part with."

"You're in luck. I just happen to have one of Jack Daniels's get I ain't sold. Had some interest, though."

Jack Daniels is Owen's Jack Russell terrier that's a lush. He got his name as a pup when he drank antifreeze. They give him Jack Daniels fer a antidote, an' he got hooked.

Owen's bitch ain't a purebred, but she comes from great

huntin' dogs on both sides, too.

"How much you askin'?"

"Two hunerd."

Some folks'd think two hundred dollars was way too much fer a mutt—'specially since you can get 'em free most anywhere. But a dog as talented as a Willis was somethin' else. I figured I could talk 'im down if I didn't rush, so I jus' nodded. "It weaned yet?"

"Barely."

"Let's have a look."

We went out to the barn, where Owen had turned one of his box stalls into a kennel. When I leaned over the door, the bitch got between me an' her litter an' growled like a momma bear for all she was no bigger'n a possum. Owen told her to lay down, which she did, still growlin'. Then he went into the stall an' come out with a puppy small enough to fit in your pocket an' cuter'n a baby duck. Owen handed him to me an' he settled into the crook of my arm like I was his mother.

I knew Owen wasn't gonna let me have this two hundred dollar dog for the fifty I had in my pocket without I promised him a favor of some sort, so I said, "What'd I have to do to get you to come down on your askin' price?"

"You offerin' to take a bribe, Sheriff?"

"You know I ain't. But there must be somethin' else you need."

He thought about it an' nodded. "Get someone to take my niece out on a date an' you can name your price."

"She must be homely as a hyena if it's worth that much."

"No. She ain't. She's just shy an' innocent."

I wondered did he mean skittish an' simple. "How

old is she?"

"Seventeen."

"She still in school?"

"When she ain't helpin' out at home."

"It might take me a while to think of somebody who ain't got a record or a serious drinkin' problem. An' I only got fifty bucks."

"I hear that. Gimme the fifty an' your word, an' you kin take the pup with you."

"What's this niece's name?"

"Cheryl."

"Your sister's kid?"

He nodded.

Owen's sister was a handsome woman and her husband wasn't bad lookin'. I figured their offspring couldn't be too homely. I shifted the pup over to my other elbow an' offered Owen my hand. "You got a deal."

We shook on it, an' I paid 'im. Then he walked me an' the pup back to my cruiser.

"Hear they're thinkin' a puttin' a new Cheap-Ass Likkers here in West Wheelin'," Owen said, as I was settlin' the pup on my front seat.

"That's the rumor."

"I been in one of them stores. Sell stuff so cheap you'd think they didn't have to pay for it."

"I hear ya."

"How'd you s'pose they do that?"

"I'd have to think on that. Much obliged fer the pup."

He just nodded. "What're you gonna call him?"

"I ain't sure. Mebbe Priceless."

. . .

Mary Lincoln come out on her porch an' offered me coffee same as last time. A few minutes later, when we was settin', dunkin' home made doughnuts, she axed, "What can I do for you today, Homer?"

"I ain't sure if you can do anything," I told her, "seein' as how you don't want to get attached to no dog."

She waited fer me to get to my point.

"Thing is, ma'am, I got this orphan pup needs a home. An' I can't take him home with me 'cause I got a mean jackass at my place'd trample him to death as soon as he look at 'im."

"I'm sure you'll find someone to take it. You must know hundreds of people in the county."

"I reckon—"

At that point, right on schedule, Priceless got tired of bein' by hisself an' started lettin' me know what he thought about it.

"What on earth is that?" Miz Lincoln asked.

I got up an' got Priceless outta the car, holdin' him like I wasn't sure I wouldn't break him. "This is the pup I was tellin' you about."

Like I figured, Miz Lincoln couldn't stand to watch me manhandle a baby dog. She charged right up an' took him from me, holdin' him like a human baby, talkin' baby talk. After a couple minutes of that I put my hands out to take him back.

"I got to be on my way, ma'am."

She give me a suspicious look, then nodded like she'd figured it out. "You thought if you could sucker me into holding this puppy, I'd offer to adopt it."

No use denyin' it. "Guilty. The way you talked about your old dog, I figured you'd do right by this one if you'd just give him a chance."

She looked like I'd just tried to stick her up. "You take me for a sucker?"

I felt my heart sink. If she wouldn't take the dog I'd have to give it to Nina. Or worse yet, Skip.

"No, ma'am. Just someone with a soft heart."

Priceless seconded my opinion by lickin' her face an' waggin' his whole body.

The look on her face softened. "It just so happens..."

I held my breath.

"... you guessed right this time. I'll take him."

"I can't tell you—"

"Don't bother. And don't even *think* of trying it again."

• • •

My next job, 'fore I could get back to real crime solvin', was to stop by Wilma Netherton's an' set her mind at ease about the rats.

"Wilma, I think we got your rat problem licked. Miz Lincoln's got one of Jack Daniels' get."

"Well," she said. "Well. The place still looks like a dump."

I shrugged. "Mebbe, but none of it's garbage. Most of it's material people'd pay money for if they needed it."

"Well, ain't it against the law to run a material yard on a farm?"

"That's something I'd have to look into."

"See that you do."

evidence by the carton

When I picked Rye up at the Grassy-ass, I got me a sandwich to go, an' we headed back to the office. There was a fella waitin' out front in a car you could tell a mile off was undercover law enforcement. I parked the cruiser in the sheriff's spot, an' he got out with a great big Charmin toilet paper carton. Rye an' I got out to see what was *that* about.

"Sheriff Deters?" the strange cop said.

"Guilty."

"You were looking into the death of Henry Ames?"

"Yessir."

He nodded. "I'm from the Oraville Police Department. We checked out Ames's residence per your request."

"Yeah?"

"We found his landlord cleaning out his room, getting ready to toss all his stuff. The Chief thought you might want to look it over." He handed me the carton.

"Much obliged."

I passed the box to Rye, an' the Oraville cop gave me

a chain of custody sheet. "According to the landlord, Ames didn't have any next of kin," he said. "When you're done with his stuff, you can pitch it."

I nodded. He started towards his car an' we turned to go into City Hall.

"Hold on a minute," the cop said.

I waited.

"That's not all." He went back to his car an' dug out another carton, which he handed to me. I peered in his window an' seen two more Charmin cartons on the back seat. The officer seen me lookin' an' said, "That's right. And there's more in the trunk."

I shook my head an' put the box I was holdin' on top of the box Rye was holdin'. "Why'n't you take these up to the office an' keep an eye on 'em?"

Rye said, "Sure thing," an' took off.

The Oraville officer stacked the cartons from the back seat on the curb next to my cruiser an' opened his trunk. Sure enough. There was three more boxes—smaller, but heavier—in there. He took 'em out, one by one, and handed 'em to me. Then he closed his trunk an' stuck out his hand.

I put down the last box an' shook, an' he got in his car.

As I watched him drive off, I wondered how was I gonna get the five boxes up to the office without losin' sight of any of 'em. I finally had to deputize two passersby to help.

Up in my office, Rye opened the boxes, one at a time, an' hauled out the contents while I took inventory.

The investigatin' officer had included a note with the chain of custody sheet, sayin' Ames's room had come furnished an' had a kitchenette, so—thankfully—there wasn't any furniture or kitchen equipment. The TP cartons was mostly clothes. We went through the pockets—found a couple lottery tickets an' receipts, a rabbit's foot, an' a roll of antacids. There was a Louisville slugger, which I'd bet Loomis never used fer playin' ball; a fishin' tackle box full of truck fuses an' replacement bulbs—stuff he used to keep his truck up; some DVDs, CDs an' video games; an' a video game player.

In all seven boxes we only found one item of interest—a small ledger book with pages labeled Nags an' Drags. There was dates, an' numbers that I figured must represent money even without any dollar signs. The numbers added up to a considerable sum, though—if it *was* money—there was no clue as to where it might be located. We hadn't found any bank books or statements, no check book or ATM card, no numbers that might lead to off-shore accounts.

"This another dead end, Homer?" Rye asked.

I shrugged. "Probably *would* be a waste of time to show his picture around Churchill Downs."

"You think 'Nags' means he was bettin' on horses?"

"Mebbe. But since we caught him haulin' horses no one seems to want to claim, my guess is he was in on some sort of horse truckin' scheme."

"What do you s'pose 'Drags' means? Drugs?"

"At this point, I have no idea."

We put everything but the ledger back in the cartons an' sealed 'em up. Then I put in a call to the state cop shop. "You got any other reports of missing or dead horses?" I asked the feller that answered the phone.

"Not that I've heard. But you'd better talk to Sergeant Underhill." He put me on hold an' I waited about five minutes 'fore I heard Underhill say, "Deters?"

"Speakin'."

"There's a state cop just over the line who collects weird. He might be able to answer your horse question." Underhill gave me his name an' phone number an' wished me luck.

. . .

Sargeant Bilford of the Kentucky State *Police* told me he'd collected reports of six other horse hijackin's or crashes endin' in horses or their carcasses turnin' up missin'. He promised to fax me his reports if I'd oblige him with a copy of my case.

His reports covered hijacks in Kentucky, Tennessee, Indiana an' southern Illinois of horses goin' to auction or dog-food plants. When I marked off the locations on my big US map, they made a circle around the nearby town of Looney.

I decided to have Rye head over there an' have a look around. Looney was a close little community—everybody, including the police chief, was first—or closer—cousins to one another, so I asked Rye to go undercover.

"What'm I supposed to be doin' there, Homer? Case the local law asks."

"House huntin'."

"Huh?"

"Lookin' at real estate. An' you got to ask about local nuisances like sewage treatment plants an' dog food factories 'cause your uncle bought next to one an' lost his shirt."

Cheap-Ass Likkers

Since I was outta leads an' tired of paperwork, I moseyed across the street to the post office to see about takin' Nina's crime report. She an' the Reverend Elroy's wife was in the middle of discussin' the new Cheap-Ass Likkers store Roy Peterman was tryna put over on the town. Bein' naturally opposed to politics, I tipped my hat an' walked right back to City Hall. But the ladies'd give me a idea. I got in my cruiser an' headed for the highway.

With my pull-over lights flashin', it took twenty minutes to get to the nearest Cheap-Ass outlet. It'd been in business a little over six months, but I'd never set foot inside. I figured it was time to see what all the hoopla was about.

The place was big an' clean' and well stocked, an' Rye was right about the prices. Everything 'cept the imported stuff seemed to be retailin' for wholesale prices. The clerk who rushed over to help me didn't look old enough to drink, much less sell likker. So, first thing, I asked to see his ID.

His driver's license looked okay, but after fallin' for

Loomis's fake Ames ID, I looked real close at the kid's.

An' sure enough, it had the same tell-tale signs.

Technically, I was outta my jurisdiction, so I put the kid's license in my shirt pocket an' pulled out my cell phone.

The kid said, "Hey!"

I held up my pointin' finger. "Just a sec."

He stood there openin' an' closin' his mouth like a fish on a dock while I rang up the State *Police*. He turned white as a fish fillet when he heard me ask for Sergeant Underhill.

When Underhill come on the line, I said, "Dan, 'member that slick counterfeit we was discussin' recently?"

The kid looked like to pass out.

"What about it?" Underhill said.

"I believe I just turned up another one."

"Where?"

I told him. He said he'd be along directly. I put the phone back in my pocket.

The kid said, "Mister, can I have my license back?"

"Sheriff."

"Sheriff?"

Just then, a guy in a white shirt wandered up. "Is there a problem?"

"You the manager?"

He nodded.

"I guess hirin' underage kids could be a problem."

"Who're you?"

"Sheriff Deters."

"You're out of your jurisdiction, sheriff. Sonny, get back to work."

"Stay put, Sonny."

'Fore the manager could mention jurisdiction again, I

told him, "Let's just call this a citizen's arrest."

The manager started wavin' his arms in the air like, *Whoa!*

I snapped my handcuffs around one of his wrists and swung his arm around behind his back 'fore he knew what hit him. I give the cuffed arm a little twitch upwards an' said, "Put your other arm behind you. An' Sonny, don't you move."

When I had the manager's second hand cuffed, I patted him down an' said, "I was just gonna arrest Sonny, but you had'a interfere."

"I didn't—"

"You got the right to remain silent."

He shut up. I pulled out the fake ID an' asked Sonny, "Where'd you get this?"

Sonny put on that stubborn, teenaged face I'd seen Skip make so many times. "At the driver's license place."

I thought I caught him sneakin' a look at the manager. "What place would that be? It wasn't the department of motor vehicles."

Sonny didn't answer.

I decided to wait for Underhill so we could separate the prisoners an' play good cop/bad cop on 'em. Meantime, I made like Sheriff Redneck—shooed all the customers outta the store an' turned the OPEN sign to CLOSED.

"You can't do this!" the manager kept sayin'.

We was *all* pretty happy to see two state cop cars pull up.

The manager greeted Underhill with, "Thank God you're here!"

Which clued Dan into what part he'd been assigned. He jumped right into his good cop act. "What seems to be the problem?"

"This guy—" the manager didn't seem willing to admit I was a peace officer. "—came in here and took Sonny's driver's license and handcuffed me."

"What do you have to say for yourself, Deters?"

"Well, Sergeant, when I'm questioning a suspect, I don't like to be threatened or interrupted."

"You're out of your jurisdiction!" The manager looked like to bust a gut. "If you even *are* a cop."

Underhill looked at him. "The *sheriff* has the right to go out of his jurisdiction to investigate crimes."

"What crime?"

I said, "Your boy, Sonny, had a phony ID in his possession."

"It looked real enough to me."

"Which is why you're not bein' arrested for hirin' a minor." I looked at Sonny. "You ain't 21, are you?"

Sonny blushed an' looked down at the floor. "I want a lawyer."

I shook my head an' looked at Underhill. "They're learnin' younger an' younger every day. Think they might be watchin' too much TV?"

• • •

When we got Sonny to the state cop shop, Underhill told me, "Deters, you're spending so much time here we're going to have to give you a desk."

"I hear that."

"How do you want to play this?"

"Let's get his date of birth an' see if he has a real license so we know are we dealin' with a minor. If we don't have to get his parents involved, we can put the fear of God in him. Mebbe he'll give up where he got that fake."

Which is how it went down. Sonny *did* have a real driver's license identical to the fake in all the particulars except his D.O.B. Under pressure, he admitted he'd got the phony ID from Lester, another kid who worked at Cheap-Ass. Lester was a real hard case with a *ex*tensive juvenile record. As for Sonny, we had forty-eight hours to hold him, so we did—to keep him from givin' Lester a heads-up.

It took about a hour to get a warrant to search Lester's premises, another hour to toss the place. We found Lester an' eighteen fake IDs he hadn't got around to delivering. Using our good cop/bad cop routine, Underhill an' I got him to give up his supplier—a computer geek in Tennessee.

Underhill passed the geek's name along to the Tennessee Department of Safety, an' started the paperwork on Sonny an' Lester.

'Fore I headed out, I said, "Tell me more about these likker heists you been havin'."

"You haven't got enough crime in your own jurisdiction?"

"Mebbe they're related."

missing mail

Friday mornin', after feedin' the jackass an' droppin' Skip at school, I finally got back to the post office to take Nina's crime report.

"Sheriff!" Nina calls me that when she's teed off.

"Yes, ma'am?"

She don't like bein' called "ma'am."

"Good thing it wasn't a murder."

"I'm here now. What can I do fer you?"

"Ain't you supposed to enforce federal laws same as county ones?"

"Yes, ma'am."

"Well, openin' other people's mail is a federal offense."

"You'd know that better'n me. You're the expert on post office matters."

"Well, take my word. It is!"

"So?"

"So somebody's been openin' someone else's mail, an' I want you to arrest 'em."

"You'll have to be a tad more specific. Who's been openin' whose mail?"

"Heck if *I* know."

Most of the time, Nina's a model of good sense an' practicality. But sometimes she gets crazy as a squirrel.

"Then how'd you know anybody's been openin' someone else's mail?" I asked.

"'Cause of this!" She handed me a bunch of catalogs an' open envelopes with the addresses tore off. "Ed Smithson found these dumped in a ditch near the Soames's driveway." Smithson is one of West Wheelin's two postal carriers. "Weren't the Soameses done it, an' it ain't their mail."

"Well, it was probably just someone too cheap an' lazy to take their trash to the dump."

"Then I want you to arrest 'em fer litterin'."

"Nina, I ain't got time for this."

"What if it's a gateway crime?"

"What do you know about gateway crimes?"

"Just what I learned from readin' your *po*lice magazines. It's a little crime that leads to bigger ones if it ain't stopped."

"How'd you figger dumpin' junk mail in a ditch—which is litterin'—is gonna lead to—What's it likely to excalate to?"

Nina shrugged. "Dumpin' bodies in a ditch?"

I just shook my head. There's no use arguin' with her when she's got her mind made up. "I'll look into it—when I got all this other crime under control."

Nina patted my arm. "I knew I could count on you, Homer."

• • •

Which may be why I found myself stoppin' a hour later when I spotted West Wheelin's other postman makin' his rounds. I rolled down my passenger's side window and said, "Hold up, Len." Then I put the cruiser in park, put on my hat, an' got out.

Len gimme a suspicious look an' said, "What's up?"

I took out my pen an' notebook an' parked my butt against the side of the cruiser. "Miz Ross ask you about the mail that was dumped in a ditch?"

I could tell by the sour look on his face she had. "I didn't have nothin' to do with that."

"I didn't say you did. That don't mean you can't shed no light on the problem."

"How?"

"She show you the stuff?"

"Yeah."

"You recognize it?"

"Mostly just regular bulk mail. Get tons of it. All the time. An' some first class envelopes. Opened."

"Anything specific you can tell me about it? Where it come from? When it shoulda been delivered?"

"It *was* delivered. A week ago. I ain't responsible for what someone done with it after that."

"Who was it from?"

"Damn near everyone—everyone sends out flyers now-a-days."

"'Member any in particular?"

"Pick'n' Save—had a good deal on box pizza. An' Best Buy."

I nodded to encourage him. I was gettin' a inklin'— something I just couldn't quite put my finger on—that I was onto somethin'.

"An' Cheap-Ass Likkers. They was sellin' Bud fer a song."

"You remember what day that was?"

"Hadda been Wednesday. That's the day the Walmart flyers always comes out."

"Anything in particular stick out about Wednesday?"

"Not that I recall."

"Thanks, Len." I handed him my card. "You think of anything that might lead to gettin' this dangerous fly dumper off the streets, I'd be obliged if you'd gimme a call."

• • •

I'd just got back to my office when Sergeant Underhill called. "Tennessee Highway Patrol picked up our counterfeiter and squeezed him 'til he squawked."

"Do tell."

"Seems he kept pretty good records, including a sale to one Henry Ames. Had Ames's picture in his computer. Care to guess who he looks like?"

"Sam Loomis?"

"Bingo. By the way, the lab's done processing the evidence in that case. When do you want to pick it up?"

I didn't. We don't have a real evidence locker at City Hall. And my office was already filled with cartons of stuff from the Loomis case.

"Any chance you could fax me a list and hold onto the stuff for the time being?"

"I guess so. But you owe me. Big time."

Rye's Looney report

Rye was done with his undercover assignment when he come into the office later that mornin'. He took off his hat an' said, "Looney don't come *near* to describin' it."

I waited.

He shook his head. "Town's just a speed bump on the state road—gas station-convenient store, hardware, Baptist church, bar, feed'n' seed, an' a little greasy spoon. Stranger sticks out like a black guy at a Klan rally 'cause every one of them Loonies looks alike. They gotta all be clones—like somethin' outta Twilight Zone."

"Set down an' start at the beginnin'."

Rye grabbed a chair an' turned it around, straddled it, an' leaned his arms on the chair back. "I done like you said—went in undercover. With a dozen jugs a White Lightnin' under a tarp in my truck."

"*That* ain't what I told you to do."

"Well, think on it, Homer. You told me to preten' I was house-huntin'. But who in his right mind'd relocate to Looney?" Don't make no sense. So I improvised. Went undercover as a moonshine man. Worked, too. Seems my reputation *pro*ceeded me. Didn't take but a hour to unload my whole inventory."

"How long'd it take you to learn what I sent you to find out?"

"Not too long. After I went through all my stock an' took orders fer future deliveries, I showed Loomis's pi'ture around. Told folks he messed with my sister an' I'd be obliged to know where I could get my hands on 'im."

"Ah huh."

"Have some faith, Homer."

"That mean you found somethin' out I can use?"

"Nobody'd seen him for a while, but he used to pass through Looney regular, deliverin' livestock to the pet food plant."

"What kinda live stock?"

"Horses, mostly."

"That musta been where he was headin' when he overshot his turnoff fer Grover. Wonder what kinda scam—"

"Why ain't whoever was s'posed to get them horses lookin' for 'em?"

"Mebbe 'cause the BLM guy sent another shipment. Problem is, the other shipment arrived almost 'fore the first one was lost. How do you s'pose he knew to do that?"

Rye grinned. "Bet Nina could beat it outta him."

"If she finds out what he was up to, she'll beat him to death." I pointed at Rye. "Don't you dare tell her."

Rye held up his hands. "I ain't crazy."

"Tell me more about this pet food plant. You didn't list it as one of the *amen*ities in Looney."

"Ain't in Looney." I waited. "It's just outside the city limits. In fact, it's across the county line. But half the Loonies work there."

"They make a lot of—What, exactly, *do* they make?"

"Some kinda special gour-met stuff. Mostly ship it overseas."

"Where overseas?"

"Loonies didn't say. But don't they eat horses in France?"

I shrugged.

"What do we do, Homer?"

I set down at my desk an' turned on my new computer. "We figure out which animal rights agency to sic on 'em. Then we get back to work findin' out who done Loomis in."

Don Firenzi

I spent the rest of the afternoon goin' over the lab reports an' the evidence list from the Loomis killin'. The list—a log book an' papers Loomis'd been carryin' when I arrested him; his keys an' fake license; an' the steering wheel an' assorted bits of his burnt-up truck—didn't add nothin' to what I knew already. The lab reports was almost as unhelpful.

One of 'em—on the truck—stated the lab rats had found another log book—half-burnt—in the cab's headliner. That sounded promisin' so I swung by an' collected it along with the official log I'd confiscated when I arrested him. Just for the hell of it, I picked up Loomis's keys too.

Back at the office, I spread newspaper over the desk top an' took the burned log out of the evidence bag. It made the whole room smell like burnt trash. I laid the book on the paper an' studied it.

It was different from the log I'd seized when I arrested Loomis. I could tell from the dates an' locations which trips he was deliverin' horses, puttin' in twice as many hours on the road as the law allowed. Same for the other trips, but there was no way to tell what he was haulin' those times 'cause there was no addresses. I had to wonder why Loomis bothered keepin' two sets of books, 'specially such confusin' ones.

I studied the keys next. One was fer the truck—no surprise there, an' one looked like a house or room key. I had the number for Loomis's landlord from the Oraville *po*lice, so I called Loomis's landlord an' asked what kind of lock Loomis'd had on his front door. Landlord named the same brand as the house key. "I switched the lock out, though," he said. "It won't fit that key no more."

"What'd you do with the old lock?"

"It's here."

"Don't s'pose you could send it to me."

"Why'd I want to do that?"

"To avoid me havin' to get a federal court order to search your premises."

"Fer what?"

"Fer evidence of a conspiracy. Ames was a alias for one Sam Loomis. An' he was involved in a interstate fraud ring."

"I didn't know—"

"Best way to clear yourself is cooperate with my investigation."

I didn't have the authority to investigate interstate anything, but I was bettin' Loomis's landlord didn't know that.

I musta guessed right, 'cause he said, "What do I gotta do?"

"Just pack up that lock an' send it to Sheriff Deters, West Wheelin' City Hall, along with a notarized statement that it was the lock you took off the door of the room you rented to Henry Ames."

"It's gotta be notarized?"

"Yeah. So if you lie in your statement we can get you fer perjury."

I could almost see him turnin' white 'fore he said, "Where do I have to go to get it notarized?"

"Any licensed notary will do—your bank or where you get your fishin' license'll be fine."

"And that'll get me off the hook?"

"Long as you don't lie."

"All right. I'll do it."

'Fore I hung up, I gave him the City Hall address an' told him to sign his name on the package tape.

One of the other keys on Loomis's ring was a Brinks key, probably fer a fancy padlock. The other looked like a safety deposit key, but there was no way to tell where either the padlock or the box might be located.

I decided to sleep on the problem. I locked the books an' keys up in my safe an' called it a night.

• • •

Saturday mornin', I let Skip sleep in. I watered the jackass an' moved him to the back fence, then picked up Nina fer breakfast.

We settled at a table at the Grassy-ass, an' Maria served coffee an' took our orders. "Homer," Nina said, "what do you know about this new guy drives a plaid truck?"

"He's wanted in Highwood, Illinois."

"Fer what?"

"'Tempted murder."

Nina's eyes widened. "How come you ain't brought him in?"

"Wasn't much of a attempt. Feller I talked to said he caught his wife sleepin' with another man an' bricked 'em into the house—covered all the doors and windows. But I don't think he was really tryin' to kill 'em 'cause he left 'em a few little holes for air."

"I see whatcha mean," Nina said.

"Weren't too bright," I added. "If he'd just shot 'em, he coulda got off on temporary insanity. He'd be a free man."

"But it's your job to arrest him," Nina said.

"No, it's the Highwood Police Department's job."

One of the things I love about Nina is she's more curious than a litter'a kittens, but she has the sense to know when to butt out. Now, she said, "He's a bricklayer?"

"Says 'Masonry' on his truck."

"Ain't Father Ernie lookin' fer somebody to tuck-point the church?"

• • •

After I dropped Nina at the post office, I took her advice an' mentioned the church tuck-point job to Firenzi. He musta followed through, 'cause just under a hour later I got a call from Father Ernie—wantin' me to check on Firenzi's background.

"Didn't he give you references?" I asked.

"Yes," Father Ernie said. "His former employer praised him, and his parish priest spoke highly of him. But Mr. Firenzi was pretty vague about why he moved here."

"Well," I said. "It's only hearsay, but I got it on good authority that he had a bit of wife trouble. Shouldn't have nothin' to do with how well he can lay bricks."

• • •

Lunchtime, I was waitin' for my take-out in a back booth at the Grassy-ass when Nina come in. I was about to say hello when Mary Lincoln followed her through the door.

Nina said, "Howdy, Mary."

Mary stopped an' shoved her hand out.

Nina shook an' pointed to a table near the window, across the room from the booth where I was hidin' out. "Can I buy you a cup a coffee?"

"That'd be very nice. Thank you."

The two of 'em sat down, an' started visitin'. I just sat there wonderin' if I should get up an' announce myself or just sneak out the back. I didn't mean to eavesdrop, but the place was nearly empty—just the two ladies, an' me, an' a few serious eaters shovelin' down their food—an' it was real quiet.

After Maria'd served coffee an' took their orders, Nina said, "You ever been married?"

"Why do you ask?" Mary said.

"I recently been asked to be a wife. I'm wonderin' what I'm gettin' into."

I wondered if Nina was gettin' cold feet.

Mary said, "Surely you have married friends you can ask."

Nina nodded. "But friends an' relations use-ly tell you what you want to hear. Strangers is more honest—when they talk to you at all. 'Sides, you're vouched for."

"By whom?"

"Father Ernie. Don't worry. He didn't spill no secrets, just said you was a Christian—that's better'n bein' a Catholic. He said you do good fer the town."

"How nice of him."

"More like just honest."

"I'm afraid I've never been married. I doubt I could give you advice."

"You ever been serious 'bout anyone?"

"Once. Long ago. Who's the lucky man?"

"Homer—Sheriff Deters."

"Congratulations. He's very nice."

Just then, Maria come out with my order. I grabbed it an' skedaddled 'fore Nina and her new best friend noticed I was listenin' in'.

dead Harlan

When I come into my office Monday mornin', I found I had a visitor—the Reverend Elroy's mother in law, Hera Latham. She stood up from the chair where the mayor's secretary had her parked an' said, "Sheriff, gypsies's come to town! You got to do somethin'."

Closest we've ever had to gypsies is some travelers come through town once. They'd filed a complaint with me when they got took for two thousand dollars by our local sleight of hand expert an' amateur card shark. Gordie MacTavish is a retired college professor an' a statistics expert who'd once confessed over a jug of White Lightnin' that he'd been banned in Las Vegas for countin' cards. When he explained to me how card countin' works, I had to wonder why they could ban him for it—seemed to me like just good card playin'. Anyway, when I told them travelers, there weren't no law 'gainst card countin' in Boone County, they left in a huff. I ain't seen a sign of 'em since.

Which is why I asked Hera how'd she knowed they

was gypsies.

"Why, she's put up a sign offerin' to do physics readings. An' she's even got a gypsy name—Madame Romany."

"Where'd you see this sign, ma'am?"

"Next door to the Grassy-ass."

I thanked Hera for doin' her civic duty. An' after she left, I put a Post-it on my filin' cabinet to remind me to follow through.

Quittin' time, I was fixin' to wander over to the post office an' invite Nina to dinner when Festus called to tell me he'd found another body in a ditch. "Looks like Harlan, Sheriff."

"I'll be right there, Festus. Don't touch nothin'."

• • •

It was Harlan all right—what was left of 'im. He was lyin' face up in the ditch, and he had a surprised look on his face—like death wasn't what he expected. He'd been a big man—six-foot-five or so—an' heavy. An' he'd had a beer gut looked like he was about to birth a bull calf. Now his body seemed smaller, like bodies always do before they start to bloat—like the dead parts are less by a considerable amount than the livin' man.

But Harlan was a *whole* lot different—seemed like half of him was missin'. It took me a minute to figure out what was wrong with this pi'ture—b'sides Harlan bein' dead. His beer gut was completely gone.

"Festus," I said. "You heard any talk lately 'bout Harlan bein' on a diet?"

"That what killed him, Sheriff?"

"Ain't likely, but he seems to've lost a lotta weight since

last time I seen 'im." I took out my cell phone an' punched in Doc Howard's number. When he come on the line, I said, "Mr. Coroner, we got a body."

"That's what you said about that Indian skeleton, Sheriff."

"This one's all here. Pretty much."

Doc sighed. Or mebbe it was just bad reception on the phone. "Give me half an hour," he said. Soon's he had the address an' directions, he hung up.

I warned Festus not to run his mouth about the case an' sent him up the road to wave off gawkers. Meantime, I set to work photographin' the scene an' collectin' evidence. Time Doc got there, I was nearly done.

Doc took a look an' shook his head. "Has the cemetery filled up since the last time I was there?"

"Not so's you'd notice. Why'd you ask?"

"People seem reluctant to make use of it lately."

"I hear that. How long you figure he's been dead?"

Doc tugged on one of Harlan's fingers, then tried to lift up his arm. The fingers was like putty, but the arm was stiff as cord wood. "Rigor has set in," he said. "And started passing off—between twelve and twenty-four hours."

I couldn't wait no longer. I tugged the edge of Harlan's shirt loose an' looked underneath. Guess I musta stepped on Doc's toes, so to speak, 'cause he said, "Do you mind?"

I ignored that. Under Harlan's shirt was a long red line of stitches where Harlan'd been cut open and sewed back together. "What do you make of this, Doc?"

Doc forgot he was pissed off as he took a close look. "The victim had surgery recently."

"That what killed him?"

Doc frowned. "I wouldn't think so." Then he got real

business-like an' said, "Ask me tomorrow. You can transport him now."

"Ain't that the coroner's job?"

"I'm deputizing *you.*"

Which is how Festus an' me come to roll Harlan into a body bag an' stow 'im in the back of Festus's squad.

• • •

First off, I had to notify the widow. Harlan an' his missus lived in a tidy white house with spot lights in the yard shinin' on old truck tires—painted blue an' white an' planted in the center with red flowers. The house had a lighted porch runnin' 'round the front an' sides. White-painted coffee cans on the steps was decorated with American flags and had the same red flowers growin' in 'em.

I parked in front an' admired the landscapin' fer a spell to give Miz Harlan time to notice she had a visitor. Then I got out an' put on my hat an' went up to the door.

Miz Harlan opened it 'fore I got onto the porch. She told the black an' white dog that was warnin' me off to be quiet, then said, "Good evening, Sheriff. What brings you out this way?"

I didn't beat around the bush. After askin' about her health, I said, "Sorry to have to break the bad news, ma'am, but Harlan's dead."

Miz Harlan's a big woman, six foot tall an' heavy. She took it pretty calm. "You sure, Sheriff?"

"Yes, ma'am."

"What of?"

"Don't know, 'xactly. He been ailin' lately?"

She got a funny look on her face—like she had two different ideas an' didn't know which one to mention.

"Just the facts, Miz Harlan."

"Harlan'd die if anyone found out—Oh, Lord!"

I guessed it'd finally hit her. Harlan *had* died.

I waited. Tears run down her cheeks, an' she sniffed like she was tryin' not to cry out loud.

Then she got herself in hand an' said, "He paid some quack down in the city to cut out all his belly fat. He figured it was the quickest way to lose weight. He was worried about his heart."

"Was he havin' problems with it?"

"No. He had a good heart." The way she said it, I didn't figure she was talkin' health-wise.

a canvass an' a autopsy

Miz Harlan told me Harlan'd gone out to work right after breakfast an' she hadn't seen him since. He didn't have any enemies she knowed of, didn't owe no money—'cept to the bank, an' nobody owed him. I waited with her 'til her family showed, 'long with Reverend Elroy an' Father Ernie. Then I started canvassin' the neighborhood.

Doin' a canvass in the country ain't no walk in the park. It's miles from one house to the next, so potential witnesses is few an' far between. When you do track 'em down, they usely ain't happy to cooperate—'specially after dark. An' they might like you well enough, but that don't mean they'll talk.

Most nobody'd seen Harlan for a couple weeks, an' not a soul had anything against him. That they'd admit to. While I was at it, I asked if they knew how our skeleton come to be in Silas Hanson's ditch. Nobody had any ideas 'bout that either, though Mother Henshaw—who was ninety an' forgetful—allowed as how Injuns lived in these parts long ago. I filed that away as interestin' but not particularly useful.

It was late, time I called it quits an' went home, tired an' hungry. The house was dark when I pulled into the drive— no Skip, but the jackass let out a "hee haw haw haw" they musta heard all the way to the interstate.

• • •

Next mornin' after we'd ate, I dropped Skip at school, then headed over to the Rooney place.

"What brings you out this way, Homer?" Martha said.

"I was wonderin' could you gimme some advice?"

"Surely, if I can. Come on in. Ben'll be glad to see you."

The three of us settled at the kitchen table with mugs of coffee an' a plate of fresh, home-made donuts. Ben don't talk since he had his stroke, but he's come to be a great listener. An' he used to own mules 'fore he was sheriff, so he an' Martha know somethin' about 'em.

"Martha, can you tell me if there's some way to get a jackass to go forward? 'Sides pullin' 'im by the tail?"

Ben gave a wide grin an' shook his head—made his whole upper body sway back an' forth.

Martha squeezed Ben's forearm, then told me, "Sometimes you have to tack 'em—like a sailboat. Pull 'em off balance to the right, then pull 'em to the left. All together, they'll take a few steps in a more-or-less forward direction. It's easier if you just train them to follow you, but that takes longer."

"I guess it would."

"You thinkin' of buyin' a jackass, Homer?"

"No way! Man'd have to be crazy. But there was a jackass in that truckload of mustangs we confiscated, an'

Mars Boone wouldn't touch it. So *I* got 'im."

Martha was too polite to comment how that made two jackasses livin' at my place. 'Stead, she said, "It sounds like you're gonna be fostering the critter for some time."

"I sure ain't gonna keep him. But I'm stuck with 'im for the time bein'."

"It might be easier, in the meantime, to hire Bello Willis to train him."

Most nobody but me knows Bello's short for Bellerophon. He's been a horse whisperer since he was eight—the first time he clapped eyes on a horse.

"I don't want to spend no more'n I hafta," I told Martha.

"Well, time is money, Homer. And it sounds like you're already spending quite a bit of time."

"You got that right. An' he's ate up my lawn—front an' back—an' half a Mrs. Shaklee's roses. I'm gonna hafta pop fer a load a hay, too."

Ben made a noise that sounded like he was stranglin'— laughin' his head off.

Martha patted my arm. "You'll figure it out, Homer. But give a thought to hiring Bello. Save yourself more aggravation."

I thanked Martha for the advice an' let her give me a bag a donuts for the office. On the way to Doc Howard's, I stopped at Mars Boone's an' arranged to have a dozen bales of hay delivered to my back yard.

• • •

Doc was nearly done, time I got to the morgue. I suited up an' joined him in the autopsy room.

"What'd I miss?" I asked him.

"The gentleman's head, heart, and liver."

"What killed him?"

"He was burked."

"Huh?"

"Someone sat on his chest so he couldn't breathe."

"That'd be murder, then."

"It would."

"Anything more you can tell me about the killin' or the killer?"

"Well, Harlan was a big man, in good health generally. Whoever did it was probably pretty large or very strong or quite heavy."

• • •

Took me a couple hours to run down Bello Willis. He was shoein' a mule for one of the sharecroppers lives on the outskirts of town. I figured either I'd come to the right place or that mule was drugged heavy 'cause it was standin' real still an' damn near holdin' its foot up fer Bello to nail the shoe in place.

I waited till he was done an' had set the next shoe in the fire to heat it 'fore I said, "Howdy, Bello."

"Afternoon, Homer. How's your jackass?"

I looked at the mule, which seemed to have gone to sleep standin' up, with one rear hoof restin' on its rim. "You ever worked with donkeys?"

"Now'n then. You lookin' to have that one you got gentled?"

"He ain't that un-gentle, just stubborn. Anything you

can do about that?"

"Only way to take the stubborn out of a jackass is to shoot him. But maybe I could train him to be more cooperative. I'd have to meet him to know for sure."

"I'd be obliged if you'd do that. ASAP."

"I guess you would be. I heard he's been auditionin' for the choir."

"Who'd you hear that from?"

Bello just grinned. "Donkeys're like cats. They won't work to please you. But they can be bribed."

"Yeah? Well, I ain't found this'n's price yet."

"I'll see what I can do."

I'd been watchin' the mule—still dozin' with his ears swingin' round like military radar dishes, an' his tail shooin' away imaginary flies. I musta looked hopeful when I said, "When can you start?"

'Cause Bello said, "I'll stop by tomorrow. But don't get your hopes up."

Nina an' Miz Harlan

What with dead bodies, mail that was missin' an' horses that wasn't, gypsies, rats, an' all the new-comers in town, I was getting' so many balls in the air I felt like a circus act. When I got into my office Wednesday mornin', I wrote a Post-it note for Harlan's case an' stuck it on my filin' cabinet, along with a reminder to find someone to take out Owen's niece. The notes made the cabinet more colorful but didn't shed much light on anything.

Next I spread my files out on my desk an' reread all the reports. Not much more I could do 'bout the dead Injun, an' the dead trucker case was already pretty cold. So I decided to concentrate on who killed Harlan.

I headed across to the post office.

Nina had a line of customers, so I staked out a spot at the end of the queue. While I waited, I amused myself by studyin' the wanted posters Nina'd gussied up to draw attention to 'em. She'd put a bonnet on a bank robber, an' wrote "D.J. Smith is a wuss," on another. An' she'd turned

Arliss McCoy's face highlighter yellow.

When it come to be my turn, I hitched my thumb towards the posters an' said, "Ain't it vandalism to deface government documents?"

Nina gimme a disgusted look. "Not if you're a government supervisor. You just come over here to her-ass me?"

I give her a "Gotcha" grin. "No, ma'am. I come over to ask what can you tell me about Harlan?"

Nina crossed her arms and leaned over the counter on her elbows. "It true you found 'im in a ditch?"

"No. Len Hartman found 'im an' flagged Festus down. Surprised he didn't report it to you yesterday."

"He knows better'n to do *anything* 'fore he finishes his route. You think it's a coincidence—Harlan bein' left in a ditch an' that ole Injun bein' found in a ditch? Think there's somebody here-abouts don't like Injuns or Injun lovers?"

"Harlan was a Injun?"

"No. But nobody knows—knew Harlan was a Injun *expert.*"

"What kinda Injuns was he expert on?"

"I dunno. Whatever kind used to live around here 'fore Ole Hickory run 'em off."

"Nina, you're a genius!"

"Well, *yeah*. Wait! What're you talkin' about?"

"Tell you later. I gotta talk to Miz Harlan."

. . .

Miz Harlan had black bunting decoratin' her porch, an' the red flowers in the tire-planters and coffee cans was dead. Seemed like Mother Nature'd decided to mourn Harlan, too, though most likely, Miz Harlan just hadn't had the heart to keep up waterin' 'em.

The front door was open a crack, and when I come up to it, the dog didn't sound the alarm—not a good sign. I rung the bell an' knocked, but didn't wait too long fore I drew my gun an' made a cautious entry.

"Miz Harlan?"

Didn't get a answer, so I went through the first floor lookin' out fer burglars or home invaders—though they usually wait for the funeral to add insult to the bereaved's injury by breakin' an' enterin'.

The place had a abandoned feel. Things were outta place and just dusty enough to embarrass a house-proud woman like Miz Harlan. No sign of the dog, either. In the kitchen, the drain-rack was empty, the sink full of dirty dishes.

"Miz Harlan?" I called out again. "You home?"

Still no one answered.

I went upstairs—two steps at a time, but careful—so as to be on balance if somethin' jumped out at me. Nothin' did.

I found Miz Harlan in a bedroom—the one she'd shared with her husband, I'd've bet. There was two dressers an' two chairs—a rocker an' a recliner. Miz Harlan was sittin' on the edge of the king-sized bed, with the dog curled up on her feet. Dog put his head up an' stared at me. Miz Harlan stared at the open closet door, still as Lot's wife. She looked like a bitty girl holdin' her blankie, but it was a man's brown suit she had smothered in a bear hug.

"Miz Harlan?"

She didn't move.

'Fore I stepped in front of her, I put my pistol away an took off my hat. "Miz Harlan?"

She come aware with a jerk. "Sheriff!"

"Yes, ma'am."

The dog jumped to his feet an' put his head on her lap, keepin' a eye on me.

"Your door was open," I said. "You okay?"

It took her a long time to say, "No, Sheriff. I'm not."

I waited. Dog whined.

After a while, Miz Harlan took a shuddery breath like someone who's all cried out. "I can't do this, Sheriff."

"What, ma'am?"

"They want me to put some clothes together for Harlan and bring them to the funeral home." She held the suit out at arm's length, then let it drop on her lap. "I can't...."

I shooed the dog away an' took the suit from her, laid it on the bed. "Lemme help you."

"Would you?"

"Sure." I pointed. "This the suit you want?"

She blinked like she didn't understand the question. I stepped over to the closet an' looked inside. The only other suit was a black one. I brought it out an' held it up. When she didn't seem to notice, I touched her arm. "You like this'n or the brown one?"

When my question finally penetrated, her eyes widened. "Lord! Harlan only wore that for funerals."

She realized what she'd just said an' buried her face in her hands, sobbing. I put the black suit down on top of the brown one and sat next to her. The dog trailed back an' put his head on her lap, an' the three of us sat there until she was cried out. When she stopped cryin' an' started snifflin', I handed her my handkerchief.

"I been with Harlan most of my life," she said. "I was

only fifteen when we tied the knot. I'm fifty-four now."

I just patted her arm.

"I don't know how I can go on."

"You got friends an' kin, ma'am. You ain't alone."

"But I can't even drive! Harlan always took me everywhere. He never seemed to mind." She dropped a hand onto the dog's head, an' he wagged his tail till his body shook them both. "Harlan was my best friend."

I didn't tell her she could learn how to drive. Or that she'd make other friends. First she'd have to learn to live without Harlan.

"You just got to take it one thing at a time, Miz Harlan. How 'bout we start with Harlan's suit?"

She sniffed an' nodded. "He hated that black suit."

"Then how 'bout we let him wear his brown one?"

"I've rumpled it all up."

"I'll run it by the cleaners. He got shoes to go with it?"

She nodded an' pointed to the closet. I dug out a pair of brown shoes an' a white shirt—thankfully the only color he'd had. The tie took longest. Harlan'd had two favorites and his widow couldn't decide which he'd want to go out in.

I said mebbe we could toss a coin for which he'd wear an' put the other in his shirt pocket. She went along with that. So Harlan's outfit was assembled.

When she went in the little girls' room to put cold water on her face, I let the dog out an' called Nina.

"How 'bout you round up some church ladies to keep a eye on Miz Harlan till she can pull herself together?"

"She tell you about the Injuns?" Nina demanded.

"Not yet."

I hung up.

When Miz Harlan came outta the little room, she seemed a mite better. So I asked her about Harlan's hobby. She brightened up considerable.

"Oh, Harlan was an expert on Native Americans. There was nothing he didn't know about the local tribe."

"He ever get into it with anybody about that?"

"I don't think so. He didn't talk about it—most people around here aren't too sympathetic."

"I hear that. He have anything to say about the Injun skeleton turned up in Silas Hanson's ditch?"

"Just that he was trying to figure out where it came from."

"Had he?"

"Not that he mentioned. But you're welcome to look through his notes if you like."

She led me to Harlan's office. It had a computer, fax an' printer, an' walls covered with maps an' pictures of Injuns and Injun artifacts—bow an' arrows, lances, beaded belts and feathered God-knows-whats.

I didn't see no notes, but Harlan'd maybe had 'em on the computer. When I asked about it, Miz Harlan said I could go through it if I liked, or take it with me. She didn't have no use for it. "I wish I could be more help, Sheriff," she said. "Harlan used to tell me about all this, but I'm afraid I didn't listen very carefully."

"You been plenty helpful, ma'am."

'Bout then, the door bell rang, an' the dog started barkin'.

"Miz Harlan, you decent?" Nina called out.

Miz Harlan said, "Oh. Company. I have to—Take as long as you like in here, Sheriff. Harlan'd be pleased you took an interest."

Mary Lincoln an' Wilma Netherton

On the way to drop off Harlan's suit, I stopped at Mary Lincoln's place to see how she an' Priceless was gettin' on. When I pulled up, they was in the yard, gardnin'. Least Mary was—pullin' weeds. Priceless was diggin' 'round the piles of junk, waitin' fer a rat to show its nose. He stopped when he spotted the cruiser, an' he started barkin' when I got out.

Mary said, "Quiet, Priceless."

An' he was. He come up to me waggin' his tail an' sniffin' my boots, then went back to his rat hunt.

I said good mornin'. Mary took off one of her gardnin' gloves an' shook my hand, then offered me coffee.

"Much as I'd love to stay, ma'am, I'm on a schedule."

She nodded an' waited.

"It occurred to me that you mighta found some old mail amongst the things you picked up off the roadways."

She shook her head. "Sorry."

"You find anything suspicious? Even a little off?"

She thought on that a minute, then nodded an' marched over to a pile of rusty metal scrap. I followed. After a minute of shiftin' stuff around, she handed me a pair of rusty old license plates. From outta state. That seemed a tad off.

"You remember where you got these, ma'am?"

"In a ditch. Down the road from the house of that man who was found dead."

"Harlan?"

"That's it."

"An' you didn't think to report you found 'em?"

"Well, no. They were expired, so I thought someone just dumped them when he got new ones."

"You mind if I take 'em?"

"Of course not. And if I find any more, I'll call you immediately."

"Much obliged."

My visit was cut short at that point by a call from Martha Rooney.

"It's Wilma again, Homer. She's called three times last hour and a half."

"Ten-four. I'll talk to her."

Martha must've got yet another call, 'cause Wilma was on the porch when I drove up. She didn't even wait till I got out of the cruiser 'fore she started in.

"Sheriff, I thought you were going to look into her—" Wilma hitched her chin towards the road. "Running an illegal material yard over there."

"An' I will. Soon's I clear up some of the serious cases I got pendin'."

"Runnin' an illegal business isn't—What serious cases?"

"I guess it ain't no secret by now. Harlan's been murdered."

Wilma's eyes got big as cow pies. "No!"

"'Fraid so. An' I'm still lookin' into that truck crash in Car Wrecks. An' Nina Ross reported someone's been stealin' mail—you wouldn't know nothin' 'bout that, would you?"

"No! No, of course not!"

"So you can see where I got a few things to take care of 'fore I can get to your problem."

Wilma looked like she'd been pole-axed. But she wasn't gonna concede. She pulled herself together and said, "How do you know some of that stuff across the street isn't stolen?"

"Don't none of it match anything I got reports about."

I thought she was gonna blow a fuse. She stood there gettin' redder an' redder, openin' an' closin' her mouth like a fish. Finally she said, "Oh you're worthless," an' stormed back into her house.

• • •

After I dropped Harlan's suit at the undertaker's, I swung by the state cop shop an' had 'em run the plates Mary Lincoln'd found. Turned out they come off one of the hijacked semis, so it seemed like I was makin' progress on somebody's case.

"You haven't lost your touch, Vergil," Sergeant Underhill told me.

"That's nice. What are we talkin' about, exactly?"

"Your hunch about Loomis's truck was right on the money."

I waited.

"Stolen from an independent over-the-road trucker a year ago. He didn't raise enough hell to keep us on point about it. Lucky for him, it was insured."

"Loomis's name ever come up in one of these liquor hijackin's?"

"Not unless he was using another alias."

"Or he just wasn't caught."

Bello Willis

Skip was stayin' over night at his cousin's an'—since my sister's even less inclined to put up with shenanigans than me—I was able to head home fer a beer an' a shower 'fore I went to spend some quality time with Nina.

When I got to my place, Bello Willis was there, leadin' the jackass around in circles an' figure eights—gettin' the critter to go forwards! Impressive. It was such a pleasin' sight, I just stood an' watched.

After a bit the jackass had enough—he planted his feet and wouldn't budge. Bello hauled off an' punched him in the shoulder.

"Hey!" I yelled.

The jackass started forward, but Bello stopped him an' just stared at me. The jackass stood patient as a carnival-ride pony as Bello yelled back, "What?!"

"What'd you hit him for?"

Bello give me a don't-you-know-nothin' look. "He's a jackass. 'Fore you can get him to listen you got to get his attention. You questionin' my work, Sheriff?"

His tone said I could get another trainer if I was, so I put my hands up an' said, "Wouldn't dream of it."

Bello nodded. "Looks like you're the one needs trainin'. Can't just anybody own a jackass. You gotta at least be smarter'n a goat."

I let that one slide.

Bellow said, "When's your next day off, Homer?"

"Sunday."

"I'll be here at seven."

"In the mornin'?"

He nodded.

Just then, Mrs. Shaklee come bustlin' outta her house with a stack of papers. "Oh, I'm glad I caught you, Sheriff. I got a eviction notice I want you to serve."

"Is that so?"

'Fore I could ask on who, she shoved the papers in my hand an' stalked back to her house.

I watched her go, then I looked at the top paper. An' I could see why she skedaddled so fast. The notice was on me, givin' me two weeks to pack up an' clear out along with my smart-mouth kid an' my big-mouth jackass. I had to read it twice 'fore I could believe it.

I looked up to see that Bello's jaw'd dropped. "I ain't never heard'a you been speechless afore, Sheriff. Mind if I have a look?"

I shook my head an' read the thing again.

Bello let go of the critter's lead rope an' took the papers outta my hand.

"Hey," I said. "He's gonna take off. An' I'll be in even deeper shit."

Bello gimme a look, then glanced at the jackass. "We got a understandin', him an' me."

I don't know was he pullin' my leg and the critter was just too stupid to notice he weren't anchored to anything, or was everything I'd always heard about Bello true. In any case, the jackass just stood like a statue until Bello finished readin' the papers an' handed 'em back.

"Ash Jackson's place is still empty, Sheriff. His pappy might make you a deal on it if you hit 'im up 'fore word gets around that you're desperate."

Bello picked up the lead rope an' started toward the back yard. He didn't even have to tug on the rope. The jackass followed him just like a old dog. An' neither of 'em give me another look.

• • •

Nina ain't a bad cook—hell, anybody can read, can cook. An' Nina sure can read. But seein' as we both work, we eat out a lot. So soon as I picked up my jaw an' had a shower, I collected Nina an' we headed fer the Truck Stop.

Hardsetter's—the truck stop's official name—was jumpin'. As usual at suppertime. Half a dozen big rig drivers was chowin' down, along with several West Wheelin' families, an' folks I figgered was refugees from the Interstate.

There wasn't any tables free, so Nina an' I took seats at the counter an' studied the menu board. Charity hustled over to take our orders.

• • •

We was halfway through our appetizers, when Rye slid in on Nina's other side. He said, "Howdy," to both of us, then asked why was I lookin' so down all of a sudden.

"You want the whole list or just the last straw?"

"Mebbe you better be specific," Nina said.

"I'm gettin' evicted."

"You? You're the one does the evictin'. How—"

"Yeah. An' I ain't figured out who killed Harlan or that trucker. Or caught the hijackers. Or found somebody to take them horses off the county's hands. An' Wilma Netherton's been ridin' me to do somethin' about her new neighbor, an' Mrs. Latham's been bitchin' about gypsies…"

"What gypsies?" Rye demanded.

"Ain't no gypsies. Mrs. Latham just don't like that new lady entrepreneur moved in next door to the Grassy-ass. Wants me to run her off."

"Well she will want," Nina said.

"Yeah, she'll get over it," Rye said. "An' Wilma'll find someone else to bitch about."

"But the horses…"

"Sell 'em," Nina said. "Ain't you allowed to do that with unclaimed property?"

"They're gonna be hard to sell if you can't put a halter on and lead 'em around a auction ring."

Rye shook his head. "So just run 'em in a truck an' haul 'em off to the dog food fact'ry."

"Rye!" Nina half shouted. She punched him on the upper arm

Rye rubbed his arm an' shook his head, but he had more sense than to complain or argue with Nina. "So what's he s'posed to do with 'em?"

"Hire Bello Willis to gentle 'em."

"Whose gonna pay fer that?" I asked.

"You can pay Bello with the money you'll get when you sell the horses."

"I doubt we'll get enough to pay Mars fer their keep, much less to hire Bello. It's costin' a hundred dollars a day."

"So—"

"Not to change the subject much, but I got a more immediate problem."

"Which is?"

"Where'm I gonna go when I evict myself in two weeks time?"

plantin' Harlan

A law enforcement rule a thumb is killers often show up at their victim's funerals. I ain't dealt with enough murders to know is that true, but on the offside chance it was in Harlan's case, I put on my Sunday suit 'fore I headed over to the funeral parlor. I didn't want my uniform to scare off whoever killed Harlan—if he decided to show up. I figured *he* was the right pronoun in this case—Harlan was a pretty big man an' there ain't many females in Boone County could pull off tippin' him over an' weightin' him down heavy enough to burke 'im.

With Festus patrolin' the streets an' Rye writin' down license plate numbers in the parkin' lot, I was free to study the folks that come to pay their respects. I brung Skip along to eavesdrop on the general gossip 'cause no one but mothers an' school teachers takes any notice of kids who ain't makin' trouble, an' I didn't figure Harlan's killer fit into either of those categories.

"I'm deputizin' you," I told Skip. "Keep a ear up fer

anyone trash-talkin' 'bout the deceased."

Skip seemed pleased as a dog with a new trick.

The viewin' was held at the Hanekamp's Funeral Home from 4 to 9 p.m. The funeral director had Harlan fixed up nice, lookin' like he really *was* sleepin'. Reverend Elroy steered Miz Harlan to a seat in the front row of chairs an' hung around for a while passin' time with his flock. Miz Harlan sobbed into her hankie while half the ladies in West Wheelin' come up to put a arm around her or to pat her on the shoulder an' offer her a Kleenex.

I kept a eye on the men.

The usual suspects was all there—Mayor an' Pappy Jackson; councilmen Cramer an' Andrews, lookin' fer votes; Roy Peterman an' Silas Hanson; an' most of the volunteer firefighters. I wasn't surprised when Father Ernie showed up, or Bello an' Merlin Willis, but I wondered what brought Don Firenzi 'cause I reckoned he hadn't been around long enough to've made Harlan's acquaintance. I knew the six local Injuns who come in together was friends of Harlan's. You could tell they was Injuns, 'cause they all had long hair—'cept Stanley Redwine who don't have any, an' five of 'em wore head bands. Stanley Redwine wore a bear claw necklace, too. 'Part from that, you'd a never guessed they wasn't six good ol' boys in Levis an' work shirts. None of the men—townsfolk or Injuns—acted 'specially broke up or suspicious. An'—Skip told me later—none of the ladies done either.

Most of the men went up front fer a look at the body. Some—Catholics mostly—crossed theirselves or kneeled down in front of the casket or both. They'd walk over to the widow an' mumble somethin' about how sorry they was or how Harlan'd be missed—even men who'd never said a word to him since grammar school. Then—'cept for the Injuns—they'd make their way out back where a jug of West Wheelin' White Lightnin' was bein' passed around.

'Bout suppertime the crowd thinned an' I had a chance to ask about Harlan's sudden popularity.

"Curiosity," Father Ernie told me. Harlan wasn't one of his flock but he always went to viewin's to offer condolences or help, or the loan of chairs or a coffee maker. "Word is that Harlan had changed quite a bit before he passed away."

"That so?"

"You can't blame people for indulging their curiosity."

"Guess not. But it makes it harder to figure out who mighta done him in. You know if anyone had a beef with him?"

Father Ernie shook his head. "I'd've said that—after Silas Hanson—he was the most innocuous man in the county."

I nodded an' changed the subject. "How's that new brick mason workin' out?"

"He did a fine job on the church so I recommended him to Reverend Elroy."

. . .

Next mornin', after droppin' Skip at school, I was back at the funeral home. Not bein' family or close friends with the deceased, I was there in my official capacity—in uniform an' in my cruiser, which I parked in front of the hearse that was stationed out front.

Reverend Elroy showed up shortly afterwards with Miz Harlan an' two of her female cousins. A few minutes later, all the Injuns that had been at the viewin' pulled up in a brand new Chevy Silverado crew cab an' piled out. I wondered was they part of the Reverend's congregation 'cause I'd never noticed 'em around on Sundays.

Elroy led the procession inside and stood by while Miz Harlan said her final goodbye to Harlan. Then they sat down an' the funeral director closed the casket.

'Bout ten o'clock, the Reverend got up in front an' said, "Harlan was a good man, a member of our congregation all his life..."

He went on like that long enough to make me wonder would he ever quit? What the widow thought of his speechifyin' was pretty clear—she sniffled an' wiped her eyes continuous. The cousins nodded an' said, "Amen," every time Elroy paused to get his breath. What the Injuns said was nothin'; so what they thought wasn't easy to guess. They sat in the second row of chairs an' looked straight ahead—didn't say a word.

When Elroy finished at last, the cousins said a very loud, "Praise the Lord!" The Injuns all nodded. I felt like praisin' the Lord myself that Elroy'd finally run outta steam.

But he wasn't done; he stood back up an' invited those present to say a word. One of the cousins went up to the front and said, "I didn't know Harlan all that well, but I ain't never heard a bad word on him." That's all she said. Then she went back to her seat.

Stanley Redwine got up but stayed standin' in front of his chair. "Harlan was a good man," he said. "A good friend of the People." Then *he* set back down.

Nobody said anything more for a good bit. When it was obvious no one else was gonna chime in, the Reverend signaled to the organist—his mother in law, Hera Latham, and she played Amazin' Grace—only a little off key.

The funeral director scarcely waited fer her to finish 'fore he motioned to the Injuns, who lined up an' carried the coffin out to the hearse.

After Harlan was securely stowed, we got in our vehicles—the Reverend Elroy in his car, Miz Harlan an' the cousins in the funeral director's limo, the Injuns in their truck, an' I led the procession out to the cemetery with my flashers blazin'. Rye an' Festus was waitin' along the route an' they got outta their cruisers an' saluted as the parade passed 'em by. All in all it was more attention than Harlan'd got in his entire life.

· · ·

The burial was a anticlimax. Everybody stood around the gravesite waitin' for instructions. Reverend Elroy said a quick prayer. The cemetery guy hit the switch to lower the casket into the hole. We all—'cept the Injuns—threw a handful of dirt in on top.

Miz Harlan insisted on watchin' the cemetery guy fill in the hole—which he started doin' with a shovel. That got old pretty quick, so he fired up his backhoe to finish up. Then the Reverend hustled Miz Harlan an' her cousins into the limo, and the rest of us got in our vehicles an' went back to work.

a burglary

"Sheriff," Martha sounded breathless. "Get out to Harlan's quick! There's been a rob'ry. Reverend Elroy sounded hysterical."

"Is the bad guy still on the premises?"

"They didn't go inside to see, thank Jesus."

Without waitin' to hear the rest, I put my flashers on an' hit the gas. An' radioed Rye an' Festus to join me at the scene.

When I got there, the Reverend was waitin' with Miz Harlan an' the cousins in Elroy's car. Elroy got out an' hurried over to meet me.

"Thank God you're here, Sheriff."

I didn't figure God had as much to do with it as Elroy did—dialin' 9-1-1—but all I said was "Burglar still around?"

Miz Harlan was outta the car by then. "The Reverend wouldn't let me go in an' see," she said. "The front door was open. So we just called you."

"Good thinkin'. You all wait here while I go in an' make sure the burglars is gone."

"Sheriff," Miz Harlan added, "my dog's missin'."

"I'll keep a eye out for him."

At that point, Rye an' Festus pulled up, an' I sent them around to watch the back while I checked inside.

On the porch, it was easy to see how the civilians knew to call. The door was part way open. The stile an' jamb was busted on the knob side, an' there was a big boot print on the center rail. I pushed the door open all the way an' entered. Carefully.

Inside, I pulled my sidearm an' cleared the first floor. Drawers an' cabinets was open, the contents rifled. Furniture'd been relocated. No sign of who done it. No dog.

Then I climbed the stairs as quiet as I could an' checked the second floor as well—same results except I found Miz Harlan's jewel box dumped out on the floor an' dresser top. I couldn't tell was anything gone, but when I went into the office, I *did* notice Harlan's computer was missin'. An' there was no sign of the dog.

It seemed to me, as I headed downstairs an' checked the cellar, that the burglar'd been pretty considerate. Most times thieves go through a place, they trash it, dumpin' everything an' smashin' stuff outta sheer cussed meanness. Nothin' here was broke but the front door.

I went out back an' told my deputies, "Ain't a robbery, just a simple house-breakin'."

Neither of 'em had any trainin' in processin' crime scenes, so I sent Festus back on patrol an' Rye out to start canvassin' the neighbors.

Back out front, I asked the Reverend an' the cousins to keep waitin' in the car while Miz Harlan come in to see if anything else was gone.

She took her time, gettin' madder by the minute—'specially when she come across her jewel box. But as she picked her baubles up from the dresser an' floor, her mad turned into puzzlement.

"I don't understand, Homer. There doesn't seem to be anything missing." She held up a small diamond ring—gold with fancy carvin' on the sides. "This is my engagement ring. Don't know why they didn't steal it. It has a real diamond."

"I'm thinkin' they wasn't after your jewels, Miz Harlan. You missin' any cash?"

"Oh, I never keep cash layin' around." She patted the handbag she had clamped firmly under her arm. "I keep it in my pocketbook."

"Yes, ma'am."

She took one more look around her room an' shook her head, then headed for Harlan's office.

"The computer's gone!" She looked around as if to catch the thief sneakin' out. "And my dog. He was on the porch when I left home this morning. Oh, if they've hurt him...."

Almost on cue, the dog started barkin', sounding pissed off but far away.

Miz Harlan was off like a shot—down the stairs an' across the yard to the barn.

She was about to open the door when I caught up.

"Wait up, Miz Harlan. Lemme get that."

I opened the door, an' the dog come out like a swarm of wet hornets. Till he spotted Miz Harlan. Then he liked to wag hisself silly sayin' hello.

· · ·

I took the break-in serious. I dusted the house for prints—weren't any—an' took a few pictures, mostly for show. Then I got on the phone to the state cops to ask 'em to keep a eye out for the missin' computer. After which I called Nina to tell her what happened—didn't even have to *ask* her to round up someone to help Miz Harlan with the broken door. Then I picked up Skip at school an' dropped him at my sister's.

"I sure hope you catch these bastards soon," he told me as he was getting outta the cruiser.

"Why? You miss takin' care of the jackass?"

"Naw. I was sorta fond of bein' a only child."

• • •

Later that evenin', when I went 10-7 fer supper at Nina's, she said, "Homer, I mentioned your housin' problem to Hazel Wrencock."

"Lord, woman, it'll be all over town by mornin'."

"Hazel can keep a secret if she thinks she'll get a commission. Don't you want to hear what she told me?"

"It matter if I do?"

Nina punched me in the arm, but not real hard. "Ash Jackson's place is on the market."

"That ain't news. It's been for sale since he bought the farm. An' Pappy Jackson wouldn't sell it to me if I was the only buyer in the state."

"He might if he didn't know it was you buyin' it."

"Like that's gonna happen."

"Hazel said you could get your lawyer to make a blind offer. Pappy don't have to know who's makin' it as long as you got the cash."

Nina knows everybody's business in West Wheelin'. So she knew I had enough saved up to buy a small place outright.

"I don't happen to have a lawyer, Nina."

"Well you could get one."

"I s'pose."

"You got something on your mind, Homer. Spit it out."

"I was just wonderin' could I get dessert with that coffee?"

Happens I could.

layin' a foundation

When I got to City Hall next mornin', Donatello Firenzi's blue plaid truck was parked out front. Firenzi was sittin' on the runnin' board, whittlin' a frog out of a stick. His big ol' coon cat was sunnin' itself on top of the pickup cab.

Firenzi spotted me an' stowed his knife an' whittlin'. "Morning, Sheriff."

I nodded. "What can I do you for, Mr. Firenzi?"

"I'd like to start by thanking you."

"For?"

"The good word you put in for me with Father Ernie. I'm not sure why because you and I have never so much as had a conversation. But I appreciate it."

I nodded an' waited.

"What made you take such a chance on a stranger?"

"No chance involved. I run your plates an' done a little background check."

I thought Firenzi turned a shade pale at that. He swallowed an' said, "Then you must have talked to the

Highwood police."

I nodded. "An' if they show up to claim you, I'm gonna hafta let 'em haul you away."

"But you're not—"

"You ain't broke no laws here I know of. An' as long as you keep your nose clean, what you done in some other jurisdiction don't concern me—if you get my drift."

"I believe I've learned my lesson."

"Good. What was that other thing you wanted to ask me?"

Firenzi looked surprised—like I'd just read his mind. But he got over it real quick an' said, "I'm looking for bricks to replace some that are missing from the Baptist church façade. I thought you might be able to point me toward someone who's tearing down a brick house or barn."

"I take it you already been to Home Depot."

"And the material yard. Neither has anything that won't stand out like a sore thumb."

I didn't have to think long to come up with somethin'. "You might could talk to Mary Lincoln—over on Route C. She's got a lot of stuff she might be lookin' to part with. Mebbe even some bricks."

Firenzi said, "Thanks, Sheriff." He peeled the cat off the cab an' stowed it inside, then drove off in the direction of County Road C.

● ● ●

Forty-five minutes later, as I was fixin' to cross the street to say howdy to Nina at the P.O., Mary Lincoln stopped her old, orange Ford in front of me. When she got out an' come around the back of the pickup, I noted she was wearin' the usual overalls an' boots, as well as man-sized leather work gloves. An' she had a orange T-shirt under her Levis jacket.

"I've got something for you, Sheriff," she said. She lifted what looked like the remains of Harlan's computer outta the truck bed an' rested it on the edge of the tailgate. "Is this the computer you're looking for?"

The thing didn't look much like the one I'd seen in Harlan's office—more like somethin' someone'd took a baseball bat to.

"Unless it's got Harlan's name on it somewheres, I can't say for sure." She nodded. "How'd you know I was lookin' for a computer?"

"The man with the plaid truck told me. Mr. Ferrari or Fernando…"

"Firenzi?"

"That sounds right."

"He say how he knew I was huntin' it?"

"He said there was a notice in the post office this morning when he went in to pick up his mail."

"I see. Where'd *you* get it?"

"At the dump."

"An' you collected it because…?"

"It should be recycled or rebuilt, or whatever they do with tech trash these days."

I wasn't sure they did anything with tech trash in Boone County 'cept bury it—whoever *they* was—but I didn't want to seem too clueless. So I just said, "Yes, ma'am."

Miz Lincoln give me a accusin' look, so I added, "Mary. I'm obliged you brought it in."

"You're welcome, Homer."

"Did you handle it without your gloves at any point?"

"No. I always wear gloves to pick things up. And I'm aware one shouldn't get fingerprints on evidence."

I nodded. "Glad to hear it."

I put on a pair of the rubber gloves that law enforcement always carries these days and relieved Miz Lincoln of the computer.

As I put it in the trunk of my cruiser, she said, "Homer, what can you tell me about Mr. Firenzi?"

"Not much. But I hear he's a pretty good bricklayer."

"I see. Well, thanks."

"Thank *you*, Mary."

She got in her truck an' drove off. I shut the trunk on my evidence and headed to the post office to see what Nina'd got up to.

• • •

There was a line at the P.O.—seemed like half a West Wheelin' was buyin' stamps or mailin' packages. I got on at the end an' amused myself readin' Nina's doctored wanted posters while I waited my turn. One of the posters was changed from "armed and dangerous" to "can't hit the broad side of a barn. Only dangerous if you're a innocent by-stander." An' one of the posters had a note added: "If you find a computer, take it to the Sheriff." That explained everything 'cept how Nina come to know what I was lookin' for.

Myra Boone was first in line with her new grandbaby on her hip. Nina ooo-ed an' ahh-ed over the kid an' got him smilin' 'fore she forked over the stamps Myra'd come in for.

Next three patrons was West Wheelin' citizens purchasin'

stamps or money orders; a feller I didn't recognize was collectin' his mail addressed to "general delivery." Nina made him show his ID an' noted the particulars 'fore she handed it over. Roy Peterman was droppin' off a box of postcards advertisin' his plan fer changin' the zonin' on his farm, an' Councilman Cramer's secretary was mailin' a certified letter.

When it come to be my turn, Nina said, "Mornin', Sheriff," just like she hardly knew me.

I looked around. Mrs. Nichols was stickin' stamps on her letters at the side counter an'—most likely—waitin' fer me to tell Nina my business.

"Mornin', Miss Ross," I said. "Pretty day, ain't it?"

Nina come back with, "It shore is." She stole a look at Mrs. Nichols 'fore she added, "How can I be of service?"

"You got any more of them American flag stamps?"

Even though she knows exactly what stamps she's got and precisely how many, Nina said, "Lemme check." She made a big enough show of huntin' 'em, that Mrs. Nichols gave up an' handed over her letters an' flounced out.

Nina said, "I thought she'd never leave," 'fore she grabbed my shirt front an' pulled me across the counter fer a kiss.

Which lasted a long time.

When we finally come up fer air, Nina asked me, "What do you need, Sheriff," an' the way she said it didn't leave no room fer doubt—I'm a lucky man! "I *know* you don't need no more stamps."

"What I need, you ain't allowed to hand out in here."

"Well, how 'bout at my place? Tonight."

"You're on. An' meanwhile you can tell me how you come to know I was lookin' fer a computer."

"Confidential informant."

"Ah hunh. Well you tell Festus next time he talks about police business to a civilian, he's gonna get time off without pay."

"You wouldn't do that."

"You wanna put money on it?"

"Festus was just tryna be helpful. An' anyway, I ain't a civilian. You deputized me, 'member?"

I nodded. "You can take that notice down." I turned to go.

She called after me, "That all you come in here for—just to harass me?"

"Naw. Came in for the kiss."

targetin' truckers

After I left the P.O., I dropped the computer Mary Lincoln'd give me off at Best Buy. I asked Merlin Willis to check if he could see was the trashed computer Harlan's an' what might be on it. At a guess, whoever damaged it was either a frustrated first-time computer user who'd lost it an' kicked it to death, or a thief who didn't know enough about computers to destroy 'lectronic evidence 'lectronically.

On the way to Best Buy, I had to pass Cheap-Ass Likkers, which made me think about my previous encounter with the manager there. I was still thinkin' 'bout it when I come outta Best Buy, so I pulled into the Cheap-Ass parkin' lot an' thought about it some more. The lot was half-full— somewhat surprisin' for the middle of a work day. I watched customers come an' go for a while. Mostly they was local folks, same ones shopped at Walmart an' Costco an' Sam's— people who love bargains or can't afford not to hunt 'em. It occurred to me I hadn't seen Cheap-Ass Likkers on Sargeant Underhill's list of hijacked shipments or heard of even one liquor store hold-up at a Cheap-Ass establishment since the chain infested our county. Curious. An' bein' inclined to satisfy my curiosity, I parked the cruiser an' went inside.

The store manager was behind the register, conferrin' with a check-out woman who looked older than Nina's granddad. When he spotted me the manager put his hands up an' spread his fingers wide.

"All my employees are legal, Sheriff. I checked their licenses with the state police."

"Glad to hear that."

He put his hands down—slowly—an' stepped out from behind the counter. The lady started ringin' up the next customer, a farmer in bib overalls an' a dirty white tee shirt.

"What do you want?" the manager asked me.

"We been havin' a whole lotta hijackin's 'round here lately. I just wondered if you-all ever been hit."

He knocked wood on the countertop an' said, "No, thank God."

I nodded, but as I walked out I wondered was he lyin'. 'Cause the countertop was made outta Formica.

• • •

Skip was leanin' against the back of a flat bed farm truck parked on the road shoulder by the West Wheelin' Grammar School drive. When he spotted my cruiser, he grabbed his backpack an' stepped to the rear passenger side door. He opened it an' threw the pack on the rear seat, then slammed the back door an' jerked open the front one.

"I'll drive."

"Day after I'm elected Pope."

Skip got in an' shut his door. "Father Ernie know you're dissin' his church like that?"

I didn't get to answer 'cause just then we was rudely interrupted by the crack of a huntin' rifle comin' from the direction of the interstate.

"Yikes!" Skip reached over to switch on the pull-over lights.

"Put your seat belt on," I said. Soon's he did, I put the pedal to the floor.

The *po*lice radio was unusually quiet as we headed for the highway. Which is pro'bly why Skip reached for the mike. I beat him to it, but I didn't use it. "No use makin' a federal case of it 'fore we know it ain't just someone huntin' varmints."

When we come in sight of the highway, I could see a familiar pick-up parked on a hill above the right-a-way. It was parallel to the road an' half hid by a stand of fence-pole trees. I let up on the accelerator an' shut off the lights.

"What're you doin'?" Skip demanded.

"Hard to sneak up on a feller all lit up like a disaster response."

"Who we sneakin' up on?"

. . .

Willy Donner was just puttin' his rifle back in the truck when we stopped behind it on the dirt road that skirted the trees.

"Hold it, Willy." I put the cruiser in park an' told Skip to stay put. I put my hat on as I got outta the car, an' put my keys in my pocket.

Willy waited with the gun restin' in the crook of his arm,

pointin' down. He looked uncomfortable as a man caught with his pants down around his ankles. He didn't look at me as he said, "What's up, Sheriff?"

I put my hand on the butt of my sidearm an' nodded at his rifle. "I'm gonna have to take that in for evidence."

"Evidence of what?"

I give him the look my Ma used on me when she caught me up to no good. "You know what."

Willy thought for a second or two, then shrugged.

I kept my eyes on his, didn't say nothin'. Eventually, he shifted the rifle an' handed it to me, stock first.

"Much obliged." I removed the shells an' put 'em in my pocket 'fore I locked the gun in my trunk. Willy followed me to the cruiser an' watched. After I closed the trunk, he kept starin' at it, like a dog does when you close the fridge on a treat.

I kept quiet an' waited. Out the corner of my eye, I could see Skip squirmin' inside the cruiser. Willy looked at Skip—no help there. Willy looked to either side of me and at my boots. He looked over at the highway, then down at his feet. He kicked the dirt of the roadbed. Finally, he glanced up at me an' said, "What?"

"Why'd you do it?" I wasn't sure what he'd done, but he didn't know that.

"I couldn't help it." I waited. "What'd they expect, puttin' them big red targets on the sides?"

What he was talkin' about hit me like a highway head-on. "I expect you to remember that there's people drivin' those trucks. An' people drivin' all around 'em. An' unless the trucks are full of bricks, your slugs could tear through the trucks and kill someone."

"Aw… I didn't think—"

"Yeah. Well I'm keepin' your gun 'til you learn to think."

"You ain't gonna arrest me?"

"Not unless someone signs a complaint."

He looked relieved, then annoyed. "What'm I gonna use to run varmints off?"

"I suggest you get a dog."

He sighed an' nodded.

"Oh. An' Willy, if anybody turns up shot in Boone County, you're gonna be at the top of my suspect list."

• • •

"Why'd you take his gun?" Skip asked me when I got back in the cruiser.

"Some people are too dumb to own a gun."

Skip ain't dumb hisself, so he knowed I wasn't gonna tell 'im what Willy done. But he wasn't gonna let it go without givin' me some grief. "How'm I gonna grow up to be a sheriff like you if you won't teach me about the job?"

"Time you're growed up enough to be sheriff, it won't be legal to be like me. 'Sides, they got schools for sheriffin'."

He slouched down in his seat and stared out the window for the rest of the trip. When we got home, he grabbed his pack outta the back seat and told me, "You'll have to take care of the jackass, Pappy. I got homework."

• • •

Merlin Willis called me 'fore I had a chance to change into my street clothes. He'd got the information off the computer.

So I headed over to Best Buy.

The machine he brought outta the back didn't look any different than the wreck I'd brought in.

I hadda ask. "Ain't that the same one?"

"Yeah. You didn't say to fix it. An' last time I hadda testify about computer evidence, the lawyers chewed my ass fer tamperin' with evidence. So I didn't turn it on. Just took out the hard drive an' copied it." He handed me a thumb drive. "You can just plug that into your office computer an' read the data off it."

"Much obliged, Merlin. What do I owe you?"

He thought on it for a minute. "A favor."

"I ain't fixin' any tickets."

He put up his hands like 'I surrender.' "Nothin' like that."

"Like what, then."

"You know any girls?"

"Most every girl in Boone County."

He blushed. "I mean—you know a girl I could fix my brother up with?"

"Which brother?" Merlin's got a half dozen. "An' don't you get hit on by every girl comes in here?"

"Bello. An' he ain't old enough to mess with any of them. 'Sides, he's shy. Girl comes around, he disappears like cash at a gun show."

I laughed out loud. Kid wasn't scared to climb aboard a buckin' bronco. Or punch a mule in the head, but he was.... "Normal," I said. "How old is Bello?"

"Sixteen."

Sixteen rang a bell. Where had I heard sixteen lately?

From someone else I owed a favor.

"Lemme get back to you on that."

. . .

I swung by the high school on my way back home. The principal was still there an' wasn't surprised to see me—way things are with kids these days, I spend a lotta time at the school.

"What is it this time, Sheriff?"

"Could I have a quick look at the last three yearbooks?"

"Is this in regard to a criminal matter?"

"Not unless curiosity's a crime."

She looked like she didn't believe me, but she took the books off her shelf an' handed 'em over. "You can sit here at my desk, Sheriff. Take as long as you like. Lock the doors on your way out."

"Thank you, ma'am."

Happens it didn't take long to find the student I was huntin'. Owen Rhuddlan's niece was quite a good-lookin' girl.

. . .

Saturday mornin', I let Skip sleep in while swung by the state cop shop.

Trooper Yates was at the front desk. When he spotted me he called out, "Heads up. Here comes trouble."

"That's Sheriff Trouble to you, Yates."

"What do you need, Sheriff?"

"You had any complaints about vehicles bein' shot at on the highway?"

He shook his head. "Not recently. You know something we oughta know?"

"I know I ain't lookin' to stir up trouble. You had

any more hijackin's?"

Yates shook his head, then knocked wood on the Formica counter.

I pointed to where he'd knocked. "Lemme know if that works."

deputy Willis makes a bust

Sunday mornin', Bello Willis showed up at one minute after seven. Skip was still in bed, an' I was up but half asleep when I opened the door.

I nodded at Bello an' glanced at the jackass—tied to the back bumper of my cruiser, eatin' the front-yard grass. When he spotted me, he let out a *hee-haw* loud enough to wake the whole neighborhood.

"Can you train him not to do that?" I asked Bello.

He laughed. "We're trainin' you today."

Which is what we did for the next hour. Gettin' a jackass to cooperate ain't much different from collarin' belligerent drunks—mostly you have to get 'em thinkin' that what you want 'em to do is their own idea. Sometimes that involves whackin' 'em with a two-by-four—or a police baton—to get their attention.

By the time Skip crawled outta the sack and stumbled out on the porch, I had the critter followin' like a pet dog, stoppin' on *whoa* an' startin' on *gee*.

Even Skip seemed impressed. "Way to go, Homer! You're smarter'n a jackass."

"You try it, Smarty-pants."

Skip musta been watchin' us out the window, 'cause he got the jackass to start, an' stop, an' walk in circles— everything but curtsy.

• • •

While Skip was walkin' the jackass around back, I axed Bello would he like breakfast or a drink.

"White Lightnin'?"

"When you're twenty-one. Meantime I got milk, water, soda, an' lemonade."

"Soda."

Skip come back then, an' I sent him inside to get us all a beverage. I wasn't unhappy when he come back an' said he was goin' back in to get breakfast. It gimme a chance to tackle Bello on a matter unrelated to four-footed critters.

"Bello, you gotta girl?"

"None of your business, Homer."

"I ain't tryna be personal. Just wonderin' if you was still fancy free."

He looked out at the front yard an' thought about it fer a while. I sipped my soda.

Finally Bello said, "I tell you, you promise not to laugh?"

I kept a perfectly straight face an' crossed my heart.

"I'm too scared to get near a girl to ask one…."

"Know just what you mean. I met Nina Ross when she was sixteen. Took me 'til last spring to get the nerve to ask her out."

Bello looked like I'd just told him I was from Mars.

"No shit?"

"On my daddy's grave. You think you're the first man got speechless around a woman?"

"I didn't think...."

"Well, you ain't."

"But why'd you care? You don't hardly know me."

"'Cause I got favor to ask."

He jus' waited, lookin' skeptical.

I said, "You know Owen Rhuddlan's niece, Cheryl."

Bello looked like he'd been gut-punched. He nodded.

"Owen axed me to find some upstandin' young feller to take her out. I figgered you fit the bill."

Bello swallowed an' said, "Ain't a feller in the whole school got the guts to even talk to *her*."

"She that dangerous? Or crazy?"

"You seen her?"

"Her pi'ture."

"She makes the most beautiful movie actress in Hollywood look like a old hag."

"She got a lotta friends?"

"I dunno."

"Well, you seen her hangin' out with anybody?"

"No."

"It ever occur to you she might be shy? An' lonely?"

That set 'im back. He though a minute an' said, "No-o."

"Well, you might find out if you ask her."

"Jus' go up an' say, 'Miss Cheryl, are you shy? Or lonely?'"

"No. Jus' go up an' say, 'Hi, Cheryl. Nice day, ain't it?' Then let her talk back. She might tell you somethin' about herself if she thought you was interested."

"Why'd she care if I was interested?"

"Well, she's a girl. An' most girls are interested in horses at some point. An' you're the local expert. Ask her if she likes horses."

"What if she says no?"

"Ask her what she *does* like. Then listen."

"An' if she says, 'Yes?'"

"Offer to take her ridin'."

"What if she don't know how to ride?"

I give him a gimme-a-break look.

"I should offer to teach her." I nodded. "But I don't know how to teach ridin'."

I give him another look. "If you can teach a jackass manners, you can teach a halfway intelligent human how to ride."

Bello chugged the rest of his soda an' handed me the can. "I'll think on it."

• • •

When Rye come in to work next mornin' he told me, "I think I got a line on your truck hijackers." He pulled his report outta my inbox an' dropped it on the desk 'fore he made hisself at home in my guest chair.

I didn't even look at it. "What's the story?"

"I was gettin' bored, jus' sittin', waitin' fer speeders to happen by, when I noticed a semi—the trailer had a new coat a paint—slowin' to avoid a car cuttin' him off. Tractor was pretty *on*remarkable—as they say. So I had another look with them nifty *bi*noculars you gimme."

Rye paused, prob'ly to let me appreciate his quick

thinkin'. I nodded an' waved my hand in a sideways circle to speed 'im along.

"Trailer didn't have no DOT numbers, an' the plate was a temporary. So I lit up an' pulled 'im over. Axed to see his papers.

"He gimme a pretty good fake license an' a *in*surance card coulda been real, an' axed me to give 'im a break 'cause he jus' picked up the trailer fer a truckin' concern, an' if he had any problems he'd be out of a job.

"I axed him to get out an' open the trailer for me. That's when he tried to rabbit an' I hadda get physical."

"You hurt 'im bad?"

Rye looked offended. "I didn't hurt 'im. Jus' turned 'im over to the state boys."

I waited fer Rye to tell me what he *did* do. He was saved from havin' to confess by the bell—the phone ringin', anyway. I put up a just-a-minute finger an' answered it. "Sheriff Deters."

"Deters, this is Yates. You want to tell me where you keep your crystal ball?"

"Might if I knew what you was talkin' about."

"When you were in here asking about hijackings you brought up Cheap-Ass Likkers."

"And?"

"They claim they got hit last night."

"You check to see they really did?"

"No, but that semi your deputy pulled over last night was full of liquor cases with Cheap-Ass shipping labels."

"Ain't that a coincidence."

"How's that?"

"Just day before yesterday, their manager tole me they'd

never been held up."

"And I take it you don't believe in coincidence?"

"Sure I do. An' UFOs, an' honest politicians. An' that Elvis is alive an' workin' at 7-11. Them shippin' labels say where the goods was comin' from?"

"No, but you're telling me to look into Cheap-Ass Likkers. I can take a hint. Thanks for the heads up."

He hung up an' I told Rye what he'd said.

"Myself," Rye said, "I was beginin' to think they'd made a deal with the devil."

"How's that?"

"Think about it. What else can you make of a chain that can sell goods below Walmart? The only outfit around here never gets hijacked?"

"I see what you mean."

"Actually, Homer," he added. "Cheap-Ass Likkers *is* the devil."

pinnin' down a case

I couldn't help myself. Even though the truck hijackin's was the state cops' business, I kept thinkin' about 'em. And wonderin' how they related to my barbecued trucker an' the Lower Fork Distillery.

George Usher, the County Attorney was havin' lunch at the Grassy-ass when I finally run him down. I waited till he lowered his mornin' paper 'fore I moseyed over with my coffee mug an' set down across the table.

I could tell he weren't happy to see me even before he said, "What is it you want, Sheriff?"

"There's a distillery just this side of the county line that seems to be makin' likker outta thin air an' water. Don't guess I could get a warrant to search the place?"

"Not without probable cause. What's it to you if someone's makin' moonshine? You aren't ATF."

"Well, might be hard to convince a jury, but a trucker who was usin' a alias 'cause he lost his license was workin' for this outfit. He was murdered after bein' caught in some scheme I ain't figured out yet, which mighta involved a stolen truck he was drivin' with phony papers."

"Was the trucker on or about the premises you're so hot to search when he was killed?"

"Nope."

"Was there evidence that this company was involved in his death?"

"Nothin' concrete."

County Attorney shook his head. "You got too many might-ases and maybes, Homer. Come back when you got the scheme figured out for sure, and I maybe, might, possibly can get you a warrant."

• • •

Right after I finished my sack lunch, I locked up my office an' headed over to the state cop shop.

When I asked at the desk fer Sergeant Underhill, the trooper on duty directed me back to his office. The sergeant was at his desk, sittin' back in his chair, feet up, studyin' the big area map on the wall next to his desk. He'd marked all the likker truck hijack locations with red push pins. Perfect. I set down across from him an' pointed to the map.

"Think you could mark all the local Cheap-Ass stores with a different color?"

"I could if I had a reason."

"Humor me."

Underhill shrugged. He pulled up a list of the store locations on his computer screen an' marked 'em on the wall map with green pins. "What're we seeing here?" he asked when he was done.

"Seems like more'n a coincidence that this Lower Fork Distillery is central to all them Cheap-Ass Likkers stores. Whose delivery trucks ain't been hijacked. 'Till I asked if they'd had a hijackin'."

Underhill looked thoughtful. "And it's central to all the other liquor stores whose trucks *have* been hit."

I nodded. "Do tell. But how'd we prove anythin'?"

"Yeah. This guy your deputy just nailed is well versed in the art of demanding a lawyer. He's never gonna talk. So any case we could make would be purely circumstantial. And Cheap-Ass Likkers's general manager swears he's not missing a shipment."

"That's only 'cause he didn't check with his bosses 'fore you asked him about it. If he was smart, he'd a claimed he'd been hijacked. That'd divert suspicion *and* he coulda got his shipment back." I stared at the red and green push pins on the map tryna get the cuffs on a idea.

"Too bad we don't know where the hijackers might hit next," Underhill said. "We could set up to catch them in the act."

"Good idea. You got any other color pins?"

"For?"

"I wanna play pin the tail on the varmints."

He shook his head like I was hopeless but he dug out a box of different colored pins. "Anything else you need?"

I waved a circle around the map we'd been decoratin'. "How 'bout a list of all the stores in this area that sell likker?"

He picked up his phone. "Let me see what the state liquor board has."

While Underhill made his call, I got up an' studied the map. Most of the stores whose trucks got jacked was close enough to the interstate for a quick'n' dirty get-away. An' the Cheap-Ass stores was all close to a highway exit or a high-traffic mall or the main drag of a fairly prosperous town.

Underhill left the room for a minute. When he come back, he dropped a pile of papers on his desk, then set down an' shoved three pages of addresses my way. "We don't have the manpower to stake out all these places," he said, leafin' through the pages he'd kept fer himself. "Not even those that haven't been hit yet."

I glanced at the pages an' handed 'em back. "Mebbe we don't hafta stake out too many."

He sat back and took a just-show-me pose.

I started pullin' white pins outta the box, shovin' 'em his way. "Start markin' the addresses of the stores that ain't been hit."

He only had to think a second on that. When he'd used up all the white pins and a few yellow ones, we studied the distribution.

He pointed at the white pins. "Most of these are pretty isolated."

I swapped a few of the white pins fer yellow ones.

"Except for those you just changed," he added.

"And?"

"And *those* have the same approach/escape characteristics as the stores whose deliveries *have* been hit."

"Just what I was thinkin'."

"So we'll only need five or six surveillance teams to cover them."

I nodded.

"Vergil, you *are* a genius!"

I didn't comment on that—seemed like pretty standard

*po*lice work to me.

"How long do you think we'll have to stake out these places?" Underhill said.

"How long between hits so far?"

"About two weeks."

"How long since the last one?"

"Ten days—if you don't count the truck your deputy stopped, which nobody reported hijacked."

"There you go." I stood up an' put on my hat. "Have fun."

a Injun raid an' misdemeanor court

Wilma Netherton was standin' on her porch next mornin', gettin' redder by the minute. I stood at the bottom of her porch steps, wishin' I'd put on my bullet-proof vest 'cause Wilma's words was comin' at me like triple-ought buck shot.

"Sheriff, you got to do something!"

"I have," I said. "Like I told you, Miz Lincoln's got herself a rat dog. Not only ain't there no rats across the road, there ain't gonna be."

"That's not what I called about."

I waited.

"That whole place is an eyesore."

"Ma'am, if ugly was again' the law, half a Boone County'd be in jail."

I wasn't sure makin' Miz Lincoln's house "disappear" would satisfy Wilma, but I thought long an' hard on how to do it as I drove back to town.

• • •

If that wasn't enough excitement fer one day, the phone started ringin' soon's I got back to my office. When I picked up, Mayor's secretary said, "Homer, there's a band of Injuns headed your way. An' they're all madder'n Geronimo."

'Bout ten seconds after I hung up, my door flew open, an' half a dozen men swarmed in—five of the six Injuns from Harlan's funeral an' their lawyer. The Injuns was dressed in cotton shirts, Levis, an' work boots. The lawyer wore sunglasses an' a three-piece *I*talian suit so shiny it like to give me eye strain.

I stood up but stayed behind my desk. "Afternoon, gents. What kin I do fer you?"

The lawyer done the talkin'. "It's come to our attention that you've got the remains of a Native American in your possession."

"I wouldn't say that, exactly."

"What would you say? Exactly?"

"I got human skeletal remains that was illegally dumped in a ditch, which is a crime. When I get who did it, I'll see the remains is properly buried."

Stanley Redwine piped in, "That's not good enough, Sheriff. Those remains are our ancestor. We want them back."

"You sayin' you lost 'em?"

"No, of course not."

"You got some way to prove you're related?"

The lawyer said, "DNA tests will show—"

"When they do, I'll consider your request." I didn't think it'd be a good time to bring up the question of who might be gonna pay fer a DNA test.

"We need the remains to do the test."

"Like I said, when I get who dumped 'em, I'll be happy to talk about it. Meantime, the remains is evidence."

"We'll see about that."

Soon's they were out the door, I got our local circuit court judge on the phone.

"Can someone get a writ a habeas corpus fer a corpse?"

"That would depend on the circumstances."

I s'plained about the John Doe case an' the judge said, "I think you're on fairly solid ground, Homer, but that won't stop them from filing a motion to get possession of the bones."

"With any luck, I'll have the case solved 'fore that."

Before I could hang up, the judge said, "By the way, Homer. There was a lawyer in here earlier asking for a subpoena."

"And?"

"He's suing you for harassment."

"Do tell. What'd you advise me to do about it?"

"I'm a judge. I can't advise you. You need to get yourself a lawyer."

"I'm in the middle of a murder investigation, Judge. Actually, two murder cases an' a body dumpin' an' a burglary. An' Nina's got me lookin' into a mail hijackin'. I ain't got the time." I didn't add, or the money, 'cause I didn't think it'd be relevant.

"Well, then, if I were your lawyer, I'd advise you to avoid being served."

"An' if you was my lawyer, I'd say I 'preciate the advice."

I spent the rest of the afternoon wonderin' what I was gonna do fer housing in another week. An' what to do about Wilma Netherton's complaints.

. . .

Next mornin' I was on my way to court, to testify against all the law-beaters I'd ticketed last month. Right in front of the court house, before God an' half the speeders in Boone County, Ed Smithson hocked an' landed a goober the size of a fried egg on the street.

I grabbed my ticket book an' rolled down the window of my cruiser. "Hold up, Ed."

He stopped; I got out an' started writin'.

Ed said, "What'd I do?"

I pointed to the slop on the pavement. "I s'pose, technically, that's litterin'."

"You crazy? Man's got a God-given right to hawk now an' then."

"Mebbe, but spittin' in public's unsanitary an' again' the law."

He made a 'gimme-a-break' face an' said, "Camels spit an' cobras spit."

"So do cads—an' them last two're low critters. What's yer point?"

"It's my constitutional right!"

I handed him the ticket. "You show me where it says so in the Constitution, an' I'll tear this up."

"I ain't votin' for you next time around."

I just shook my head an' parked my cruiser.

When I got inside the courthouse, I seen Roy Kilgore sittin' in the front pew, an' I got a inspiration. Kilgore didn't bother to contest his citation fer litterin'. Hell, he'd dumped all the trash from his car right in front of the court house to protest the last sentence the judge handed him fer litterin'—

musta been thirty witnesses. The judge always made him do community service—highway litter pick up, an' since he was in court fer somethin' nearly every month, there wasn't all that much litter left to collect. 'Specially with Miz Lincoln on the job. So mebbe he figgered on a light sentence this time, too.

If so, he figgered wrong.

'Fore the judge could pronounce his usual sentence, I stood up an' asked could I have a word.

His honor musta been gettin' tired of Kilgore, too, 'cause he said, "Sure, Homer. Shoot."

"We pretty much got a handle on the litter problem, your Honor. An' Mr. Kilgore don't seem to be gettin' the point. Mebbe we oughta try givin' him a couple days hard labor."

"What did you have in mind?"

As I told him, I could see his smile gettin' brighter an' brighter. An' Kilgore looked glummer an' glummer.

Which is how—a hour later—I come to be supervisin' while Kilgore dug in a line a bushes on the parkway in front of Mary Lincoln's house.

Just before I finished up at Mary Lincoln's, I got a call on my cell from my sister Penny.

"Homer, I can't watch Skip for you tonight. Junior's in a play at school and I don't have a ticket for Skip. The school is *not* going to let him in without one."

"Well, thanks anyway, Penny."

"You're *not* leaving him home alone."

Since Penny's in charge of the county's child welfare services, I said, "'Course not," even though Skip is thirteen, an' that's old enough to babysit younger kids. Anyway, he wouldn't be home alone—there was the jackass.

• • •

When Rye come in off his shift, I was unwindin' in my office with two fingers of West Wheelin' White Lightnin'. I figured it was close enough to quittin' time to ask him to join me. He poured hisself a stiff one an' set down an' put his feet up on my desk.

After a spell, I said, "Rye, what's your opinion of Cheap-Ass Likkers's business model?"

"Classic, Homer. Jus' like them big box stores. They come in an' undercut the locals, put 'em out of business. Then they can charge what they like."

"'Cept, could be, Cheap-Ass don't have to pay fer their inventory."

"No shit! No wonder I can't compete."

further investigatin'

After Rye took off, it come to me that my BBQed trucker, Sam Loomis, had stole back his own truck 'cause he musta knowed sooner or later we'd be onto his fake IDs and the fact that his truck was stolen property. I wondered how he thought he could get away with it—a semi's pretty hard to hide. But then again, he *had* got away with it. The whole two years he'd been drivin' it. An' someone—or a ring of someones—had been makin' big rigs disappear pretty regular. All of which made me wonder if Loomis'd had anything to do with *that*.

I still hadn't located any of the money he musta made by drivin' twice as many hours as the law allowed an' sellin' stolen horses to the pet food fact'ry. Unless he was gamblin' it all away, he musta stashed it somewhere. His safety deposit key—which'd been settin' in my office safe fer two weeks—was a big clue, though followin' it was gonna be a tad difficult. It didn't have no bank name on it, an' my investigation hadn't turned up a check book or debit card or mention of any bank.

I pulled out all the papers I had, an' went over 'em again. A monthly receipt from a Leonard's Garage gimme pause. It had a phone number on it, so I called an' asked fer Leonard.

"You got him."

"You happen to know a Sam Loomis?"

"Who *is* this?"

"Sheriff Deters, Boone County."

"Why're *you* asking fer this Loomis?"

"Police business. You know 'im?"

"No."

"How 'bout a Henry Ames?"

"What's *he* done?"

"Got hisself killed."

"Aw, shit!"

"Friend of yours?"

"Naw. He owes me—owed me—two months' rent."

"Fer what?"

"Parkin' his pickup truck in my garage."

"You still got it?"

"Till he settles up."

"Well that truck may contain evidence of who killed him. Be obliged if you'd just keep it safe 'til I have a chance to go over it."

"An' confiscate it?"

"Only if it can prove who killed him. An' even then, only 'til after the trial."

"What about the contents?"

"You got a mechanic's lien on anything that ain't evidence."

"When you comin' to look?"

I checked my watch—'bout time to fetch Skip from school. An' I didn't want to keep him up half the night with police business. So I said, "First thing tomorrow."

"That a promise?"

"Yessir. An' I hope when I get there, I don't find your fingerprints inside the truck. Or signs you been into it lately."

"Why's that?"

"It'd make you a accessory after the fact."

"Well I didn't kill him—I can't collect rent from a dead guy."

"Yeah. Well, he was mixed up in some bad shit. Which is why he was killed."

• • •

Skip wasn't anywhere in sight when I got to the junior high. I called his cell an' his home room teacher answered.

"Skip's got detention, Sheriff."

I couldn't keep my disappointment outta my voice. "What'd he do?"

"He locked a classmate in a locker."

"The kid okay?"

"He is, but Skip needs to understand that's not an acceptable way to settle a dispute."

I sighed. Real loud. So she could hear I wasn't questionin' what she said. "I hear you. What time's he detained 'til?"

"Five-thirty. And please be punctual. My husband's coming for me at five-forty-five."

"Ten-four."

It occurred to me I hadn't clapped eyes on the county's new horses since Mars Boone hauled 'em off. Since I had two hours to kill, I decided I oughta swing by an' have a look. Time I pulled outta the junior high drive, I had another thought an' I detoured past the high school.

. . .

I had to use my phone to locate Bello Willis; he agreed to meet me in twenty minutes 'round behind the school. Guess he wasn't keen on explainin' to his buddies why he was talkin' to the Law.

I pulled off on the back service drive an' cut the engine— made like I was workin' radar. After a bit, Bello opened the front passenger door, slid into the seat, an' scrunched down so only the top of his head was showin'.

"What'd you need, Sheriff?"

Since we was already on a first-name basis, I figured "Sheriff" was his way of lettin' me know he didn't appreciate bein' contacted at school. An' I guessed I'd have to arrange bus service fer Skip when he moved up to ninth grade.

"Just wonderin' if you was makin' progress with Cheryl."

"Why you takin' such a interest in my personal life all of a sudden?"

I just shrugged an' waited.

"I got as far as askin' her if she likes horses."

"And?"

"I'm stuck again. She does, but I don't happen to have a horse just now."

I said. "How'd you like me to *give* you a horse?"

"Why'd you wanna do that?" Obviously, the kid wasn't born yesterday.

"Well, happens I got a few more horses than I know

what to do with."

"An' you're just gonna gimme one?"

"I was thinkin' more along the lines of you could have one if you do me a favor."

"I knew it. Rye said you're the sharpest horse trader in the state. I didn't know he was talkin' real horses, though. What kinda favor?"

"You heard about them mustangs the county got saddled with?"

"Ye-ah."

"You been out to see 'em yet?"

"Nah. My truck's broke. Boone's is too far to walk fer horses so poor nobody'll even claim 'em."

"I gotta go out an' check on 'em. How 'bout you come along an' gimme a expert opinion on whether we oughta sell 'em fer dog food."

That got 'im. "You can't do that! Not horses!"

I shook my head. "May not have a choice. They're mustangs—wild animals. Can't sell 'em fer ridin' horses. An' there ain't enough yuppies 'round here to sucker into buyin' 'em fer pets. Hell, they ain't even broke to lead."

"Let's go see 'em. I'll bet you fifty bucks I can have the lot of 'em—how many is there?"

"Two dozen."

"I can have 'em all followin' like carnival-ride ponies in a week."

"Is that a fact?"

"Damn straight!" He gimme a closer look an' got a God a damn-you-! expression on his face. "You been plannin' on that, ain't you? You knew if I thought you was gonna…"

"You're the horse whisperer. If you can't make somethin'

of 'em, they're just dog meat."

He shook his head.

"Look, Bello. You need a horse or two. I need them nags gentled enough to auction off by Oktoberfest. If you can do that, you can have your pick of the bunch—any two you like."

He got a stubborn look on his face but finally said, "I better look at 'em 'fore I make any promises."

"Just you, Ace."

I dropped Bello off at the high school an' swung by the junior high to pick up Skip, who was waitin' on the school's front steps. He dragged hisself over to the cruiser an' got in an' put on his seat belt without lookin' at me.

I didn't say nothin'. I also didn't start the engine.

After a long silence, Skip said, "*What?*"

"You plannin' to explain?"

"I done my time. I don't hafta talk about it."

I didn't see any point in arguin', so I started the car an' headed toward the highway.

"Where we goin'?" Skip demanded.

"To work."

He looked like he wanted to ask about it, but just shook his head an' slumped down in his seat.

• • •

It was gettin' on dark when I spotted a semi pulled off on a side road not far from the Interstate exit. Wouldn't a crossed my notice if we hadn't had so many hijackin's of late.

I pulled up behind it, put on my pull-over lights an' got outta the car.

"Stay put," I told Skip. "An' call fer back-up."

"Who's on tonight?"

"*I* am. So call the state cops."

"Ten-four."

I put my hand on my gun butt an' walked around the curb-side of the truck, got as far forward as the fifth wheel an' stopped dead. I started to pull my gun, but I was distracted by what I was seein'—the trailer's landin' gear was deployed an' the tractor's brake lines disconnected. Seemed like I'd caught someone in the middle of detachin' the payload.

'Fore I got my weapon clear of my holster, I was further distracted by the sound of a pistol bein' cocked. An' a round bein' chambered in a semi-automatic. An' a gravelly voice demandin' that I—

"Freeze!"

I froze.

"Put your hands up an' turn around. Slow!"

I done what the voice said an' found myself starin' down the barrel of a 9 mm semi-auto. An' outta the corner of my eye, I seen two other pistols pointed my way—a old fashioned Colt .45 an' a .25 caliber Saturday night special.

"Looks like your luck just ran out, Marshal," the gravel-voiced bad guy told me. White guy, five-eight or so, with brown eyes an' yellow hair. If he hadn't had a beak like a eagle, I'd a took him fer one of the Jackson clan. He was wearin' coveralls—like a mechanic at some fancy car dealership. They all was.

I said, "Sheriff."

"Huh?"

"I ain't a marshal. I'm the sheriff. An' you-all got some explainin' to do."

He stepped around to my right side an' poked me in the ribs with his gun. "I don't have time for comedy." He took my sidearm an' stepped way back, shovin' my gun in his belt. Then he pointed at the ditch between the truck an' the field next to the road. "Get over there."

The other two turkeys put their guns in their waist-bands an' watched the show. I took my time, hopin' Skip'd got through to the state boys, an' that he had the sense to stay outta sight.

Unfortunately, the truck was only three good steps from the ditch. Took just a second 'fore I come up against it an' turned to face the firing squad.

Leader pointed his pistol at me one-handed, arm's length an' sideways—like some TV gangster. I had to fight myself not to laugh.

His finger tightened on the trigger. "Your luck just ran out, *Sheriff*."

The unmistakable sound of someone pumpin' a shotgun made his jaw drop. Everybody turned toward the sound. An' froze.

"Drop your weapons!" Backed up by the shotgun—my shotgun—Skip shoulda been terrifyin'. He had the gun to his shoulder an' his finger on the trigger. His feet was nearly shoulder width apart, left one slightly fo'ward. He stared at the leader with both eyes wide an' hard.

But Skip's only thirteen. All three bad guys laughed.

"You got to be kiddin', boy," the leader said.

Skip kept the gun on *him*.

"Not boy, asshole! Skip *Jackson*."

It was the first time in six months I'd heard him admit to bein' related to the badass Jacksons. He was signed up at school as Skip Deters.

Leader hesitated just a second 'fore he said, "You gonna shoot *all* of us?"

The other two took the hint an' started movin' away from each other.

Skip held the shotgun perfectly still, pointed straight at the leader's chest. "Just you, Ace."

Skip looked meaner than a baby rattler, an' all eyes was on him. None of 'em was really payin' me no mind. Which give me the chance to step toward the nearest badass an' drop him with a boot to the hamstring, just above his knee. His leg went out from under him; I caught his arm as he went down an' relieved him of his .45. I pointed it at Leader.

The sound of the hammer comin' back as I cocked it caused him and his remainin' buddy to spin around again. An' freeze. Again.

"You may have doubts about Skip, gentlemen, but you *know* I'm gonna shoot if you don't drop your guns."

When they did, I had 'em all down on the ground an' had Skip cover 'em while I retrieved my sidearm, put cuffs on the three of 'em, and searched for other weapons. Then we sat 'em in a row an' he kept a eye on 'em while I looked in the truck. Found the driver tied up in the trailer like a spider's dinner. He was pretty happy to be rescued.

I sent him to sit in his cab so I could inventory the trailer. I'd just got up on the tailgate when Skip yelled, "Sheriff, cavalry's arrived."

• • •

The state boys took control of the hijackers, the scene, an' the case, but Skip an' me had to go in to make statements. When we was on the way, back in my cruiser, I asked Skip, "How'd you get the shotgun out without the key?"

"Fer me to know an' you to figure out."

I give him the look, and he said, "I seen where you keep the spare key in your office. Had it copied one day when you was out."

"How long ago was that?"

"Three months."

I just nodded. I didn't ask him for the key, just waited.

Finally he said, "I locked that kid in the locker so he would know how it feels. Weren't no big thing—principal's got all the locker combinations."

"You got yourself detained just so some kid'd know how it feels to be stuck in a locker?"

"No. No! How it feels to get jacked around by someone stronger'n him. I told him if I heard him pickin' on another little kid, I'd lock him in standin' on his head."

"Think that'll work?"

He shrugged.

"I guess you can keep the shotgun key. Fer emergencies."

He nodded.

"An' gimme your word you won't brag to your Aunt Penny or no one else 'bout what went down tonight."

"Pappy! I ain't *crazy!*"

• • •

When we got to the State Police station, Sergeant Underhill listened to our stories an' told me, "Nice work, Vergil." Then he turned to Skip. "Son, it seems to me you watched *Stand By Me* a time or two too many." Skip just grinned.

Underhill set Skip up in his office so he could do his homework while I sat in on the interviews. Truck driver's story sounded just like all the other truckers' stories we'd heard since the beginning of the hijack epidemic. He'd got flagged down by what he thought was a lady with car trouble who turned out to be a guy in a woman's coat an' hat with a pistol. The car drove off an' the guy an' his accomplices tied the trucker up.

The hijackers didn't have no story at at all. Every one of 'em lawyered up soon as he was brung into the interview room.

"Well," Sergeant Underhill said, "we'll just see if a night in a cell loosens up their jawbones. Meanwhile, we'll look into what kind of records they all have."

While his men was doin' that, Underhill an' Skip an' I adjourned to the diner 'cross the road from the station. The food was good an' plentiful, an' Skip was happy as a crow on a roadkill when we finished off with chocolate malted milk shakes. When he was done with his, he put his glass down an' burped, then asked Dan, "Why'd you call Pappy Vergil?"

Dan laughed. "Long story, son. One you'd best ask your dad to tell you. Next time you got insomnia."

Loomis's stash

Tuesday mornin', right after I dropped Skip at school, I
headed over to Okra, West Wheelin's white trash sister city,
to follow up on my promise to check out Loomis's pickup.
The place was remarkable tidy for a Okra establishment—
red brick with new roofin' an' fresh-painted doors, clean
windows, a yard clear of trash, an' a parkin' area without
derelict vehicles. Leonard was out front jumpin' the battery
on a Chevy Tahoe. Tall guy—six -one or -two, brown hair,
red face, an' clean navy coveralls. He didn't seem to notice
my cruiser till he got the Tahoe started an' come up for air.
Then he said somethin' to the kid who was helpin' 'im and
ambled over to my car.

"You must be Sheriff Deters."

"Guilty."

He didn't introduce hisself, didn't need to, 'cause his
coveralls had Leonard stitched above the left breast pocket.
"Guess we might as well get it over with," he said—didn't
say what, just turned an' headed towards his buildin'.

I got outta the cruiser an' followed him into a shop as clean an' orderly inside as out.

He pointed to a ten-year-old Ford F-150 that didn't show any evidence of pride. "All yours, Sheriff."

'Sides bein' covered with mud from some off-road excursion, it was rusted where it'd been scraped an' dented. The windshield was cracked, the rear bumper hangin' on outta habit, an' the license plate sticker expired.

Leonard shook his head like he didn't understand, either, how a man could drive such a wreck. "Keys're in it," he said. "Just gimme a receipt fer anything you take." He wandered off as I pulled out my latex gloves an' put 'em on.

The truck bed was full of empty cans—beer, Red Bull, an' soda, as well as assorted rubbish an' tools so old an' rusty nobody'd bother to steal 'em. Inside, the cab was littered with more empties plus fast food trash an' crumpled cigarette packs. After lookin' it over, I backed out an' dragged one of Leonard's trash bins over to the door, started shiftin' the trash into it. I checked out all the crumpled store bags for receipts that might clue me to where Loomis shopped— Cheap-Ass Likkers, Safeway, an' various truck stops an' fast food places along the interstates. There musta been another bushel of trash under the seat. Behind the seat was rubber boots, a ratty jacket, a shovel, an' half a dozen unmatched gloves. In the jacket pocket, along with loose change an' stale cigarettes, I found a cash register print-out from a sportin' goods store for a box of 9 mm ammo. So far, I hadn't found a gun. I put the jacket, boots an' gloves on the floor of the front seat, an' the print-out in a evidence bag.

Without the trash, the search went easier. I emptied the glove box into one of the paper sacks I carry in my cruiser for evidence collection—'cept for the registration. I noted the particulars on that 'fore I put it back where it come from. I checked under the seat with the mechanic's mirror I carry for vehicle searches. It's a little round thing mounted by a swivel on the end of a metal rod. It let me see the 9 mm pistol Loomis had tucked into a holster wired to the under side of the driver's seat. The gun went into a evidence bag, too, an' the evidence bags went into the trunk of my cruiser.

I was about ready to turn the truck over to Leonard, when I noticed a crumpled paper sack wedged against a support strut under the seat. I eased it out, smoothed it up, an' opened it. Found I'd hit pay dirt! Inside was a crumpled bank deposit receipt, stained with what looked like coffee from a cup it must've shared the bag with. But I could still read the bank name an' account number. Bingo!

• • •

The bank was in Okra, too, an' the bank manager told me I'd have to get a court order 'fore he could even confirm that Sam Loomis—or Henry Ames as they likely knew him— had a account there. I didn't argue.

I beat feet back to West Wheelin' an', right after lunch, I walked into the chambers of a very understandin' judge with all the necessary paperwork. Judge asked me to summarize the case—which I did. Then he signed the warrant with a flourish.

"Just be sure you let me know what you find, Homer."

• • •

The bank manager held up his hands and said, "I told you, Sheriff, you have to have a warrant."

When I handed it to him, he got a look on his face like somebody'd farted. The warrant was for the bank records of one Henry Ames, also known as Sam Loomis, or a Samuel Loomis, any an' all accounts, and the contents of his safety deposit box.

"There'll be a fifty dollar fee for opening the box," the manager told me, "because we'll have to call a locksmith."

"Happens I got the key."

• • •

As it turned out, Loomis had a savin's account with $253.17. One of the tellers printed me off copies of the last year's statements, then turned me over to the lady in charge of the box vault. Loomis's key worked just fine to get the box open, an' the vault lady was good enough to find me a cardboard carton to haul away the contents—$150,500.00 in bundles of fifty dollar bills, an' a handful of lottery tickets. She made me sign a receipt for the stuff, an' I asked her if she remembered Loomis.

"Mr. Ames is not a nice man. He's rude, and crude, and very impatient."

"Well, I don't think he'll be troublin' you again."

I stopped on my way outta the bank to have one of the tellers check the cash—to be sure was it genuine.

It was. Which answered *one* of my questions—what had Loomis done with all the cash he'd been makin'? But it posed a couple questions more. Who was payin' him to do what for all that money? An' what was I gonna do with it now that he was dead?

Nina meets two jackasses

When Skip an' me come outta the house next mornin', Nina's truck was in the drive but she was nowhere in sight. Didn't take long to find her—out back, makin' friends with our new pet, feedin' him a sandwich she musta got outta her lunch. The jackass was just eatin' it up. An' rubbin' his head against her, gettin' hair an' slobber all over her uniform. She didn't seem to mind.

She said, "Mornin, boys."

I give her a peck on the mouth.

Skip got all red an' muttered, "Mornin', Miss Nina." To me he said, "I'll wait in the car."

Soon's he was outta sight, I give Nina a proper hello. Didn't come up fer air till the jackass tried to take a bite outta my duty belt.

Nina said, "Whew! Guess you're glad to see me."

"When ain't I ever?"

The jackass started nibblin' on my gun butt. I slapped him, an' he backed up fast.

"Don't hurt him, Homer! He's just jealous."

"You belong to me now. He ain't got the right to be jealous."

Nina blushed an' changed the subject. "Homer, where we gonna live?"

"Well…we could move in with you an' Grampa."

Nina didn't look too pleased.

I said, "Out with it."

Seemed like she was gauging what I'd think 'fore she said, "Grampa ain't too fond a teenagers."

I knew she was thinkin' of the time Angie Boone stayed with 'em—stole Grampa's twenty-gauge. An' that wasn't all Grampa weren't fond of. "Or Jacksons," I added.

Nina knew I wasn't gonna throw Skip to the wolves by sendin' him back to his natur'l family. Not even to marry her. So I said, "We'll just have to get our own place."

She brightened.

I said, "'Cept who'd take care a Grampa?"

She frowned an' thought on that.

Jackass helped me out by head-buttin' me up against her. I let my fingers wander up her arms, to her neck, an' down… Nina blushed an' pushed me away, then looked around to see was anyone watchin'.

I grinned. "Mrs. Shaklee won't gossip much."

"Homer, be serious! I'm tryna think."

So I put my hands up an' stepped back, an' while she was thinkin' I got the jackass fresh water an' a half a bale of hay.

"He's cute," Nina said. "What ever made you keep a jackass fer a pet?"

"He ain't mine. An' he ain't a pet. An' we ain't keepin' 'im."

"Well, don't get all bent outta shape."

"You think of someone who could stay with Grampa?"

"Matter of fact, I did."

• • •

Lunchtime, I called Nina to see if she wanted to join me at the Grassy-ass, but she told me she was busy. I hung up an' looked out my office window to see just how long the line was at the post office. No line. Nina'd put her *Out to Lunch* sign on the front door, an' her truck was gone from where it'd been parked earlier. I figured she'd tell me what *that* was about when she was ready.

I was just walkin' toward my office door when Hazel Wrencock, the real estate lady, come through it.

"Sheriff, Nina Ross told me you're lookin' to move. Soon. That true?"

"It is if Nina says so."

"What kind of place are you looking for?"

I thought about Mrs. Shaklee an' said, "Somewhere there ain't no close neighbors."

"Rent or buy?"

"Buy, if it ain't too much."

"How much is too much?"

"What's available?"

"Why don't we go over to my office and look at the listings?"

"I'm kinda workin' today."

Hazel looked around like she might see somethin' in the office that'd make me change my mind. She spotted my computer an' her eyes lit up. "Or we could just go on line and check a few listings on *your* computer."

. . .

Time my lunch break was over, I hadn't got anything to eat, but I'd looked at listings for every place for sale in Boone County.

"Well, Sheriff," Hazel said, "have you seen something you like?"

"Yeah, but Pappy Jackson ain't gonna sell it to me."

"Ash Jackson's place?" The one Pappy'd inherited when his son Ash bought the farm. "Why ever not?"

"Pappy an' me been on opposite sides of most everything long's as I can remember. An' he holds it against me that I didn't arrest the person that shot Ash."

"Well, if you have the money to buy the place outright, he wouldn't have to know until you took possession."

"What do I gotta do to set *that* up?"

. . .

I didn't have to hunt Nina down after work. One minute after I watched from my office window as she closed up the P.O., she come through my office door like a firefighter on a rescue mission. So it wasn't surprisin' that she started in the middle without so much as a "howdy."

"Homer, Hazel Wrencock said you fixed on a place, an' you're ready to sign! That true?"

I figured Nina'd been spendin' too much time with Hazel—she was startin' to sound just like her. But I didn't say so.

"Yes, ma'am."

"Well, *hoo*ray!"

I held up my hands like 'I give up.' "'Fore you get all excited, it's Ash Jackson's place."

She thought on that a minute, then said, "Well, we can have it fumigated. An' mebbe Father Ernie can perform one a those exor-circumcisions."

"You mean a exorcism?"

"What I said."

"You ain't bothered by it used to belong to Ash Jackson?"

"Heck no. I allus thought it was wasted on Ash. An' it's got a nice big yard. An' shade trees."

"But it ain't real big."

"It's got two bedrooms, so Skip won't have to sleep on the couch. An' when we have kids, we can add on."

"How come you're so damn obligin'?"

"Don't swear. I ain't obligin', just ready for us to have our own place." She moved real close—close enough to get a rise outta me, if you get my drift.

Don't know where that woulda took us if my radio hadn't come to life all of a sudden.

"Homer, where you at?"

I took a deep breath an' backed away from Nina. Slow an' careful. I picked up the radio mic. "That's, 'what's your 10-20?' Rye."

"I'm down in the parkin' lot."

Nina clapped a hand over her mouth to stifle a laugh.

I just shook my head an' said, "10-4."

"I'm fixin' to punch out," Rye added. "You need anything 'fore I take off?"

"No, Rye. Have a nice evenin'."

I put the mic back an' wrote myself a note on a Post-it to go over radio protocol with Rye sometime soon. Nina read it over my shoulder.

"What's sometime soon, Homer?"

"That's after I figure out who killed Harlan an' Sam Loomis—a.k.a. Henry Ames—an' nail them truck hijackers; an' unload the jackass an' the mustangs; an' nail the turkey that left the Injun bones in Silas Hanson's ditch. Oh, an' buy a house an' move in."

"You're stallin'."

"What do you mean?"

"All them Post-its you got stuck on your filin' cabinet—your to-do list—none of 'em ever get done."

"Those're why I ain't makin' any progress—too many to keep track of. An' some of 'em ain't solvable."

"Like which?"

"Wilma Netherton is never gonna be happy 'til I run Miz Lincoln outta town. Which I ain't gonna do."

She nodded, like that was perfectly reasonable, an' laughed. "That reminds me. Hera Latham asked me to ask when you're gonna do somethin' about that gypsy."

"That what you come in here to tell me?"

"No. Damn! I almost forgot."

"What?"

"To tell you my cousin Elsie's comin' to live with Grampa."

"That's good of her."

Nina give a sarcastic grin. "More like shrewd—she won't be payin' room or board. How soon can you get the deal done for Ash's place?"

"What's your rush?"

"If I have to live with Elsie, you'll have another murder on your hands."

. . .

"You an' Skip comin' for dinner tonight?" Nina asked me after we'd finally said a proper hello, then come up for air.

'Fore I could answer, my phone rang. I held up my pointin' finger, said, "'Scuse me," an' picked up the receiver. "Sheriff's office. Deters."

Skip's voice said, "Pappy, can I go bowlin' with the cousins?"

"*May* I go bowlin'."

"Huhn?" I waited 'til he got the point an' said, "*May* I go bowlin'?"

"There gonna be adult supervision?"

"Aunt Penny. An' she said I could stay over after."

"Okay. Have fun." I didn't have to ask about his homework. I knew Penny was usin' the bowlin' expedition as a incentive fer *her* kids to do theirs.

Skip said, "Thanks, Pappy," an' hung up.

I turned to Nina. "Where were we?"

"You was about to tell me if you're comin' over fer dinner."

"I'm workin' tonight." Nina looked like her dog just died so I added, "Don't mean you can't ride along."

"Thought you gotta be law enforcement."

"You're still deputized but I can do it again if you don't feel official."

Nina hauled on the gold chain around her neck, an' dangled the ring I'd give her in front of me. "I ain't gonna feel official till we find Rye a girl, an' I can wear this on my finger."

. . .

Nina went home to change, an' I called the state cops to see if they'd made any headway tracking down the gun I'd brought 'em yesterday or convincin' the hijackers we'd caught Monday night to give up their bosses.

No joy on either count, Sergeant Underhill told me. The gun'd been bought legally at a gun show in Virginia by a feller who'd since passed away. Virginia state cops were tryin' to track down how it came to be in Loomis's hands. The hijackers wasn't talkin'. They'd been arraigned an' would have to post one million dollars for bail. Each. Judge musta been gettin' tired of hijackin' cases. Needless to say they'd be on ice fer a while.

"Good," I told Underhill. "Mebbe the chill'll loosen up their tongues."

"One can only hope," he said. Then he hung up.

. . .

Nina was rarin' to go when I picked her up half a hour later. Time we'd made one circuit of the town, she was bored with law enforcement, ready to tackle somethin' else.

"Homer, you had a chance to talk to Rye yet?"

"'Bout what?"

"Women."

"It's all I can do to talk to him about deputy-sheriffin'."

"Well, you need to ask him what kinda woman he's lookin' for so we kin help him find her."

I shook my head. "Why don't *you* ask him?"

'Fore she could come back on that, I spotted a semi

pulled over up ahead an' said, "Hold on a minute."

Nina looked to see what was important enough to interrupt us solvin' Rye's problems.

The truck driver was leanin' one elbow against the curbside of his trailer, facin' the truck cab an' holdin' a cell phone up to his ear.

I put on my pull-over lights an' stopped the cruiser right behind him.

Nina said, "Homer, what—?"

"Stay in the car."

I grabbed my sheriff's hat and got out, put on the hat an' started towards the driver. I seen exactly when he noticed someone comin' up on 'im. He jumped—like someone poked him with a cattle prod—an' turned around real fast.

I said, "Evenin'. You havin' trouble?"

He said, "Later," into the phone, then turned it off an' put it in his pocket.

"No, sir. I just stopped to make a call. Reception ain't too good in the truck."

Judgin' by the number of truckers that fly through here with their cell phones glued to their ears, I thought that a mite suspicious. "Mind showin' me your license, registration, an' insurance card?"

He fished his wallet outta his back pocket an' thumbed through it. He handed me a new-lookin' CDL—accordin' to which his name was Goodson Wooten—an' a valid-lookin' insurance card. I *eggs*amined them *very* carefully—they seemed okay—an' handed 'em back.

"Registration, Mr. Wooten?"

"Sonny." I waited. He said, "In the truck. I'll get it."

I followed him up to the cab an' waited while he climbed

up and reached out his registration, which also looked okay. "Hand me down your manifest and log book while you're at it."

"What've I done?"

"Well, for one thing, you ain't usin' your hazards. That's a safety violation. But I'm willin' to cut you some slack if you cooperate."

He shrugged an' produced the requested items. The manifest said he was haulin' plumbin' fixtures; the log looked okay. I handed 'em back an' was about to cut him loose when we heard the back doors of the trailer slam shut.

Sonny looked like he was suddenly facin' down the barrel of a 12-gauge. I turned my head just enough to see Nina come around the back of the truck an' head toward us.

In that fraction of a second I was distracted, Wooten reached back in his cab an' come out with a .22. He pointed it at me. "Drop your gun, Sheriff!"

It was déjà vu all over again.

I said, "Nina get back!" an' took a step away from the truck, further onto the shoulder.

Nina froze. Wooten pointed the gun at her an' said, "Don't move, girl." He told me, "You don't drop your gun, I'll shoot her!"

His hand was shakin', but he seemed scared enough to shoot someone by accident. So I drew my sidearm, slowly, an' dropped it as ordered. Wooten jumped down from the cab, keepin' his gun on Nina. As he reached for my pistol, I backed away an' let my mad show, clenchin' my jaw an' squinchin' up my eyes. "Shoot her an' I'll tear you apart 'fore you can swing that toy around. You gonna shoot, better shoot me first!"

He took the hint an' swung the gun in my direction. Got off one round. Just one. It missed me by a good six inches. 'Fore he could get off another, Nina jumped forward an' cold cocked 'im. I seen rocks drop slower.

"'Mind me never to piss you off," I told her as I pulled out my handcuffs.

She grinned. "Well, *you* come up with the distraction. You almost had *me* convinced you was gonna tear him apart. Where'd you learn to do that?"

"Watchin' *Dr. Who.*"

"Dr. who?"

"That's right. On PBS. Me an' Skip never miss a episode."

• • •

West Wheelin' ain't got a proper jail, just a holdin' cell off the sheriff's office that we mostly use for scarin' the livin' daylights outta juvenile delinquents 'fore we turn 'em over to their folks. Stands to reason we also ain't got a proper interrogation room. The state boys are pretty obligin' about lettin' me use their facilities—entertainment, Sergeant Underhill calls it. So I hauled Mr. Wooten over to the state cop shop an' put him in one of *their* interview rooms.

Like most law enforcement officers, I let my suspect set an' stew fer a spell while I checked the plumbin' an' got coffee an' run his prints through AFIS an' his name through NCIC to see if he'd been caught before an' was he wanted now.

Meanwhile, Nina, Underhill, an' Trooper Yates waited around fer the show to start.

The background check showed Sonny had something to answer for 'sides the stolen truck, the contraband, an' the unlicensed handgun. Turned out he was a local boy—raised in Okra—who'd got hisself arrested fer drunk drivin' an lost his real license. 'Cordin' to the Department of Motor Vehicles, he'd *just* got the license back. Which meant if the log book I'd confiscated was correct, he'd been drivin' fer some time without a valid license.

I asked what he'd been doin' fer a livin' while his license was suspended.

"Odd jobs."

"Like what?"

"Loadin' feed. Cuttin' cord wood."

"How you been gettin' yourself to these *odd* jobs?"

"Wife drove me."

I looked up at the two-way mirror as I raised a eyebrow. I knew Underhill was watchin' an' would check the story 'fore I got the next three questions out. "That so?" I asked Sonny.

"God's truth!"

"You might wanna take care how you use the Lord's name," I said. "I seen your log book. An' your manifest don't match up with the load of likker you was haulin', which you ain't got a receipt or shippin' order for. Then there's the matter of aggravated assault on a peace officer. You're lookin' at some serious jail time."

He got paler'n a black man at a Klan rally. "I want a lawyer."

I decided we'd let him set in the state cops' lock-up a day or two, then make him a offer he couldn't resist.

likely prospects

First thing next mornin', I decided to tackle Miz Latham's complaint—'bout our new resident gypsy. The sign in her window said, "Psychic Readings, Life Coaching, Ordinary Magik." The little store Madame Romany'd took over was clean an' bright with fresh paint an' real flowers, with a rockin' chair an' a Lazy Boy, a coffee table an' Ansel Adams posters. It seemed more like a new-age coffee shop than a—I ain't sure what it was exactly.

I wasn't sure what I was expectin' Madame Romany to be like, either, but Reba McEntire at twenty wasn't it. She had long, copper-colored hair—the real thing, an' blue eyes. An' she was dressed like a hippie chick from a Woodstock poster—only cleaner. White, long-sleeved shirt with stitchin', an' bell-bottom jeans. No shoes. But no flowers in her hair.

When I come through the door, she was standin' on one foot with the other in the air, crossed over her shin. Her hands was out in front of her like she was playin' a imaginary flute. She was smilin'.

I took off my hat. Her smile got wider. She lowered her hands to her sides an' her foot to the floor, an' said, "Good morning, Sheriff. How can I help you?"

"Tell me what exactly is a psychic readin'."

"I'm afraid there's nothing very exact—Perhaps I should just give you a demonstration."

I nodded, an' she led me through a doorway in the back of the shop that was closed off from the rest of the place by a bead curtain.

The back room was painted white—no pictures. There was a small round table, flanked by two foldin' chairs an' covered with a dark blue cloth. A deck of cards sat on the middle of the table top, along with a itty-bitty clam shell, a silver dollar, a small chunk of pink quartz, a pheasant tail feather, a .38 shell casin', an' a one-inch ball of smooth-sanded wood—all arranged in a circle around the cards. Ms. Romany slid into the chair that was backed up to the far wall; she offered me the other.

I set down. Couldn't help but pick up the shell casin'. "What's this for?"

She laughed. "It's a tell."

"That tells what?"

"Something about you."

"Which is?"

She just smiled. She shoved all the junk, 'cept the shell casin', off to one side an' handed me the cards. Didn't take but a glance to see they weren't regulation. Instead of hearts an' spades, clubs an' diamonds, they had odd pictures with labels like Seven of Swords, The Tower, an' The Hanged Man.

Madame Romany watched me check 'em out, then held out her hand for the deck. I passed it back.

"When you've thought of a question you'd like to have answered," she said, "I'll ask you to pick a card."

There was *a lot* of cards, an' I had no idea how was I s'posed to know which to pick.

She shuffled them and set the deck in front of me. "Cut them, please."

I did.

She fanned the deck out, face down. "Pick one."

I did an' turned it over. The label said, "Temperance." I couldn't tell what she thought of that. Her expression didn't give no more away than a black jack dealer's at a high end casino. She said, "Have you thought of a question?"

I nodded. I'd thought of a couple.

She started layin' out the cards in a pattern that looked like some bizarro game of solitaire, studyin' each one as she put it down. An' she studied my reactions.

When she finished, she said, "What is it you want to know?"

"Who killed Harlan?"

• • •

I'd just got back to my office when Hera Latham come bustlin' in. "Sheriff, you haven't done anything about that gypsy woman."

"Yes, ma'am."

"Why not?"

"Far as I can tell, she ain't broke no laws."

"Isn't it fraud to claim you can tell the future?"

"Would be if that was what she was claimin'. Sign says, 'Readin's.' Don't mention nothing 'bout tellin' the future."

"Well, what do you think *readings* means?"

"That kinda question's outside the scope of my job description, ma'am. You want me to arrest her for 'readin's,' you're gonna hafta get the town council to pass a ordinance definin' the term an' make it against the law to do it."

Hera's mouth opened and shut, then hung open while she took it all in. She musta decided it'd be easier to get the traffic commission to convene, 'cause she finally just said, "What good are you?" an' stalked out.

Hera'd no sooner left than my phone rang. I picked it up an' said, "Sheriff's office. Deters."

"Sheriff, we got a request from the courthouse for you to serve some papers." Eleanor, Mayor's secretary. "On yourself," she added.

"Mrs. Shaklee already served me. I'm on it."

"No, Homer. This is a summons and a complaint. I guess you're being sued. And since the process server hasn't been able to catch you himself, he's asking the sheriff's office to do it."

I sighed. "I can only handle so much at a time, Eleanor. I'll get to it soon as I clear some of the serious matters I got pendin'."

"Like what, Sheriff? What's more serious than being sued?"

"Murders. An' hijackin's. An' citizens complaints about on-usual newcomers."

"What am I supposed to do with these papers?"

"Well, you ain't bein' paid to serve 'em, so just hang on to 'em till next time I stop by your desk."

"When's that gonna be, Sheriff?"

"God only knows."

• • •

Lunch time, Nina met me at the Grassy-ass an' brought up the subject of findin' Rye a woman. There's times when I feel like I'm livin' in Dogpatch. Other times I wish I was. "Sadie Hawkins Day ain't a bad idea," I told her. "How 'bout you arrange one an' we'll see which local lovely Rye lets catch him."

Nina gimme her don't-mess-with-me look. "Just tell me who's available."

"Well, there's the Homely sisters." Comfort an' Joy.

She shook her head. "Like you said, they're homely."

"Gloria Starcutter?"

"Star-crossed. If it wasn't for her bad luck, she wouldn't have any at all. Rye don't need the grief."

"Leona Hazelwood?"

"Secretly engaged. What do you think a Sally Ann Wallace, Homer?"

"She's nice enough but she's dumber'n a box a rocks. How 'bout Lucy Willis? She ain't but Rye's second cousin."

Nina shook her head again. "She's scary she's so smart."

"Well, she don't hold a candle to you in the brains department."

"I know. But I don't put on airs an' try'n' talk like I ain't from around here."

"Well, I seen him eyein' Madame Romany from across the square. She don't talk like she's from around here, but then she *ain't* from around here." I finished my coffee an' signaled Maria for the check. "I told you," I said to Nina, "I think Rye'd rather find his own girl."

Nina went on like she didn't even hear me. "How 'bout

Miz Lincoln?"

"She's too good for Rye. An' too old. An' she'd never put up with his shit."

Nina scratched her head. "What about that new lady just moved in next to the Grassy-ass? The one with the curly hair. Wears overalls." Alice Bowne.

"I don't know. Rye's kinda partial to huntin', an' that woman's one of them animal rights nuts."

"Why'd you say that, Homer?"

"Well, you gotta be nuts to turn loose a whole truckload of horses in the Truck Stop parkin' lot."

"You may be right. I'd'a just stole the truck an' turned 'em loose in a field somewheres."

"Possible she can't drive a truck."

Nina thought on that a minute, then did a one-eighty on the subject.

"Homer, you're a bachelor. You gotta get in on this too."

"Hell, no. I'm the sheriff."

"That makes you a great catch."

"You already caught me."

"The rest a West Wheelin' don't know that."

"Well, they would if you'd just wear that ring I paid so much fer."

"I gotta catch you on Sadie Hawkins Day first."

"How 'bout I just give myself up?"

"Where's the fun in that?"

I couldn't argue with that kind of logic so I just shook my head an' said, "I gotta go back to work."

• • •

"So what's this *life coachin'?*" Rye asked me later. We was sittin' in the office, comparin' notes an' windin' down fer the day with a jug of White Lightnin'. "This ordinary magic sounds like a scam. She tell your fortune?"

"She didn't tell me who killed Harlan, but she said I'd figure it out."

"That don't take no physics ability—you allus do. I was over to the post office today an' Nina asked me what I thought a her. I ain't even met the woman."

"You tell Nina that?"

"Yeah. She offered to introduce us. What's Nina up to?"

"I axed Nina to marry me."

"Aw, I was workin' up the nerve to do that."

"Yeah. Well, I axed her first."

Rye just shook his head like it was sad I'd go around behind his back. Then he looked suspicious. "So what's that got to do with Ms. Romany?"

"Nina's all worried you'll be heart-broke by our news 'less you got someone too."

"She don't trust me to find my own woman?"

I just shrugged. "You know Nina."

"Yeah. I do."

"Well, you don't have to actually get married. Just show up around town with a woman, an' I'll try to convince Nina you're as serious as you're likely to get."

Rye took a sip of his drink an' thought on that fer a minute. "Rumor has it Ms. Romany's a witch. Just like Annie Felton."

Rumor had had it Annie Felton was a witch 'cause 'fore she moved away, she'd witched half the men in West Wheelin'. But contrary to malicious gossip she weren't a loose woman. Feller offered her money to sleep with him once, an' she cussed him out an' threw him outta her car—goin' sixty through Car Wrecks. He turned up next day with a concussion an' two broken arms. Way he told it, she'd magicked him into the air an' let gravity do the rest. The story put a mortal fear of Annie into half the men who'd been pesterin' her. An' after one of the town's worst gossips come down with lock-jaw....

Rye said, "You know that expression, 'colder'n a witch's tit'?"

"Yeah."

"That's just a expression. Annie's ain't cold."

"You know that from experience?"

"Damn straight."

"How come you never mentioned it before?"

Rye held his glass up. "A gentleman don't talk about a lady."

• • •

Nina musta actually been listenin' to my idea 'bout Sadie Hawkins Day, 'cause next mornin' she come into my office an' plunked a stack of flyers on my desk.

"New to Oktoberfest, First Ever Sadie Hawkins Day Race and Wild Horse Auction." The rest of the sheet gave particulars an' invited all bachelors an' bachelorettes to join the race an' mebbe get a real, original mustang gentled by Bello Willis.

"What am I s'posed to do with these?" I asked her.

"Post 'em."

"Why can't you do it?"

"'Cause I'm gonna be plannin' the events. An' givin' a

few pointers to certain eligibles so they won't miss out."

"Match-makin'."

• • •

First off, I made it a point to stop by an' give Owen Rhuddlan one of the flyers so he'd be sure to have Cheryl show up fer the race. "It's ladies' choice, Owen, an' Cheryl can have her pick of the bachelors."

"I thought *you* was gonna arrange fer her to meet a nice boy."

"Done that. Now it's up to Cheryl."

Owen looked like I was tryna put somethin' over on him. "You hooked Cheryl up with someone I ain't even met? Without bringin' 'im by for a inspection first?"

"I ain't never met Cheryl. I arranged for a nice boy to introduce hisself to her, an' he has. Next step is fer her to catch him on Sadie Hawkins Day."

"*Next step* is fer you to bring him by here so I can see is he fit to date *my* niece."

"I reckoned everybody in Boone County knows Bello Willis. An' that he's fit to date anybody's niece."

"The horse whisperer?" I nodded. "Why'n't you say so?"

I just nodded an' tipped my hat an' said, "See you at Oktoberfest."

• • •

I located Bello in Mars Boone's back pasture, leadin' one of the mustangs around like a pet dog. When he seen me drive up, he sauntered up to the fence an' tied the mustang to it. The horse snorted and pawed, then started trimmin' the grass. Bello leaned on the fence while I got out of the cruiser. When he said, "Afternoon, Homer," I guessed I was back in his good graces.

"Bello. How're they comin' along? They gonna be ready?"

"Yeah, like I told you. Cheryl's been helpin' me gentle 'em. She's a natural."

"Glad to hear that."

"An' a keeper."

I took that as a hint to hand him one of Nina's flyers. "You wanna keep her, best show up at Oktoberfest an' let her catch you."

• • •

I deputized Rye to pass out the rest of the flyers, made a point to tell him to give one to Mary Lincoln, an' Don Firenzi, Madam Romany, Alice Bowne, an' several of the women Nina an' I'd discussed. I figured the women'd get the idea to show up if they was interested in Rye. And he needed to see any eligible woman he might want to get caught by.

"You ain't gonna tell me to give one to Billie Bonds, are you?" he said. "'Cause I ain't gonna do it."

Made me *really* wonder what was up between the two of 'em. But all I said was, "If you feel that strong about it, I'll give her one myself."

"She don't need to know 'bout this, Homer." He waved the stack of flyers. "She's got enough men to run down with all them bail jumpers an' felons. Don't be encouragin' her to go after innocent men—she might take a fancy to *you*. 'Sides, ain't you got a murderer to catch?"

a Injun protest march

The day Oktoberfest rolled around was cool an' sunny, with a few leaves driftin' down from trees as bright an' colorful as fireworks caught on film. I shined my shoes an' put on my dress uniform. Skip put on his favorite T-shirt, the one that said *Knowledge is Power/ Power Corrupts/ Study Hard/ Be Evil*. We fed an' watered the jackass an' got in my cruiser to head over to the fairground. I waved to Mrs. Shaklee as I backed down the drive.

"You got one week to get outta here, Sheriff," she yelled.

I just nodded an' waved again.

"What're we gonna do, Pappy?" Skip asked.

"Worry about it tomorrow, son."

He shook his head but he dropped the subject.

When the radio squawked, Skip beat me to the draw. "This is Deputy Deters," he said into the mic. "Over."

Rye's voice come outta the speaker. "Don't you have to be eighteen to be deputized?"

"What d'you need, Rye?" This time Skip's voice sounded

more like me than I do.

"Looks like we got a Injun uprisin' on our hands, Homer."

I took the mic from Skip. "Where are you?"

"In front a City Hall."

. . .

When we got there, the mayor was faced off against Stanley Redwine and his band along with three women an' half a dozen teen-aged boys. 'Cept for the lawyer, they was all dressed in outfits looked like costumes from a old-time western.

"Sheriff!" Mayor half shouted. "Tell these people to disperse!"

"We got a right to protest," Stanley insisted.

Mayor looked ready to blow a gasket, but I knew Stanley an' his bunch thought they had a point. An' it come back to me—my momma's lecture on why the geniuses that wrote the Constitution added all the bits about freedom of speech an' assembly an' so forth. "Homer," she'd told me, "people who can't have their say are like boilers with no safety valves."

So I said, "They got a point, Mr. Mayor. An' a right to state their grievances."

"But—"

"Long as they keep it peaceful."

I give Stanley Redwine a look, an' he nodded like a bobble head.

Mayor's mouth opened an' closed—made me think of a stranded fish.

I looked hard at Stanley. "You ain't plannin' to take no scalps or occupy no buildin's?"

Stanley put his hands up like "I surrender" an' shook his head. "'Course not."

"I got your word on that?"

Stanley looked a tad insulted but he made a X over his chest.

"Good. Then in the interest of public safety, I'll provide you with a *po*lice escort."

Stanley's jaw dropped an' he looked at his high-priced lawyer. Lawyer shrugged.

"An' my deputies'll make sure nobody interferes with your right to state your case."

"They can't have a march without a permit," Mayor chimed in.

I give him a stern look. "We'll take care of the paperwork later."

Mayor's mouth opened an' closed one more time 'fore he figured out what I was up to. Then he sighed an' nodded.

Which is how I come to be in my cruiser, with four-ways an' pull-over lights flashin' as a band of Injuns marched down Main Street in full-feathered outfits wavin' protest signs an' tomahawks.

When they passed the post office, Nina stepped out in her post-mistress uniform, locked the front door, an' got in at the back of the line. An' Rye an' Festus waved everybody who come to gawk in behind Nina. Time we got to the fair grounds, just outside town, I felt like the Pied Piper leadin' the parade.

Oktoberfest

Volunteers had gussied up the fairgrounds with punkins, corn shocks, fall flowers, an' strings of colorful gourds. Just for good measure, Halloween decorations—cardboard witches and black cat cutouts—was stuck here an' there. As the Injun parade marched in, early-bird fair-goers was stragglin' past where the Chamber of Commerce had set up—rafflin' a new Prius—an' Mayor's secretary was handin' out programs for the day's events.

I pulled off to the side an' let the parade march by, then parked. Lotta the cars in the lot had outta state plates or municipal stickers from nearby cities, an' I noticed folks from Okra an' other neighborin' towns minglin' with the West Wheelin' residents.

While I waited for Nina to grab a program from the mayor's secretary, Sergeant Underhill wandered up. He was outta uniform, an' had a handsome blonde on his arm. A strawberry blond teenage girl tagged along behind 'em. Made me do a double take.

He said, "Morning, Vergil. I'd like you to meet my wife and daughter." Underhill a family man!

To them, he said, "This is Sheriff Deters."

"Mornin', ladies," I said, an' tipped my hat.

Mrs. Underhill returned my good mornin'. The girl just smiled an' blushed. Underhill told me he'd see me later and steered them in the direction of the raffle.

Nina come back with a program an' we studied it together. First off was a post-season baseball game. We didn't have enough police for a team, an' too many volunteer firemen, so the Baptists was takin' on the Catholics with the Evangelical Congregationals supplyin' umps an' score keepers.

After that there was a 1-K marathon around the dirt track, an' games for the rug rats—ring tosses an' sack races. Then the turkey shoot an' lunch, then the horse auction. I noted that the Sadie Hawkins race was the last event of the day. "How'd you figure on that?" I asked Nina.

"Well, most of our volunteers is entered in the race," she said. "An', just in case the winners feel like celebratin' afterwards, we wanna have most of the heavy liftin' over an' done with."

"Good thinkin'."

"Father Ernie's idea. He's in charge of keepin' things on track, an' he's had lotta experience with volunteers."

We started down the concourse where all three churches had raffles goin'—fer quilts, home-made preserves an' gift cards from places like Target an' Walmart. The church ladies was sellin' apple products—home-made pie an' cider. People was crowdin' around, snappin' 'em up.

Just about every business in town had a booth with free samples or coupons. Madam Romany had her table up with the little cards an' "tells." Maria Lopez wasn't there, but her husband Jesus sat at one of his hand-crafted tables, on a matchin' chair, handin' out sweet treats he called *dulces*. Little José Lopez was playin' under the table with a wooden truck his Pa'd made an' jabberin' in Spanish to his new baby sister. He dropped the truck an' screamed, "*¡Abuelos!*" then went runnin' towards them when Martha Rooney wheeled Ben in our direction. Nina hurried up to hug 'em hello. I grinned an' said, "Mornin', Martha. Sheriff."

"It *is* a good morning, Homer," Martha said. Ben just gimme a crooked smile an' bobbed forward an' back in his wheelchair until José climbed on his lap an' patted his cheek. At that point, Nina an' I resumed our patrol.

Traffic was gettin' heavier. Men, women an' kids, teenagers and retirees, yuppies an' rednecks rubbed elbows an' other parts, crowdin' 'round the booths an' tables, watchin' the free show. Three local Bozos clowned with a genuine-lookin' mime, while a balloon-animal guy passed out giraffes an' wiener dogs. An' a juggler on stilts stepped carefully between the rug rats. Nina an' I kept movin'.

The Injuns had set up a teepee with a card table in front so they could hand out flyers. "Educational brochures," Stanley Redwine called 'em.

Farther along, Truck Towing had a spot where Dwayne Truck's model-pretty wife was signin' people up fer next semester's school bus service, an' handin' out coupons for free oil changes—filter extra.

I was surprised when we come to Mary Lincoln's orange Ford pulled up, tailgate open, with a fair sample of the junk from her collection laid out neatly. A sign on top of the cab said, "SEE IT? NEED IT? TAKE IT." Mary was nowhere in sight, but Priceless was doin' guard duty from the cab, barkin' at anybody who come near the half open windows.

Don Firenzi's plaid truck was parked along side Mary's with what looked like overflow—a neat pyramid of matchin' bricks, a pile of like-new plumbin' brass, an' gently used pipes of assorted lengths an' bores.

At the far end of the concourse, Bello Willis an' Mars Boone had set the mustangs up in the stock pen closest to the action, an' a sign invited all comers to "PICK YOUR PONY. AUCTION WILL BE HELD AT 2:00 P.M. SHARP. ALL SALES FINAL."

Nina an' I was admirin' the herd when Rye showed up in a borrowed horse trailer with the jackass.

"What's he doin' with your pet?" Nina demanded.

"He ain't mine and he ain't a pet. An' I'm hopin' some fool'll think he's cute an' bid on 'im."

Rye backed the trailer up next to us an' got out. I pointed at the jackass. "How'd you get him to go in?"

Rye grinned. "Bribed Bello to load him."

"Well, see if you can find Bello and bribe him to off-load him."

"Yes, sir. Then I'm takin the rest of the day off."

"You gonna be around." I wasn't askin'.

"Is a jackass stubborn?"

"If there's trouble, I expect you to help me out."

Rye looked hurt. "Don't I always?"

I didn't answer 'cause nine times outta ten he does.

Rye took off to look for Bello, an' Nina kissed me on the cheek. "I'm gonna help the Chamber of Commerce sell tickets," she said. "See you later."

She went, an' I ambled around lookin' out for pick-pockets an' under-age drinkin', enjoyin' the day. By 10:00 a.m. I had the feelin' God was in heaven an' all was right with West Wheelin'. Shoulda knocked wood.

One of the decoration punkins come flyin' out between the Baptist Church booth an' Jesus's table. The basketball-sized vegetable just missed a passin' teenager, splattering his shoes an' pants legs, makin' him jump backwards like a spring-loaded booby trap, then charge forward.

Jesus jumped, too, towards the source of the punkin toss. He come back draggin' a kid big enough to play varsity football an' old enough to know better. Same time, the victim drew back for a punch that woulda took Jesus out if I hadn't grabbed the kid's fist an' yanked. Kid landed flat on his back.

I stepped around him an' relieved Jesus of his prisoner. "Much obliged, Jesus."

He nodded an' helped the other kid up.

"You wanna press charges?" I asked the victim.

He looked at the bully, then looked around, then shook his head.

"Then get along."

He looked like he wanted to say somethin', but finally just shook his head again and skedaddled.

I turned to the offender. "I'm gonna let go of you, son, but don't try to run. I *know* where you live."

He gulped an' stood still.

"Let's go this way." I pointed towards the stock pens.

"You takin' me to jail?"

"I might. If you don't do exactly what I say."

We got to the livestock area an' I located a shovel kept

there for clean-ups. I handed it to the kid. "You made a mess; now clean it up."

We went back to where people was steppin' carefully 'round the pumpkin puree. I directed traffic while the kid scraped up the mess and dumped it in a trash bin. I had him return the shovel, then I herded him down to the other end of the concourse an' handed him over to Nina.

"This young man's got a twenty minute time out to serve. An' I'd be obliged if you see he serves it."

Nina blinked, but nodded.

I pointed the kid to a nearby foldin' chair. "You sit here until this lady tells you you can go. An' next time you make trouble, you *are* goin' to jail."

• • •

Didn't take long for more trouble to find me. With Rye's help.

Rye pointed me out to a fat, red-faced man, in a business suit an' tie, who charged up wavin' one of Chamber of Commerce's programs. Rye followed him, bustin'—I could see—with curiosity.

"You the sheriff?" the man demanded.

"Guilty."

"This says you're planning to auction off twenty-two mustangs."

Rye shook his head.

I nodded. "An' a jackass."

"You can't. They're U.S. Government property."

"And you'd be?"

"William Smith."

"From the BLM?"

"Yes. And I'll get an injunction to stop you, if I have to."

"Good luck with that." I pulled a folded-up copy of his fax from my pocket an' handed it to him. "You can keep this."

He read it an' stalked away fumin'. When he got to his car, he burned rubber headin' away.

"What if he gets the injunction, Homer?" Rye asked. He wasn't too keen on the auction idea an' was likely hopin' the BLM guy would just take the horses off our hands. But he'd donated a gallon of White Lightnin' to the cause, to lubricate the bidders, and he didn't want to see it wasted.

"He ain't gonna get much sympathy from the court." Judge is a good ol' boy from the next county. We may have our differences, but we're pretty much united against the feds.

Just to be safe, soon as I got back to my cruiser, I called the court clerk on my cell phone to ask what was goin' down.

"Oh, that BLM guy's come 'n' gone, Homer," she said. "Judge told him if he could prove the horses were his—which he'd have to do in court, he'll have to pay their bill. He just said, 'Forget it,' an' walked out."

• • •

The turkey shoot, which was next on the agenda, come off without a hitch. An' without anything gettin' shot but the turkeys on the targets.

Nina took the prize—as usual. An' two of the Willises come out second an' third. Nina donated her turkey, which was as big as a goat, to the local food pantry, an' that took away the sting of nobody else havin' a shot at winnin'. But

Willy Donner, who couldn't' hit the broad side of a Target truck, followed me around the rest of the afternoon, whinin' that he'd of won if only he had his gun back.

the horse auction

After lunch—which was more like a banquet with fried chicken an' mashed potatoes; biscuits an' gravy; greens an' black-eyed peas; three kinds of pie: apple, sweet potato, an' *pe*can; ice cream an' sweet tea—Nina wandered off to check out her competition fer the Sadie Hawkins race. Like she really had any. I headed to the stock pens to check on preparations fer the auction. I'd got about halfway down the fairway when Alice Bowne come tearin' out of a herd of city visitors like a border collie comin' after a stray sheep.

"Sheriff! What's he doing here?" She pointed toward the BLM guy huffin' an' puffin' towards the stock pens.

"You know him?" I asked.

"No. But I know he's up to no good."

"How's that?"

"He's a friend of the truck driver who was abusing those horses."

"How'd you know that?"

"I saw them having dinner together at a truck stop.

The night before the driver came here. They were drinking together—toasting something or other. Thick as thieves."

"You willin' to sign a statement to that effect?" She nodded. "Then I'll look into it an' get back to you." I tipped my hat an' hurried to catch up with Smith.

• • •

"Mr. Smith!"

Smith paused and turned. When he spotted who was talkin' at him, he scowled. "I don't want to speak to you, Sheriff."

"You get your injunction?"

"You know I didn't. There's not a snowball's chance in hell I'd get justice in this town."

I shook my head. Smith turned an' stalked away.

I thought about goin' after him, but decided I had enough on my plate fer one day. I could deal with Smith tomorrow.

• • •

There was a good-sized crowd millin' around the stock pens—lots of local folks an' plenty of, at a guess, city folk. Rye'd changed outta his uniform an' was handin' out samples of his best brew, in Dixie cups, to anyone who looked old enough to vote. The auctioneer, Leroy *Van*dyke Willis, was conferrin' with Bello an' Mars Boone.

Then Leroy turned on his microphone an' greeted the crowd. He had a local reputation almost as good as the *original* Leroy Vandyke, so it was a good guess most of the audience was there to be entertained, not to buy nothin'.

Leroy described the first horse, a chestnut mare, but before he could name a starting bid, Mr. Smith pushed through the crowd an' said, "I'll give you one hundred dollars for the whole sorry lot."

Leroy put a sad expression on his face an' shook his head, then he looked hard at Rye. "Mr. Willis, this gentleman's cut off."

Smith turned redder than the horse's coat as the crowd roared.

"I'm gonna start the biddin' at twenty-five dollars, Leroy said. "25? 25? 25?" A local farmer raised his hand an' Leroy said, "I'm bid 25. Now 30? Wanna bid 30? 30? I got 30! 35? 35? 35? Now I'm bid 35. 35. Do I hear 40? 40? 40! Now 45? 45? 45?

"Don't stop now! 45? Last call 40 dollars. New bidder! 45! Can I get 50? 50? 50? Sold for 45 dollars!" He pointed at the winning bidder. An' Bello hurried over to get the man's name as Leroy started describin' the next horse.

After that the bidding got fast and furious. Leroy played bidders off against each other with stuff like "You gonna let her walk off with that fine mare for *only* forty dollars?" an' "Twenty-five dollars! I seen dead horses go fer more than that."

Once Rye's second an' third round of free samples started kickin' in, neighbors who'd been rivals at anything—goin' back to high school football—started biddin' against each other like they was mortal enemies. One little black gelding went for five hundred dollars. Which made me wanna thumb my nose at Mr. Smith. Didn't have to stoop that low, though. Smith headed back towards the parking lot looking fit to kill anyone who so much as said hello.

The jackass come up fer bid last, an' it seemed like the only folks left hangin' around were just curious 'bout who'd be fool enough to buy a jackass. Leroy tried to start the biddin' at twenty-five but got no takers. "Come on, folks somebody's gotta want this cute little feller. What'm I bid?"

A little kid held up his hands and said, "I got fifty cents." His dad pulled his hand down, shakin' his head at Leroy.

A high school kid offered to pay two dollars, so Leroy started his chant with "I'm bid two dollars. Wanna bid 3? 3? Three dollars! Wanna bid 4? 4? 4?" Leroy looked at the kid who'd started the biddin'. He just shook his head. Somebody finally said, four, an' Leroy started up again with, "Now I'm bid 4? Can I get 5? 5? 5? Last call four dollars."

Somebody in the back raised his hand. Leroy said, "New bidder! Five dollars! I'm bid 5. Wanna bid 6? 6? 6?" Leroy looked around, but it was plain the novelty was wearin' thin, an' nobody was goin' over five.

"Sold! To the gentleman in the White Sox cap."

Everybody stared. The man just took out his wallet an' handed Bello a five dollar bill.

I couldn't help myself. I hadda go over an' ask. "Just outta curiosity, Mister, what're you plannin' to do with a jackass?"

"I'm going to give him to my sister."

I figured that could start a family feud, but it wasn't my problem. I was just happy to be shut of the critter. Last I seen of it, the man in the Sox cap was tryin' to get the jackass to follow him away from the auction ring.

Leroy, meantime, was advertizin' his next auction—a farm sale just over the state line, all prime equipment in mint condition. Successful bidders lined up to pay fer their bargains an' make arrangements to pick 'em up or have 'em delivered. I hung around to watch 'cause some of 'em was startin' to sober up an' wonder could they back outta the deal. I said, "All sales is final," so many times I was starting to feel like a recorded messenger. Most of the complaints went somethin' like, "What am I going to do with a wild mustang?"

"Whatever you'd do with a tame one."

"I don't know anything about taming horses."

"Well, you're in luck. We happen to have Bello Willis, the world's best horse whisperer, right here in Boone County. He won't just train your horse, he'll train you how to train it. Time you're done, your horse could be worth three times what you paid."

"I suppose he charges an arm and a leg."

"You'll have to take that up with him."

"How am I supposed to get the damn thing home?"

I felt like tellin' him failure to plan ahead on his part didn't constitute a emergency on mine, but what I said was, "You kin arrange transportation with Mars Boone."

The next guy I give my suggestions to said, "I'm not going to fool around training a horse!"

"That feller who offered to buy the whole lot for a hundred dollars might go as high as five bucks for it."

"I paid seventy dollars for that animal!"

"Well then, you might could donate it to the Hiram Walker Farm an' get a tax write-off."

Sadie Hawkins race

The Sadie Hawkins Race was set up to start in the middle of the fair grounds race track. Two lines, bachelors in one, single ladies in the other. Martha Rooney was stationed on the sidelines, half way between with a bullhorn an' a starter pistol, an' instructions to fire as soon as everybody was in position. Married townsfolk an' underage kids lined up on the sidelines with Ben Rooney, Mars Boone, D.W. Truck an' his missus, an' the Lopez family—all formin' human fences to channel the action away from parkin' lots and animal pens.

Under pressure from Nina, I took my place in line between Rye an' Bello Willis. An' I noticed Don Firenzi, Richard Truck, the Jefferson brothers—Tom an' Jeff—an' half a dozen Jacksons fillin' out the roster. Behind us was most of the women Rye an' Nina and I'd mentioned in our discussions of likely prospects. Nina was standin' elbow to elbow with Cheryl, who looked like she'd got pointers from someone—she had a rope looped over her shoulder. Wilma Netherton, sportin' a butterfly net, was lined up next to Alice Bowne, who was wearin' new-lookin' runnin' shoes.

I shook my head an' looked at Rye. "Ready?"

"No. I ain't." He looked back at the ladies' line-up an' turned white as skim milk. Made me want to see who could scare him—he'd never turned a hair facin' down the ATF or the *en*tire Jackson clan.

Billie Bonds had squeezed in between Alice Bowne an' Patrick Truck's sweetheart an' was starin' at Rye like a rattler after a mouse.

"Ready?" Martha yelled into her bullhorn. "Set..." The *bang* of her starter pistol drowned out the word "GO!"

I started walkin' towards Nina, who looked pretty disgusted that I wasn't givin' her any kinda challenge. I hadda dodge Wilma's net, 'fore Nina give up waitin' an' grabbed me by the shirt-front. She staked her claim with a kiss that musta set tongues waggin'.

Most of the other men fanned out an' took off or turned to look for the ladies they wanted to be caught by. Cheryl musta been practicin', 'cause she dropped a loop over Bello on the first try.

Tom an' Jeff Jefferson took off like them Kenyan fellers always win the New York marathon. They was outta sight 'fore you could say scat.

Rye took one look at Billie Bonds and run over to Madam Romany. "I surrender!" She looked like you coulda knocked her over with a feather. Rye glanced at Billie Bonds, then at Ms. Romany. He took her hand and brought it to his chest, closed her fingers around a handful of his shirt front an' said, "Take me. I'm yours. Please! You kin throw me back later if you change your mind."

Madame Romany glanced at the other prospects. Cheryl

had Bello, who was too young for the fortune-teller anyway. Patrick Truck's long-time sweetheart was clingin' firmly to his arm, an' Mary Lincoln was holdin' hands with Don Firenzi. The only other unclaimed single men in sight were two of the Jackson brothers, who looked like biker gangsters, an' Willy Donner.

Madam Romany nodded. "I don't know what I'm going to do with you, but okay." She let go of Rye's shirt and slipped her arm through his.

Rye looked at Billie Bonds again—like a guy who's just made it over the fence 'fore the pit bull nailed him. Billie just looked thoughtful.

I stake-out a truck

Nina didn't have a chance to do nothin' with her Sadie Hawkins prize 'cause it was my turn on the night shift. I give her a good night kiss an' a rain check, an' sent Skip home with my sister Penelope an' her kids.

Time the fairgrounds cleared out, an' all the out-of-towners had made their ways back to the interstate, West Wheelin' was quiet as the grave. Cruisin' the empty streets gimme a chance to think on all that'd went down since Handy Taylor found the skeleton in Silas Hanson's ditch, from the truck hijackin's to Harlan's murder. I figured most of them had to be connected—it was too much coincidence that our local Injun expert ended up like the long dead Injun, an' that the barbecued truck driver had been haulin' a suspicious load of horses in a stolen truck in the same general vicinity that the liquor truck hijackers was stealin' trucks as well as liquor. I was pretty sure the hijacked liquor was stashed at the Lower Fork Distillery. Unless—like Rye suggested—they was makin' liquor with a replicator. An' the booze was probably bein' sold at Cheap-Ass Likkers outlets.

Problem was how to prove it. Not even a sympathetic judge was gonna issue a warrant to search the premises or either concern's records without some probable cause. Coincidence didn't qualify. Unless we could catch the hijackers in the act an' follow 'em to where they took the loot, we was S.O.L. The state cops had been tryin' to do that since Underhill an' I cooked up the idea. So far, with no luck. It was likely too easy to spot the tails. I wondered could we get LoJacks fer all the liquor delivery trucks operatin' in our part of the state.

Next mornin', soon as Festus took over patrol, I swung by the state cop shop to ask.

"You got a great imagination, Vergil," Underhill told me after I'd laid it all out. "While you were at it, did you imagine how we're supposed to pay for a bunch of LoJacks?"

"The insurance companies—"

He shook his head. "Most of the shipments weren't insured for enough to make them care. But I think we're making headway. We're about three days past due for a hit."

"None of the fellers we nailed so far is talkin'?"

"The only one we got a snowball's chance in Hell of turning is that last one you nailed—Wooten. If we offered to overlook his driving without a license, assaultin' a peace officer, and putting in twenty-hour days behind the wheel."

"Well?"

"I'll talk to my boss—see what we can do."

"Is Wooten still in lock-up?"

"Oh, yeah."

"Let me have a word with him."

. . .

Goodson Wooten—Sonny—was a changed man. Not only had he been off his feed in lockup, he'd shed any remainin' attitude. I guess the lawyer he'd demanded to see had painted a grim pi'ture of his prospects, 'cause Sonny said he'd be happy to talk to us—even signed a waiver. An' when I asked was he ready to cut a deal, he was eager as Priceless after a rat. He was also ready to talk about the liquor he'd been haulin'.

Someone—he was fuzzy on just who—had offered to pay him to deliver it to Cheap-Ass Likkers. He was s'posed to be paid cash when the goods was off-loaded. Nothin' particularly s'picious about that. Lots a companies paid independent truckers to deliver their goods, an' sometimes they paid cash to get a better price. Truckers went along with that 'cause they wasn't plannin' on declarin' all the money or payin' taxes on it. That was the deal Sonny'd made with Cheap-Ass.

From what I'd been able to find out, apart from his problems with his CDL, Sonny was a straight-up feller. He owned his rig an' had kept up the insurance premiums—far as the *in*surance company knew he was licensed to drive the whole time his license was suspended. An' if we'd just drop the charges, he'd *still* be licensed an' insured.

I told Sonny to hang tight an' went out to dicker with the state. They was of the opinion that a turkey in a pen is worth a flock on the run.

"Nina didn't have probable cause or permission to search his load," I told Underhill. "I was fixin' to send him on his way."

Underhill wasn't convinced.

"I'm willin' to drop the assault charge," I said, "an' look the other way on the rest if he cooperates."

"Cooperates how?"

"Just goes back to work haulin' likker 'til someone hijacks his truck."

"How's that gonna help us? You gonna buy him a LoJack?"

"I'm gonna stake his truck out."

"Like that's worked for us."

"From the inside."

Underhill started to nod, then stopped himself. "What's to keep him from tippin' the hijackers off?"

"He ain't a bad man. He's a local with a wife an' a mortgage. An' I doubt he wants to spend more time in jail."

• • •

After we cut Sonny loose, I went back to the office an' reorganized my schedule, an' called my sister to make arrangements for Skip. Then I broke the news to Nina that I'd be workin' nights for the next little while. At the post office. Where she couldn't make too much of a scene. After which I threw a Mini Maglite, my little mirror for checkin' under things, an' a thermos of coffee into a backpack, an' charged up my cell phone. I had Sonny pick me up at Hardsetter's. "You got a cell?" I asked him 'fore I climbed in the trailer.

"Does a bear shit in the woods?"

"I'm gonna give you my number, an' if you see anything suspicious, I want a heads-up."

He nodded an' closed me into the back, then set out to make his first pick-up.

Inside, the trailer was pretty new an' fairly clean, but also pretty tight. No holes from damage or fer ventilation. Fortunate for me, the roof was some kinda plastic that light could shine through—though that didn't help once the sun went down, an' the doors at the back wasn't air-tight.

The job was mostly boring. And a lotta work. Half of the places Sonny picked up from wouldn't help him load the truck, an' half the places he delivered to wouldn't help him off load. Just to speed things up, an' 'cause I didn't have anything better to do, I helped him some. Keepin' outta sight, I'd bring the boxes from the front of the trailer to the doors, and he'd take 'em from there. Or Sonny would lift the boxes up, just inside the doors, an' I'd stack 'em in the front. If the load come on pallets, which had to be moved with a forklift or front-end loader, I'd make myself scarce till they was nearly done, then make like a hitch-hiker, bummin' a ride after Sonny pulled out.

Sonny's schedule varied quite a bit, though we made sure he was stickin' to the allowable number of hours. That was the only thing that saved my ass 'cause I was still Sheriff an' had family responsibilities. An' Mrs. Shaklee kept remindin' me to evict myself immediately. After a week of sleeping in the back of the moving truck, followed by days of harassment by Nina for neglectin' her, I got lucky. Sonny made a pick-up, an' I'd just nodded off when my cell phone woke me up. I turned it on and said, "Deters."

Sonny's voice whispered in my ear. "Sheriff, we's bein' hijacked. Two guys with guns—"

Then I heard, "Get out of the truck!" and the sound of

the phone hitting the truck seat. The phone didn't go dead, but what I heard next was too confusin' to make much sense of—sounded like shouts an' doors slammin'. I kept listenin' for a clue to what was goin' down now. The truck started movin', an' I could hear gears shiftin an' traffic sounds. No shots. Maybe that meant the hijackers hadn't killed Sonny.

Then someone said, "It's me. We got the shipment. Tell Wilcox we're heading back. And he better have cash this time." For a while the speaker musta just listened, 'cause all I heard was truck an' traffic noises. Then he said, "Bullshit! Tell Wilcox to tell him he can bring the money himself. I'll drop a dime to ATF before I let him stiff me again." He paused, then added, "Son of a bitch!" Softly. Like he was just commentin' to hisself.

The rest of the ride he was speechless—so to speak. I heard the radio—traffic an' weather an' Brad Paisley's latest chart-topper. An' truck noises. After a half hour, the truck slowed and I heard the driver say, "Open the gate." The truck slowed even more, then turned right and drove a little further. As soon as it stopped, I heard what sounded like a industrial strength overhead door openin'. The truck did a three point turn and backed up beepin'—not far. Then the motor cut off. The truck door slammed. Heard the overhead door again. Another door slammed, a little ways off. Then quiet.

I whipped out my cell an' speed-dialed. When I heard Underhill say, "State Police, Sergeant Underhill," I said, "Dan, I think I've run down our hijackers."

"You sound funny, Vergil. You been drinking?"

I was startin' to get high from the adrenalin, but no point tellin' him that. "Nope," I said. "Just a bad connection."

"Where *are* you?"

"Inside the Lower Fork Distillery. I think. You better check my phone coordinates for certain."

"You got a warrant for that?"

"Don't guess I need one. They kinda invited me in."

"How's that?"

"Truck I been stakin' out from the inside just got hijacked."

"You in any immediate danger?"

"Not till they decide to off-load the truck."

• • •

Which they decided to do not long after I hung up. I heard what sounded like a regular door bein' slammed. An' voices, though I couldn't make out words. Someone fiddled with the latch on the trailer doors. Light come in through the widenin' crack between 'em. I had my Sig out, aimin' it down the beam of my Mini Maglite.

The doors swung wider. I said, "Freeze!"

The guy on the other side of the door said, "Shit!" an' swung it shut.

I yelled, "Hold it!" an' aimed a little to the right of where the bad guy would be. I heard someone fumblin' with the door latch again an' I fired. Heard a yelp, then footsteps runnin' away. Then nothin' fer a while. Finally someone yelled, "Back out till Harry gets here with the rifle!" An' a door slammed.

During the quiet that followed, I dug the little mirror outta my backpack an' shoved it through the hole I'd just drilled in the trailer door, stayin' back from what I figured was the line of fire. Nobody in sight. I swung the door open slowly, keepin' the mirror through the hole, an' checked for bad guys along the driver's side of the truck. None visible.

I pulled the little mirror outta the bullet hole and held it down to check under the truck for ambushers. No legs or feet in sight. So I dropped to the building floor an' had a better look around.

The truck was parked in a dim-lit warehouse stacked halfway to the ceiling with rows of pallets loaded with liquor boxes. To the right, on the passenger's side of the truck, was a row of overhead doors, all closed tight. Probably dock doors where the semis could back up to load or unload freight. To the left and behind the truck, it looked like the rows of pallets ended in blank brick walls. There was no sounds of whisperin' or heavy breathin'.

I kept my Sig ready an' started toward the cab, watchin' for hijackers between the rows of pallets. The little mirror showed me the cab was empty. I opened the driver's door an' took a quick look inside. The key was in the ignition. Sonny's phone was on the passenger's side of the seat, half-hid by a order of French fries spillin' out of a McDonald's bag. I found some napkins in the bottom of the bag an' used 'em to clean off the phone, which I shut and an' shoved in my pocket 'fore I backed out an' closed up the cab.

The truck was just inside a big overhead door—what I'd heard activatin' earlier. Windows high up in it was reinforced with chicken wire an' painted over. So I couldn't see out or easily break the glass for a look. An' there weren't any holes to poke my little mirror through.

Next to the big door was a human-sized door with a dead-bolt lock above the handle. No key. I made my way to the door an' tried to open it. No luck. They musta locked it from the outside. There was a switch next to the overhead door, but I resisted the urge to hit it. I took out my cell an' redialed Underhill.

He answered, "Yo."

"Dan, what's your twenty?"

"We're just pullin' up outside the gate. What's happening?"

"One of 'em's goin' for a rifle."

"Where *are* you?"

"Inside the warehouse."

A reinforced panel in the overhead door suddenly shattered, and the M-80 CRACK of a rifle caused Underhill to shout, "God, dammit!"

I ran back to the semi and climbed into the cab. When I turned the key, the engine started right up. I jumped out an' hit the overhead door switch.

Nothin' happened.

My turn to swear.

"Vergil, what's going on?" Underhill sounded as close to upset as I'd ever heard.

"You see a truck come tearin' out the warehouse, don't shoot," I said. "It'll be me!"

I dropped the phone on the seat and put the semi in gear, blessin' my ma for makin' me learn how to drive one. The truck started forward, an' I shifted up slowly, so when the bumper hit I'd still be in a gear low enough to take the stress of rammin' the door. The bumper made contact. The door groaned, then screeched as the truck applied pressure a door wasn't designed to handle. Another bullet tore glass away from the wire reinforcing the building's windows and punched a spidery hole in the semi's windshield. The rifle-crack slammed my ears.

An' then the door surrendered, pulling out of its tracks and bucklin' over the semi's hood. It draped itself onto the cab as the door frame shattered an' the anchor bolts pulled free.

The truck speeded up through the doorway, an' I tried to remember the layout of the yard outside. Gravel and asphalt, mostly. Now dotted with cars and pickups. The men who was hunkered down behind 'em, facin' off against the barricade of cop cars along the fence, scrambled for cover as a new threat charged 'em from behind.

I aimed the truck at the man with the long gun. Saw the windshield shatter long—it seemed—'fore the rifle cracked again. I didn't hear the bug hit the radiator, but I heard him scream. And I saw him bounce off and roll away. And lie still. And I felt little bumps as the truck tires ground his rifle into scrap.

I hit the horn as I jerked the semi toward the still-closed perimeter gate. The sound made me feel like the captain of a ocean liner. The gate disintegrated as the big truck hit. It took me two blocks to bring it to a stop.

I grabbed my cell phone. "Get in there 'fore they burn the evidence!"

a recap for the state *police*

By the time I got turned around an' back to the scene, most of the action was over. The state cops had swarmed in an' rounded up the bad guys an' was searchin' the premises fer anyone tryna hide till the law cleared out. There was four guys in custody, not countin' the one I'd run down with the truck. *He* was still lyin' where he'd landed 'cause the state boys was afraid to move 'im 'fore the EMTs arrived. The others was cuffed an' seat-belted into the backs of four separate State Police cruisers.

I walked over to the guy I'd disabled an' was relieved to find him still breathin'. Someone I knew. Harry Wilcox. Lower Fork Distillery's uncooperative manager. Sergeant Underhill was squatted down next to him, tryna keep 'im calm an' still. When Wilcox spotted me, he passed out.

"Nice going, Vergil," Underhill said.

"What'd *I* do?"

"With our luck, scared him to death."

Far as I knew, Wilcox'd never clapped eyes on me before.

So he didn't have any reason to be 'specially scared of me. His passin' out hadda be a odd coincidence or some kinda clue. I shrugged. "Anybody heard from Sonny?"

"Don't change the subject...Sonny?"

"Guy they..." I hooked my thumb in the direction of the captured hijackers. "...Hijacked the truck from."

"Oh, him," Underhill said. "He called from a bar to report a sheriff had been hijacked. Dispatcher thought he'd been drinkin', but the bartender came on an' convinced him the complaint was legit. We sent a trooper to bring him along."

At that point, the ambulance arrived, an' the paramedics swarmed out to take possession of Wilcox. Underhill wandered off to supervise the clean-up.

I made a beeline for the evidence van an' axed one of the techs if they'd found a cell phone on any of the prisoners.

"All of 'em. Why?"

"The one who drove the truck here was talkin' on his to his boss, an' referencin' *his* boss. 'Fore we question any of 'em we oughta know who drove the truck here, who was he talkin' to, an' who was he talkin' about."

The tech just nodded an' said, "We'll get on it, Sheriff."

Just about then, a state cruiser pulled in with Sonny hangin' out the passenger side window.

"Sheriff!" he yelled when he spotted me. "Am I glad to see you!"

The car stopped. Sonny piled out an' come at me on a run. "I was afraid..." he said.

I said, "Seems like they didn't hurt *you* none."

"They scared me half to death but they just put me out an' drove off. It took me forever to walk somewhere there was a phone. Did you get 'em?"

"Mebbe. You'll have to see if you recognize any of 'em."

"D'you have my phone?"

I'd forgot I'd put it in my pocket. Strange he was more worried about his phone than his truck. I resisted the urge to hand it back to him. "'Fraid we're gonna have to hold it fer evidence."

I couldn't tell what he thought a that. He said, "What about my truck?"

"You can probably have it back when they're done processin' it."

"What about the cargo?"

"Might be some broken bottles but it's mostly all there."

He nodded. "Now what?"

"This ain't really my circus, so we'll have to wait an' ask the ringmaster."

Underhill. Who frowned when he spotted Sonny. "Thought you were going to keep your nose clean."

Sonny opened his mouth to protest; I cut in. "He was just doin' his job—How 'bout we see if he can ID anybody?"

Sonny looked scared. "They was wearing masks."

"Were they wearing clothes?" Underhill axed.

"Yeah."

"Well let's see if you recognize any of their clothes."

We done a circuit of the yard, an' Sonny looked in the windows of all the cruisers that was holdin' prisoners. Sort of. He didn't seem keen on lookin' real close. When he was done, he shook his head. *Vigorously*, as my ma woulda said. I figured all the prisoners who was lookin'—an' they was *all* lookin'—could see he was sayin' no.

If Underhill was disappointed, he didn't show it. But

I figured he'd noticed what I had—Sonny reacted to the guy in the third cruiser like he would if he'd come across a cottonmouth. Underhill signaled one of the troopers to come closer, an' told him to take Sonny to the cop shop to give a statement. Soon as they was out of earshot, Underhill said, "Maybe you ought to see if *you* recognize any of them."

I didn't have to tell him I hadn't *seen* the hijackers. *They* didn't know that, though, an' I was sure Underhill knew they didn't know it. I done the circuit the same way Sonny had, only I took the time to study each one, an' say "Howdy," an' listen carefully as he demanded to see his lawyer.

I was surprised that I *did* recognize three of the hijackers—the clowns Skip an' I'd arrested. The bad guy in the third car was the one Skip had christened "Ace."

"You fellas are slow learners," I told him. "You just made bail."

"Go fuck yourself!"

I just shook my head like he was hopeless, an' backed away an' closed the car door. Slowly. So he could tell he hadn't got my goat.

"Well?" Underhill said after he'd sent the bad guys to be fingerprinted and photographed.

I told him where I recognized the three guys from.

"Four guys. The one you didn't recognize is the guy your deputy arrested a while back."

"I'd like to know who bailed 'em out."

"Same guy bailed out your barbecued trucker."

"Billie Bonds?"

"Ah hunh."

"They better hope they get long sentences."

"Why is that, Vergil?"

"She's the only one ever made Rye break a sweat."

"She?"

"Yeah. I don't know the story, but I'll bet she'll take her loss outta their hides."

"One can only hope."

• • •

'Fore we got back to the State cop shop, I'd called to ask my sister to keep a eye on Skip an' ask Rye to mind the office.

Underhill made a phone call, an' when he got off, he said, "You're in luck, Vergil. Wilcox is going to make it. And he put enough holes in things to convince the dumbest jury in the state that you ran him down out of self defense."

"What about Sonny's truck?"

"He should be able to claim it in a day or two."

I handed him Sonny's phone an' told him where Sonny lost it an' how I'd got it.

"You think Sonny may be in on this? *You* told us he clean."

"An' he prob'ly is. But it can't hurt to check it out."

"I'll get someone on it. Meanwhile, let's see what our hijackers have to say."

"Not till we know whose numbers is in their call logs."

"Why?"

I told him what I'd told the tech—'bout the call I'd overheard right after the hijackin'.

"Well, they haven't come back with the call lists yet," Underhill said, "so why don't we go get coffee an' compare notes?"

Which is what we did. At the cafe across from the

station, the waitress served us steak an' eggs with our coffee an' left us the pot.

"Well, I ain't too bright," I said when we were alone.

"How's that, Vergil?"

"I dropped the ball on the Loomis case—which I'm pretty sure is related to this one. I got sidetracked an' failed to do a thorough canvass after his truck went missin'. Somebody might a seen Loomis stealin' it from Truck's or seen the somebody hangin' around who sabotaged the brakes. Now I'm thinkin' that someone might be one of these turkeys."

"Don't be too hard on yourself. Even *you* can't think of everything."

We tucked into our food for a while. Then Underhill pushed his plate away an' topped off his coffee. "Maybe you should lay this out for me."

"Lower Fork Distillery was one of the places Loomis delivered to, so I checked it out. Didn't seem like they was really distillin' anything 'less they was usin' a replicator."

"That what put them on your radar?"

"That an' how uncooperative the manager was when I tried to get a interview."

"And?"

"An' several people pointed out how Cheap-Ass Likkers seemed to be sellin' retail at wholesale prices. That an' they never got hijacked till I started askin' made me think hadda be a connection."

"So we have to find the connection?"

"I'm still waitin' to find out who owns both concerns."

"Maybe I can expedite that."

"I'd be obliged."

"Meanwhile, let's go interview Ace."

"You read my mind."

• • •

It was after 9 a.m. by the time we left the cafe. Sonny's truck was parked in the State Police lot, decorated like a parade float with yellow crime scene tape. Inside the station, Trooper Yates was on the desk. When he spotted me, he said, "We're having cards made up for you, Sheriff. 'Deters Demolition.'"

"Make fun all you want. I made the bust."

"We got those call lists yet?" Underhill asked.

Yates handed him a pile of papers. "Your prisoners are screaming their heads off for their lawyer. All of them want to call the same one."

"Who's that?" I cut in.

"Austin Glenlake."

"His name on the call lists?"

Yates shrugged. Underhill said, "Let's go in my office and see if we can find out."

• • •

There was five call lists with the name of the man the phone belonged to penciled in on the top of each. The lists was divided into contact numbers, dialed calls, received calls an' missed calls, with the time an' date fer each number called. Some of the called an' received numbers had names listed with 'em, some didn't. One of the numbers was on all the lists an' it looked familiar. Just to be sure, I phoned Rye an' axed him to look it up in the Loomis file.

"That's the number fer his lawyer," Rye told me when he got back to me.

What I'd thought. "Thanks, Rye."

"You comin' back to work any time soon?"

"You tired of bein' actin' sheriff?"

"Nah. Well… a guy come in just now askin' where he could find you. If I was a bettin' man I'd wager he was fixin' to serve you with papers."

"I'll be back tomorrow. But you don't have to tell the feller that." I hung up an' told Underhill, "That number's Austin Glenlake's throwaway phone."

"The jerk lawyer you arrested for bribery?"

"The same. An' since Loomis an' the hijackers all got him on speed dial, I'm thinkin' he might have some explainin' to do."

felonies an' misdemeanors

"'Fore we tackle Ace or Glenlake," I told Underhill, "mebbe we oughta see if Wilcox is awake. He might could straighten out this mare's nest."

"Good thinking, Vergil. I'll drive."

$\bullet \ \bullet \ \bullet$

We nodded to the trooper on guard outside the door, an' went in to find Wilcox hooked up to a EKG machine an' handcuffed to the safety rail on the side of his hospital bed. His nose was broke and both his eyes was blackened. He had a bandage coverin' the top half of his head, a cast on his good arm, an' both legs in traction.

Underhill led us into the room, an' when Wilcox spotted him, he turned his head towards the wall—didn't even muster enough oomph to axe fer his lawyer.

Underhill walked around the bed, so Wilcox was facin' him, an' Wilcox turned his head back towards me. Took him a second or two to recognize who was he lookin' at, after which he said, "Aw shit!"

I said, "You wanna tell me what I ever done to you?"

Wilcox glanced back at Underhill, who shrugged.

Wilcox sighed. "What kind of deal can I get if I tell you?"

"'Pends on *what* you tell me," I said. "Why don't you start with how come you know me when we never met before?"

"Somebody showed me your picture."

Underhill said, "Who?"

"Not 'til we got a deal."

"Your boss *pay* you to try'n kill a peace officer?" I axed.

"I didn't think..." Wilcox jerked his good wrist, snapping the cuff against the metal bed rail. "I better talk to my lawyer."

"That would be who?" Underhill said.

'Fore Wilcox could answer, I said, "Austin Glenlake."

Underhill didn't turn a hair. Wilcox's eyes widened like a kid's at a Freddy Krueger film.

"'Fraid you're gonna have to get another lawyer," I told him. "Court ain't gonna let a co-conspirator represent you." I wasn't sure that was the case an' it ain't my call to make. But I was bettin' Wilcox didn't know that.

Underhill musta knew—looked like he was fixin' to chew nails. But he didn't say nothin'.

Wilcox had turned whiter'n the bandage on his head. The EKG machine he was hooked up to started screamin', the squiggles on the monitor raced across the screen. Wilcox just managed to get out, "I want another lawyer!"

when a nurse come chargin' through the door to throw me an' Underhill out.

. . .

Underhill was pissed—lettin' a suspect know what you know that he didn't know you know is s'posed to be bad interview technique. I pretended I didn't notice. Sometimes, when you're dealin' with experienced criminals, it don't hurt to defy their expectations. We didn't talk till we was halfway back to his station. Then he said, "*Why* did you do that?"

"To shake him up."

"You did that. Now he's lawyered up."

"He's gonna have to have a lawyer to work out a deal anyway. *Now* we know for sure Glenlake's in on the scheme, not just representin' the players."

"Yeah. Well, since you seem to have taken over this show, just tell me what we're planning to do next."

. . .

Back in Underhill's office, we studied the telephone lists, one of which was for Wilcox's phone. He'd made plenty a calls to Glenlake, but that didn't prove nothin'. Either man could claim attorney-client privileges an' no doubt would. The fact that Wilcox had made long calls to all four hijackers— 'specially Ace—an' vice versa, was somethin' but not much. So was the fact that all five of our prisoners had been caught red-handed. But all we really had on Glenlake was Wilcox's over-reaction. Which wasn't gonna be admissible in court.

"You get anywhere on who owns Lower Fork?" I axed.

"So far, just a nest of Chinese boxes. We're not the Fed, you know."

Which give me a idea. "Mebbe it's time to cut *them* in on this."

"I'm listening."

"ATF owes me fer runnin' down who killed their agent last spring. An' they'd *love* to shut down a outfit's cheatin' 'em outta their excise."

Underhill pushed his desk phone towards me an' said, "Sic 'em."

After I'd laid out the scenario fer my "friend" at ATF, I called my lawyer an' axed would it be conflict of interest for him to represent a guy I was gonna charge with tryna kill me. I thought Underhill, who was listenin' in, was gonna bust a pipe.

Lawyer told me "probably" and axed for details; I told him about Wilcox and how we had him on enough charges to send him up fer several lifetimes. But we wanted him to cut a deal an' cooperate. So he needed a honest lawyer. Who the county would reimburse.

"I doubt there's enough money in Boone County to pay *my* fee for a case like that, Homer, but I'll find him someone. When's he going to be arraigned?"

"Well, he ain't leavin' the hospital fer some time, so I guess soon as we can arrange fer a court to come to him."

When I hung up, Underhill said, "You are out of your cotton-picking mind!"

"So I been told. We ready to lay this out fer the prosecutor?"

• • •

Which we did. At his office. George Usher, the Boone County prosecutor, shook his head. "We haven't even charged these guys yet."

Underhill laughed. "We haven't even questioned any of them."

"They lawyered up," I protested. "An' we don't know who's master-mindin' all this."

"Well, your clock is ticking," George said. "Charge them with the hijacking and attempted murder and we can go from there when you guys get your stuff together."

Underhill an' I both nodded.

As we headed for the door, George said, "Keep me posted."

• • •

Stead of callin', the ATF elected to show up in person—all three of the clowns that invaded my office last spring—in the same suits, with the same attitude. I was sittin' back in the corner of Underhill's office, mainlinin' coffee when they come through the door, so they didn't notice me right off.

"We're here to take charge of your prisoners," the one in the gray suit told Underhill.

"And your evidence," the one in the brown suit added.

Underhill wasn't any more intimidated by their act than I'd been. "I'm afraid you'll have to wait until we're done with them. We have them on attempted murder of a police officer among other things."

Which trumped failure to pay likker taxes.

"But that'll be a lot sooner," I chimed in, "if you got us that information I requested."

The three of 'em turned together like well rehearsed line dancers. They kept their faces straight—don't think any of 'em had another expression—but I could see they was dismayed.

"What are you doing here?" Gray Suit demanded.

"Cooperatin' with a brother law enforcement agency. Just like you're plannin' to do."

Gray Suit looked like he was fixin' to bust, but all he said was, "Fine." He turned to Brown Suit, who turned to Blue Suit. Blue Suit took a envelope out of a inside jacket pocket an' put it on Underhill's desk.

Gray Suit said, "We expect copies of all your reports." Then the three of 'em turned in unison an' stalked out.

Underhill waited 'till the door closed 'fore he broke out laughin'. "You all right, Vergil."

"Mebbe. Let's see what they brought us 'fore we celebrate."

Underhill opened the envelope an' spread the contents out on his desk. Ten sheets a paper. Each sheet was a summary of the incorporation paperwork fer a different company. Top sheet was fer Lower Fork Distillery, which seemed like it belonged to a AAAce Distribution Corporation—in a other state, which appeared to belong to... An' like that fer all ten of the companies, the last of which was located in one of those offshore countries that don't share info with U.S. law enforcement agencies. Underhill pointed to a paper halfway through the pile.

"This one owns Cheap-Ass Likkers. You struck gold, Vergil. Here's our connection."

"Does it connect Cheap-Ass to Glenlake?"

"That'd be too easy."

I just nodded. Underhill picked up his phone an' dialed. After a bit he said, "Did you manage to access those emails?" Guy on the other end must a said yes, 'cause Underhill said, "Thanks," an' hung up the phone. He turned on his computer an' brought up a folder. Inside was a bunch of emails. "From Wilcox's phone," Underhill said. "We looking for anything in particular?"

"Yeah, anythin' with a picture attached. Or anythin' to or from Ace or Glenlake's phone."

Underhill opened one of the messages an' said, "Bingo!" My picture was showin' on the screen.

I grabbed Underhill's phone an' dialed the county prosecutor. When he said, "County Attorney's office. George Usher speaking," I said, "This is Sheriff Deters."

"I was just going to call you. Three ATF agents were just in here to file a complaint. Where do you get off cutting me out of the loop on this hijacking conspiracy?"

"George, I'm just tryna get to who killed Samuel Loomis."

"The trucker? What's he got to do with the hijackers?"

"He was drivin' a stolen truck, makin' deliveries to the bogus distillery."

"Why didn't you say so earlier?"

"I did. You told me to get back to you when I had something concrete. Think I finally got it."

"What?" George didn't sound quite so pissed off. Which was promisin'.

"Loomis had the same lawyer—Austin Glenlake—on speed dial. Same as all the hijackers we nailed.

"If he's good, that proves nothing more than that he has a reputation as a shark."

"He's the one I arrested for tryna bribe me."

"And?"

"He emailed a picture of me to the guy who runs Lower Fork."

"Is that all you've got?"

"He had long conversations with all the guys we nailed—before they was arrested. An' he left the message, 'get rid of the moonlighter' on one of their cell phones."

"Have you questioned this guy?"

"Can't. He's lawyered up. An' Glenlake's his lawyer."

"Not if they're co-conspirators. Have your hijacker call another attorney—or we'll have a judge appoint a public defender, and we'll see if we can make a deal."

• • •

Ace was *really* unhappy when we gave him the bad news. He *wanted* Glenlake. When I told him he'd have to call somebody else, or talk to a public defender, he looked ready to cry. Told me he didn't *know* anybody else.

It was late afternoon time we'd got a judge to appoint Councilman Andrews to advise Ace on his rights. Then the four of us—Ace an' Andrews, me an' George Usher—set down at the conference table in the state police station to talk turkey.

The most George would offer Ace was that he'd drop some of the pissant charges an' ask the court for the minimum sentences if Ace pleaded guilty to the rest. In return, he'd have to tell us about Glenlake an' testify against him when the time come.

He sang like a mountain canary about the hijack scheme. Why not? We'd caught him in the act. Twice. I figured that'd be enough to arrest Glenlake, but we also needed enough on 'im to subpoena his papers an' phone records. George an' I adjourned to the hall outside the room so I could ax what else we needed.

"Something that proves Glenlake was more than just a co-conspirator."

"Like solicitin' murder?"

"That would do it."

I nodded an' went back in. George stayed outside to watch through the two-way mirror.

When I was back settin' across from Ace, I said, "You happen to recall a voice mail message Glenlake left you a couple or three weeks back?"

"Remind me."

"Get rid of the moonlighter?"

Ace got a little pale an' his jaw muscles tightened.

I waited.

"No."

I shook my head an' tried to look disappointed. "You was gonna tell the truth."

"I wanna talk to him," Ace said, hitchin' his thumb towards Andrews.

I nodded an' left the room. I checked the plumbin', got myself a cup a coffee, shot the breeze with Underhill an' Trooper Yates for a while.

Usher come back from wherever he'd got off to. "Well?" he said.

"My guess is he's plannin' to plead the fifth," I said.

"For?"

"Glenlake wouldn't kill Loomis hisself, an' Wilcox is too smart to get involved in a premeditated murder. The other three ain't smart enough to pull one off. That leaves Ace. Andrews won't let him admit to the murder, but maybe we can get him to say the message was about Loomis. Then you legal types can work out what to charge him with and how to sell it to a judge."

George nodded. Underhill got Ace's phone for me, an' George an' me went back in the conference room.

"I've advised my client not to answer any further questions," Andrews said. "He's—"

"I understand," George interrupted. "…That he doesn't want to implicate himself in any further malfeasance. But he agreed to cooperate, and we need to know what this voicemail was referring to."

George looked at me, an' I turned the volume up on Ace's phone an' played the voice mail.

Ace whispered in Andrews' ear. Andrews nodded an' told Ace, "Tell them."

"It was that truck driver he…" Ace jerked his head towards me, "…arrested at the truck stop. The one who fucked up hauling horses."

"Did he mean moonshiner?" George axed.

"No. Loomis was working for us. He was *moonlighting* as a horse hauler. Glenlake was afraid he'd called attention to us by getting himself arrested."

"Or that he'd talk?" I said.

Ace glanced at Andrews, who shook his head. Ace shrugged.

"Why'd Glenlake call *you*?" George axed him; Ace shrugged again. "What did Glenlake mean, 'Get rid of him'?"

Ace looked away an' said, "Fire him, I guess."

Doubtful anybody in the room believed that, but none

of us called him on it. Andrews would tell him not to answer if we did.

Andrews finally said, "That's enough." George nodded.

I took Ace back to his cell, an' George went off to get us some subpoenas.

• • •

After a judge signed the paperwork, Underhill an' I figured out which of the other three hijackers was the dumbest an' let him call his attorney. Then we sent him back to his cell an' waited for his attorney to show up.

• • •

Glenlake stormed in around suppertime, madder'n a sack full a stray cats. "You've held my clients for nearly twenty-four hours," he shouted, "without letting them call their attorney?"

"Don't get your tail in a knot, Austin," I told him. "We'll get 'em all a attorney. But you ain't it. You're under arrest, too."

• • •

'Fore I called it a night, I axed Underhill about Sonny's truck.

"Beside the windshield and bullet holes," Underhill told me, "the tractor isn't too badly damaged—just some dents and scrapes from the door and chain link fence you took out—that's on you, by the way. If the county won't pay."

We was settin' in his office with our feet up, windin' down.

I said, "Wasn't there a reward put up by the liquor distributors?"

"Yeah, but law enforcement doesn't qualify to collect."

"Mebbe we could nominate Sonny."

"It's not enough we overlooked several felonies?"

"We can't charge him with those, 'less we want the Feds after *us* for conspiracy."

"What!"

"We cut him loose without chargin' him when we shoulda threw the book at him. 'Sides, if Sonny can't collect the reward, the distributors get to keep it. An' they make enough off the poor jokers they sell booze to."

Underhill held up his hands. "If you want to nominate Sonny for the reward, that's on you. I'm not getting involved."

• • •

Roustin' Sonny from his bed close to midnight did half the job of convincin' him to talk.

"If you don't have a real good reason why you lied when you said you didn't recognize the hijackers, I'm gonna run you in for conspiracy to commit a dozen felonies."

Sonny got whiter'n the wife-beater he was wearin'. "They said they'd kill me, Sheriff. Even if the law arrested them, they'd get outta jail an' come after me. An' my wife, too."

"Ah hunh. First thing in the mornin', I expect you over to the State Police station to give Sergeant Underhill your *revised* statement."

• • •

It was after midnight when I tapped on Nina's window. Lights was all out in the house. I didn't want to wake her if she was sound asleep, an' I sure didn't want to wake Grampa Ross.

Wasn't but a minute 'fore Nina threw open the window an' leaned out.

"Evenin', Miss Ross," I said.

"Homer, you been drinkin'?"

"No, but I'm high on you."

"Horse feathers!" I didn't try to change her opinion. She added, "Thought you was workin' nights."

"Not any more. We nailed the hijackers, so I'm back workin' days."

"'Bout time."

"Skip's spendin' the night at Penny's."

"You come all the way over here to tell me that?"

"Naw. I come to tell you this's been the longest week of my life."

"S'pose you think I oughta let you spend the night."

"I don't think you oughta, but that's never stopped you before."

She nodded. "Well, don't just stand there, go 'round to the back door so I can let you in."

We barely got into Nina's room 'fore she was tearin' off my uniform. She pushed me onto the bed an' pulled off my boots, then started tuggin' off my britches. Last thing I remember was her sayin', "Homer, don't you dare fall asleep…"

who killed Harlan

"Homer, who killed Harlan?" Rye axed me next mornin'. We was havin' coffee in my office while I filled him in on all the arrests an' developments.

"Gotta been Murphy."

"Who the hell's Murphy?"

"He's the one figured out that if anything can go wrong it will. At the worst time possible."

"Why—?"

"To complicate my life. Harlan'd be hale an' whole if I hadn't had two other dead bodies an' a rash of truck hijackin's to deal with."

"You're pullin' my leg. Don't do that, Homer. You're s'posed to be showin' me the ropes, not confusin' me with foolishness."

I grinned. "Rye, if you was simple, I'd buy that, but you ain't."

"We talked to everyone Harlan knowed, Homer. Who's that leave?"

"The invisible man."

"Huhn?"

"Too bad you don't read more, Rye. You're missin' out on a lotta neat tricks."

"Like how someone can make hisself invisible?"

Which give me a idea. I got the missin' mail outta the file cabinet—still in the evidence bag Nina'd insisted I put it in when she give it to me. Didn't take me long to dump the bag out on my desk an' dust it all fer prints—found a few dandies. I lifted 'em with tape an' 'tached each one on a numbered evidence card, then handed the cards to Rye. "Run these by the state cop shop fer me, will you?"

"Aw, they'll laugh me outta Boone County."

"Ask 'em to check 'em against Harlan's fingerprint's an' run any that ain't Harlan's against their data bases."

"You think it was Harlan's mail?"

"I think it's too much coincidence—all this stuff bein' dumped in ditches. We catch who dumped the mail, mebbe we can shed some light on who dumped the bodies."

"What you gonna do while I'm doin' the legwork?"

Legwork. Rye was learnin' the lingo. I was impressed. I said, "I'm gonna mosey over to the post office an' see if I can't get 'em to give me some elimination prints."

• • •

"Ain't there laws against self-incrimination?" Nina said, when I told her what I had in mind.

"Ain't self-incrimination if you ain't done nothin' wrong."

"An' what if I have?"

"Have you?"

"'Course not!"

"Well, then…?"

"How you gonna get Len an' Ed to go along?"

"Gonna appeal to their sense of civic duty."

"Good luck with that."

• • •

Luck didn't have much to do with it, as it turned out. Both West Wheelin' postmen were happy to prove they weren't involved in the misdirection of U.S. mail, 'specially when they come in from their routes an' found me fingerprintin' Nina. I run the print cards by the state police an' got results 'fore I closed up fer the day. Len Hartman's prints was all over the evidence. I called Nina an' she confirmed Harlan's place was on Len's route.

• • •

I cornered Len next mornin', just as he was climbin' into his mail truck.

"Got a couple questions for you, Len."

He put his hands up an' waved 'em back an' forth. "I don't wanna to get involved, Sheriff."

"Seems like you're the one seen Harlan last. You know what that means?"

"You're gonna make my life miserable 'cause you ain't got no real suspects? What's my motive?"

"I ain't accusin' you, Len. But there's a killer out there. Somebody strong an' evil enough to kill Harlan. Could be someone lives on *your* route. What if he decides he don't like the way you deliver mail? You want him on the loose?"

As he thought about that, Len seemed to get more an' more upset. "Hell, no!" he said, finally. "But what can *I* do?"

"Think back. You remember anything outta the ordinary 'bout Harlan's mail?"

"Everything about Harlan's mail was outta the ordinary."

"In what way?"

"He was always gettin' packages an' special deliveries an' stuff."

"Post office keep records of that?"

"Certified, an' registered, an' tracking. You'd have to ask Miz Ross."

"I'll do that. Much obliged." I handed him my card. "You see or hear of anything suspicious, gimme a call."

He put the card in his pocket, but from the look on his face, I figured he'd have to be dodgin' live rounds to even consider it.

. . .

"Why didn't I think a that?" Nina said, when I asked about Harlan's special deliveries. "'Course I got records. You think Harlan was dealin' drugs or contraband, an' someone killed him for it?" I give her a look, an' she said, "'Course he wasn't. I didn't say that. You didn't *hear* that."

"Think I could see the records?"

"You got a warrant?"

"How 'bout we do it the old-school way?"

"Which is?"

"You let me peek at the records an' if it comes to anything, I'll sweet-talk a judge into givin' me a warrant."

She shook her head, but pulled out a old oversized ledger book.

I said, "Thought the post office was computerized."

"S'what they tell me. But they won't let me send Ed or Len fer classes. An' that thing…" She pointed at the console that weighed mail an' dished out postage labels. "Is broke down more often than a Amtrak train." She patted the ledger. "So this is believe-it-or-not faster." She run her finger down the columns an' called out all the special deliveries Harlan'd had fer the year before he died—twenty of 'em—while I wrote down what they was an' who they was from. After which—since there wasn't another soul in the place—I give Nina a 'specially appreciative thank you.

● ● ●

Back in my office, I called everyone on Harlan's mailin' list to ask what they'd sent him an' why. Some of the folks who answered wanted to know who was I? An' what was I doin' pokin' into Harlan's business? When I told 'em Harlan had been murdered, they was to a man—an' one woman—happy to talk. Most of Harlan's special deliveries was books, most of 'em on Injuns.

The last feller I spoke to was the director of a small museum. I identified myself an' told him I was investigatin' a mail theft case involvin' the certified package he'd sent Harlan that seemed to have disappeared. "What was in it, if you don't mind my askin'?"

"An Indian artifact—a ceremonial necklace Harlan sent me for authentication."

"Was it?" I asked. "Authentic?"

"Yes. Didn't Harlan tell you?"

"Hate to be the bearer of bad news, but Harlan's been murdered."

"Why—"

"What I'm tryna find out."

The guy on the other end of the line was speechless. Or at least, real quiet until I said, "What was the necklace worth?"

"Probably nothing. It was a common item, very plain and unremarkable. It wasn't what the 'thieves of time' would consider collectible. In fact, only an academic or a member of the tribe that produced it would recognize it as old or significant."

"Or Harlan."

"Or Harlan." I waited to see if he'd volunteer anything more. He did. "I can send you a jay-peg of it if you'd like."

I liked. I gave him my email address, then asked, "Harlan ever mention who might know about this necklace?"

"I believe he was quite reticent about sharing his finds with local people. He said his neighbors were unsympathetic toward Native Americans."

No kiddin'!

"Well, you hear of anyone unsympathetic enough to do Harlan in, you'll let me know?"

"I certainly will."

I hung up an' thought about the necklace until my computer dinged to tell me I had mail. The picture showed a string a little flat gray an' brown an' black beads—looked like slices of chicken bones colored with different shades of mud. They was strung together on a piece of ordinary cotton string. The message the picture was attached to said the beads had arrived unstrung, an' a expert on the museum staff had strung them together so none of them would get lost in the mail. The order of colors was "an educated guess based on similar artifacts the museum has in its collection."

I filed the photo an' turned off the computer 'fore I went to thank Nina again for her help.

• • •

She was closin' up the post office fer the day when I come in, waitin' on the fifteen folks who'd come in at five to five to get their mailin' done. I locked the door an' put the CLOSED sign up, then took my place at the end of the line—hadda get back outta line to let customers out when they was finished an' keep more from sneakin' in whenever the door opened.

When there was finally no one left but Nina an' me, I give her a proper kiss. Lasted a while.

We finally come up fer air an' Nina said, "Whew! You can close up fer me any time."

"Come to thank you fer your help."

"Somethin' else I can help you with?"

"Matter of fact…" I give her another kiss, then got serious. "I'd be obliged if tomorrow you let out I had a break in Harlan's murder."

"Who done it?"

"I ain't prepared to say yet. Just let it slip that I'll be out at Silas Hanson's place Saturday afternoon, wrappin' up some details." No one in Boone County is better at keepin' secrets than Nina. But also ain't a soul can get the word out faster.

"You know who done it an' you ain't gonna tell me?"

"All in good time."

"You don't know yet, do you?"

"You're welcome to come by Hanson's Saturday an' see."

makin' connections

Just after quitin' time, next afternoon, Rye an' me was celebratin' us solvin' Rye's first homicide case with a jug of West Wheelin' White Lightnin'. We was settin' up in my office with our feet on my desk when the mayor come in. Rye shoved a chair over towards His Honor an' passed the jug.

"Don't mind if I do," His Honor said. He took a pull an' passed the jug to me. After a while, he said, "Looks like you got everything worked out 'cept who killed Harlan an' where that skeleton come from that Festus found in the ditch."

"I'm workin' on those," I told him. "Did Roy Peterman have a EPA report done on that property 'fore he petitioned the county for a zonin' change?"

Mayor shot me a gimme-a-break look. "'Course he did."

"Well, if I can have a look at that report, an' the engineerin' study he was s'posed to have done, I may be able to solve the mystery of our ancient Injun."

"How's that, Homer?" Rye asked 'fore the mayor could.

"Rather not speculate 'fore I take a look at the

284

EPA report."

Rye nodded. He's known me long enough to figure I wasn't eager to share my hunches with the mayor.

"Do what you gotta do, Sheriff," Mayor said. "An' meantime, how 'bout you pass me the jug."

. . .

First thing next mornin', I moseyed over to the county records office an' commandeered the file on Peterman's zoning request. He'd had to prove to the EPA his plan wouldn't exterminate any endangered critters or put nothin' harmful in the air or water. The file contained a bunch a reports on soil conditions, drainage, an' so forth. After lunch, I looked 'em over—couldn't make a whole lot of sense of 'em, so I decided to get some technical assistance. I made photocopies of all the reports, includin' the ones Doc Howard an' his experts made on the skeleton, an' I headed to the University.

. . .

Doc's office hours is from one to three p.m. I timed my visit late enough that he'd be done dealin' with the most pressin' student emergencies, not so late I'd miss him if he left early. He was just fixin' to leave.

"Not another body, I hope, Sheriff."

"Same one."

"*Which* same one?"

"The dead Injun."

"I assure you, there's nothing more we can do with it."

I nodded. "I was hopin' one of your geologists might could take a look at a couple reports. See if there's any similarities."

"Let's see them."

I handed over the photocopies, an' Doc shuffled through 'em. After a bit he said, "Curious." Then he stood up an' gathered up the papers. "Come with me."

I followed him halfway across the campus to the Geology department, to the office of Professor Ostler. Doc tapped on the door, then barged in without waiting for a invite.

Ostler was short an' round as a corn-fed possum an' just as cranky. "What?" he demanded.

Doc didn't pay no attention to his temper. "George, take a look at these and tell me if they mean what I think."

Ostler blinked like the same fat possum in headlights, then took the papers Doc was holdin' out. He studied 'em a while, mutterin' things like "interesting," "very curious," an' "fascinating!"

Finally, he handed Doc the papers back an' said, "Ninety-three percent chance the samples are from the same source as the Native American remains. You'd have to do further tests to be more certain." He glared at me, then Doc, then said, "Get the hell out of here. And next time make an appointment."

Doc didn't seem to notice his bad mood. Out in the hall, he said, "Where *is* this property?"

I told him an' axed, "Why?"

"Because the Anthropology department will want to know immediately."

"Hold on, Doc. It's private property. You-all go chargin' over there, you're liable to get shot."

"You're not suggesting I ignore what could be a significant historical find?"

"No. I'm just suggestin' you let me do my job."

"Which is, in this case?"

"Well, disturbin' a Native American burial site, failin' to make a report to the state authorities, an' illegal dumpin' is all criminal acts...."

I thought Doc was gonna bust. I put up my hands. "You kin help."

"How?"

"Get Professor Ostler to put his opinion in writin'. Then I can get a search warrant for Peterman's farm an' deputize your bone-hunters to find where the Injun bones was buried."

Which is how we come to set up a egghead posse to go over Peterman's farm the followin' Saturday mornin'.

field trip

One of the reports sent back from the University with the Injun bones stated "The soil clinging in the crevasses of the bones was inconsistent with the sand/soil of the ditch where the remains were found."

I coulda told 'em that. Why dig up a body an' drop it anywhere near where it was buried? Dumpin' it in a ditch was a hell of a way to get rid of it unless you wanted it to be found. Why there? Harlan had signed for the beads the museum guy sent back, but they hadn't turned up at his house or in the ditch where he was dumped. Where'd they go?

After I got Professor Ostler's report, I took all the paperwork from Peterman's rezonin' application and the University reports on the skeleton to the county agent to find out where in Boone County soil consistent with the trace on the skeleton might be found. Turned out, on the opposite side of Silas Hanson's farm from the ditch. An' a remote corner of Harlan's, near Hanson's, an' at Peterman's place.

Back in my office, I fired up my computer. I had to call Merlin 'bout how to work the external drive he'd copied Harlan's data onto, but eventually I managed to open Harlan's files. Most of 'em was pretty dry—kinda like readin' law or physics books—but some of it was maps. They wasn't labeled any way particularly useful to law enforcement, but I got the gist. Harlan had guessed there was a Injun burial site—or sites—in Boone County, an' had marked where he thought they might be found on his maps. He'd also marked where the beads come from that the museum guy sent pictures of. The most interestin' file was a copy of Harlan's will. He'd left his farm to his wife, but had wrote he hoped she'd leave it to his favorite tribe when she passed. I wondered had he ever showed it to her.

So I asked Miz Harlan. He hadn't, an' their lawyer hadn't got round to readin' it fer the family yet. I didn't tell her what it said—it wasn't my place. An' she'd learn soon enough. I axed her was there anything I could do fer her. She said just find Harlan's killer. I told her I wouldn't quit till I did.

Next, I went to the County Attorney to axe about laws governing Injun burial sites.

"It's too bad Harlan passed," George told me. "*He* was the expert."

"Well, we'll have to make do with a anthropologist from the University. Meanwhile, are Harlan's maps enough to get search warrants for where he thought might be Injun cemeteries?"

"Why do you need to know that?"

"It looks like Harlan mighta been killed by someone didn't want him tellin' where one might be found."

"I should think so. How're you going to execute them?

I bet you wouldn't recognize an Indian grave if you fell into it."

"You get me the warrants, I'll figger out how to search."

"Warrants?"

"For Silas's place, an' Harlan's an' Roy Peterman's."

• • •

Saturday mornin' I deputized three professors from the University, half a dozen graduate students, an' Skip, an' led them an' Rye on a scavenger hunt for old bones. Only reason Nina didn't come was she had to keep the post office open till noon.

The egghead posse found two more beads at Peterman's, signs of a "disinterment" at Hanson's, an' half a dozen undisturbed graves at Harlan's—all right where Harlan's maps predicted.

I called George to break the news, axed him to get a court order to protect the sites till the state antiquities and the local tribe could get their two cents in on the situation.

"I can't do that, Homer," George told me. "It's a state and federal matter."

"Well, who could?"

"I'll call around an' ask."

I suspected George was draggin' his feet 'cause he didn't want to get involved, so I got hold of Stanley Redwine an' axed for the number of his sharkskin lawyer. When I told him about our finds, an' the unofficial town meetin' I was convenin' shortly, he said he'd be along directly with the necessary papers.

. . .

We was done with the search by noon, an' by half-past noon, half of West Wheelin' had showed up in front of Silas Hanson's. It was kinda déjà vu. Most of the gawkers who'd been there when John Doe turned up, along with Nina, Roy Peterman—who lived across the road from Silas—our local reporter, Abner Davies, an' Stanley Redwine's band an' lawyer.

Thank goodness it wasn't a crime scene this time, 'cause everybody milled around, speculatin' an stompin' the parkway grass till I got out my bull-horn an' called fer "Quiet!"

"What's going on, Sheriff?" Mayor demanded. "Rumor has it you've made a breakthrough on your case. Which case?"

I nodded. "Both cases. I think. It seems pretty clear that whoever killed Harlan did it to keep him quiet about a Injun cemetery." I looked at Silas.

"Silas, you got the right to remain silent, but you're a God-fearin' man. An' you know confession is good fer your soul."

Silas turned two shades of white an' swallowed.

We all waited.

Finally he said, "I ain't gonna add lyin' to disturbin' the dead. I done it."

"You wanted to make it look like Peterman dumped them bones?"

"Yeah."

"But they really come from your property."

Silas nodded.

"You didn't want to lose your farm to Injun claims?"

He nodded again.

"An' you hoped I'd think Peterman done it to jam you up?"

Silas nodded again.

"Mighta worked, too, if I hadn't been so distracted by all them other things."

"Sheriff, what're you gonna do about it?" Roy Peterman demanded. "You gonna arrest him?"

"I'll think about it. Meanwhile, don't get too smug. You got some Injun remains buried on your place too."

"Prove it."

"I will, soon's the report comes from the state anthropology department." I pulled the paper the Injuns' lawyer'd give me outta my pocket an' handed it to Peterman. "Meanwhile, the state don't want you doin' nothin' to disturb the site. An' if you ain't got a alibi for the afternoon Harlan died, you'd best get you a good lawyer."

I turned to the crowd an' said, "That's all, folks. You can get the details in the paper."

Abner, who was takin' notes faster'n a court reporter, pointed his pen at me. "I expect an interview, Sheriff."

I nodded. Rye put the cuffs on Peterman an' stuffed him in a cruiser while I served the Injuns' paper on Silas. Silas looked like his best dog just died. Nina told me she'd take Skip home an' see me tonight. Then everybody headed out.

• • •

Time I got to the state cop shop, Peterman was nervous as a cat at a dog fight. Rye wouldn't tell him nothin' an' the state cops wouldn't even talk to him. I walked in; he said, "Sheriff!—"

I held up my hand to shut him up. "You got a right to remain silent, Roy. Anything you say——"

"I didn't mean to kill him!"

"Can be held against you in a court a law."

"I was just holdin' him down, tryin' to get him to listen."

"Will you shut up an' let me finish!"

He did, an' I did. He nodded when I axed did he understand, then added, "Time I noticed he wasn't breathing, it was too late."

"You just left him there for the dogs and varmints?"

"I knew the mailman would be along shortly. I wanted to talk to Harlan without his missus overhearing, so I was waiting when he came out to meet the mailman. Harlan always got to his mailbox around delivery time. I swear I didn't mean to kill him!"

An' I believed him. I didn't point out that Harlan might'a been resuscitated if Peterman had called 9-1-1. Or that Len Hartman hadn't discovered the remains 'til Harlan was comin' outta rigor. Roy was tellin' the truth as he saw it; an' nothin' was gonna bring Harlan back.

So we charged Roy with manslaughter an' called George to take over the case.

• • •

I headed back to the office just before sunset, an' I hadn't got far when Martha come on the radio. "Homer, Wilma Netherton just called. She was too hysterical to tell me what's wrong."

"Ten-four. If she calls back, tell her I'm on my way."

Wilma was on her porch, pacin' like caged hyena, wringin'

her hands an' gettin' her dogs so riled up they wouldn't stop barkin'. There wasn't a cat in sight. Smart critters.

When I got outta my cruiser, the dogs started barkin' at me. I put on my hat an' give 'em a don't-piss-me-off look an' yelled, "QUIET!"

Dogs looked surprised. An' shut up. An' lay down.

I turned to Wilma. "What seems to be the problem, Miz Netherton?"

Wilma's hand shook as she pointed towards the road. "That—That woman—Look!"

I looked. Peepin' above the line of new bushes across the road was the top of somethin' looked like a castle from a kid's story book, with four towers or spires made of gray stone studded with shiny round disks instead of bricks. A flagpole—looked like made from a broomstick—topped the tallest spire, with a pennant flutterin' from it in the breeze. I couldn't make out what was on the little flag, but it was colorful an' stood out in the last light of sunset against the bare trees in Mary Lincoln's yard.

"What's she up to?" Wilma screeched. "She can't do it!"

"Wilma, settle down! I'll go check it out. You go inside and make yourself—" I almost said a cup a coffee, but it hit me she may've had too much of that already. "…A good stiff drink."

Wilma's a Baptist, who don't drink. She opened her mouth, then snapped it shut. Then she turned around an' stalked into her house an' slammed the door.

I got in my car an' drove across the street.

It was startin' to be too dark to see, but first thing I noticed was a stake drove into the front grass with a building permit nailed to it. Second thing was Don Firenzi's plaid truck. Firenzi's cat was parked on top of the cab with its front feet tucked under its chest. Firenzi was up on a scaffold, dressed in rubber boots an' coveralls with a trowel in one gloved hand an' a plasterer's hawk in the other. I watched as he slapped mortar off the hawk onto the wall he was buildin'—looked like the wall of a castle with steel window frames set in places an' rebar pokin' up fer reinforcement. Instead of bricks, Firenzi was usin' empty bottles—blue an' green glass mostly—from a old milk crate on the scaffold. When he ran outta mortar on his hawk, he scooped more outta a five gallon paint bucket. The pile of scavenged glass bottles I'd seen on my last visit was gone.

At that point, the porch light went on, an' Mary come outta the house. "Don, how can you see what you're doing? And supper's nearly ready, so why don't you call it a day?" She spotted me an' said, "Good evening, Sheriff. Homer."

Firenzi turned around an' said, "Sheriff." To Mary, he said, "Let me just use up the last of this." He went back to layin' the bottles into the wall while Mary an' I watched. When his hawk was empty, he scraped the last of the mortar outta the paint pail an' slapped that in place, then smoothed it an' put his tools in the pail. He climbed down, went to the hose pipe an' started washin' mortar off his tools.

Mary turned to me an' said, "What brings you by so late Homer?"

"Some a your neighbors got a low tolerance fer novelty. I said I'd check to see you had all your plans an' permits in order so they could put this—" I waved at the construction. "...Outta mind. You run this whatever-it-is past the buildin' department?"

"It's a castle. Of course we did. They thought it was

unusual, but structurally sound. Do you want to see the plans?"

"That won't be necessary." I didn't add I probably wouldn't be able to make heads or tails of that kinda plans. "What made you decide to build a castle?"

"Well, the sign on Don's truck says Masonry and Whimsy. So I asked him what whimsy was, and he said, 'What would you like?' I asked for an example, and Don said, 'A castle.'"

"When she asked what I'd build a castle *with*," Firenzi chimed in, "I told her just about anything. Like the stuff she had lying around the yard, for instance."

"One thing led to another," Mary added, "and here we are."

"Well," I said, "I guess it all looks better as a castle than in piles."

"And it's much more practical, Homer. When it's finished, Don's going to rent it from me. For a studio." She looked at Firenzi an' smiled, then looked back at me. "Would you like to join us for dinner?"

"I'd be obliged, but I got a few things to wrap up 'fore I call it a day." I pointed at the castle. "Good luck with that."

Wilma musta been watchin' for me, 'cause she swarmed out on her porch as I drove up. I got outta the car—didn't bother to put on my hat—an' walked up to the porch.

"What *is* that thing, Sheriff? And what are you going to do about it?"

"I'm gonna ask you what was the first thing you done when Miz Lincoln moved in across the road."

Wilma looked confused. "I didn't do anything."

"Ah hunh. An' what was the first thing you done when the Davises moved in?"

Wilma looked even more confused as she thought about it. Finally she said, "I took them over a *pe*can pie."

"Yeah. Well, I think your problems with Miz Lincoln will end if you just take *her* a pie." I put on my hat. 'Fore I turned to go, I said, "Bein' eccentric ain't illegal in Boone County. So don't call me again 'less there's been shots fired. Or I'm gonna run you in for wastin' police time."

Last I seen a Wilma, as I backed outta the drive, was her standin' with her mouth open, watchin' me drive away.

• • •

Back at the office, Rye cracked a jug of White Lightnin' 'fore we called it a night, an' we had a drink to celebrate solvin' all our cases.

"Homer, what're we gonna do with all that money Loomis had in the bank?" Which was now burnin' a hole in my safe.

"Technically, it belongs to Henry Ames."

Rye give me a look that said, "Yeah, right!"

"Mr. Ames ain't all that competent to handle money, so I asked his daughter to take care of it for him."

"You're shittin' me!"

"I wouldn't do that, Rye."

"But it was Loomis's money!"

"Said Henry Ames on the paperwork."

"A.k.a. Loomis. Loomis didn't have no next of kin. We could use that money. We could get a new squad car. Or some laser radar."

"Miss Ames needs it more, Rye. Nursin' homes ain't cheap."

Rye just shook his head an' left the office.

movin' day

I didn't have to show up fer the closin' on Ash Jackson's old place Monday mornin'. Hazel Wrencock set up a blind sale—made it seem like she'd suckered some city feller into takin' it off Pappy Jackson's hands. All I had to do was get a cashier's check for the purchase price, an' sign the papers. Hazel come by my office after the deal was sealed to give me my share of the paperwork an' the keys to the house.

First thing I done was call up Lockout Willis an' have him change the security arrangements. Then I give the new keys to Jesus Lopez an' axed him to fix anything that was broke an' give everything a new coat of paint—inside an' out. I didn't mention anything about any of it to Skip—figured if he knew, he might be tempted to brag to his buddies at school, an' everybody in Boone County'd know about it.

Jesus done the job in three days. Found out later that Martha Rooney watched his kids so he could work round the clock. Martha took over from Jesus. She called up everybody owed me—or her—a favor. Told 'em to show up at my old place Saturday mornin', ready to work an' with all the empty boxes they could scare up. So Saturday, when Skip axed me at breakfast, "Ain't we s'posed to be outta here today?" I was able to say, "We will be."

I'd just finished washin' the breakfast dishes when we heard a commotion outside. Turned out most of West Wheelin' was congregatin' in the front yard, carryin' boxes.

Martha Rooney led the parade. "Nina said to tell you she'll be closing the post office early, and she'll meet you at the new house," Martha said.

Skip said, "What house?"

"You'll see," I told 'im.

Shortly after that, Rye and Merlin, the volunteer fire department, the Truck brothers an' Dan Underhill arrived, most of 'em in pickups. Stanley Redwine an' his band come in their Silverado. The mayor even showed up to supervise. Church ladies swarmed into the kitchen an' started emptyin' cabinets an' drawers into cartons an' crates. Jesus Lopez led most of the volunteer firemen down the basement with boxes an' totes. Mary Lincoln shoved a couple boxes at me an' said, "Put your personal effects in these, Homer. The men are going to move your furniture next."

In less than a hour, everything Skip an' I owned—except for my gun safe, which Rye, D.W. Truck, an' I had moved after dark the night before—was packed into a assortment of vehicles on its way to our new place. Martha an' Maria Lopez—who'd closed up the Grassy-ass to help—scrubbed the floors an' took out the last of the trash 'fore they climbed in Martha's van to join the convoy. The whole operation seemed like a cross between army ants cleanin' out a picnic an' a Chinese fire drill. Mrs. Shaklee stood beside her jackass-chewed rosebushes watchin' the show with her arms crossed an' her jaw set. When the house was finally empty an' clean as a old Ajax-was-here commercial, I handed her the keys an' told her I was much obliged.

Mrs. Shaklee just said, "It's about time, Sheriff," an' watched me climb in my old Dodge pickup an' drive off.

• • •

We'd pretty much got everything stowed away an' settled, an' the church ladies—from all three churches—was layin' out a pot-luck spread on foldin' tables Father Ernie'd set up in the yard, when a horse trailer pulled up. Bello was drivin', Mrs. Shaklee ridin' shotgun. Bello done a three-point turn an' backed the truck up near one of the big trees in front of the house. He jumped out an' dropped the truck-ramp while Mrs. Shaklee come bustlin' over to me. "A little housewarming gift, Sheriff," she said. She didn't smile when she said it. She *did* point towards the horse truck, where Bello was leadin' a jackass down the ramp.

The jackass. The one I thought I'd got rid of at the auction. Jackass must've spotted me or Skip 'cause he let out a *hee-haw-haw-haw* they might could hear all the way in town. Bello didn't pay that no mind as he tied the jackass to the tree an' closed up his truck. He got back in the driver's seat 'fore I could even say, "Hey!"

Mrs. Shaklee pressed the paper she was carryin' into my hand and said, "…along with a bill for re-landscaping my rental property." She turned an' stalked back to the horse truck 'fore I could think of anything to say. Soon as she was in the cab, Bello took off like a posse was after him. Which

I was tempted to arrange.

Last guest to arrive at the house-warmin' party wasn't invited. Pappy Jackson come outta his truck spitting tacks 'cause he'd finally discovered who bought the property— after he'd been bragging he'd stiffed some city guy with more money than brains.

While Pappy was standin' there rantin', jackass come up behind 'im and give 'im a shove that knocked him off balance, an' he landed face down in the free fertilizer the critter'd just laid down. Pappy got up, an' the jackass took off after him, followin' till he come to the end of his tether. A good many of the movin' crew had run afoul of Pappy one time or another, so the jackass got cheers an' applause as Pappy made a run fer his truck. Skip laughed with the rest of 'em, 'til I told him to knock off disrespectin' his birth dad. "'Sides, It ain't right to make fun of folks with disabilities. You gonna laugh at Grampa Ross cause he can't hardly walk?"

That took the fun out of it for Skip.

· · ·

Later, when everybody'd cleared out, Skip an' I sat on the porch with sodas, enjoyin' our new front view an' watchin' the jackass trim the grass.

"You ain't gonna be scared to stay out here all alone," I axed him. "When I'm on duty?"

"Heck no. 'Sides, I won't be alone. I got a vicious guard donkey to protect me."

proposal accepted

"Homer, how d'you think all this stuff's gonna work out?
Everything that's been goin' down lately?"

Nina an' me was stretched out in the sun next to the
Glass Mountain Reservoir, first weekend in November. The
grass was still green. The trees was nearly naked. We was
sittin' on one blanket, snugglin' under another. We'd polished
off our picnic lunch an' washed it down with hot mulled
cider. Skip was with Bello, learnin' how to teach horses—an',
hopefully, donkeys—tricks. Rye was on patrol, my radio was
turned off, God was in heaven, an'—far as I knew—all was
right in Boone County.

"Peterman an' Harlan was friendly, " I told her, "an'
Miz Harlan is unnaturally forgivin', so Peterman'll likely
plead guilty an' get the minimum sentence. As part of the
plea bargain George is offerin' 'im, he'll have to sell his land
to the Injuns so they can open a Native American tourist
education center."

"So no Cheap-Ass Likker stores in town?"

"I think the whole chain may be foldin'."

Nina smiled. "That should make Rye happy."

"I dunno. He seems to be takin' to law enforcement—may wanna retire from moonshinin'."

"What'll happen to Silas, Homer? Ain't what he confessed to pretty serious?"

"On the advice of his lawyer, he didn't admit to diggin' up the bones, but since he confessed to dumpin' 'em in front of half the town, we hadda charge him with unlawful disposal of human remains. The tribe'll probably settle fer him donatin' the part of his land where the remains was buried, an' the court'll probably let him off with probation. Oh, an' Miz Harlan made up a will leaving her place to the Injuns when she passes."

Nina was quiet fer mebbe five whole minutes. Finally, outta the blue, she said, "Homer, can we get a horse?"

"If you're askin', you must want me to talk you out of it."

"Why'd you say that?"

"'Cause if you really wanted a horse, you'd just go out an' get one."

"You know what I like about you, Homer?"

"What?"

"You know me better'n I do. An' you love me anyway."

What could I say to that? What I *did* say was, "Nina, you never did give me a straight answer—will you marry me?"

"Sure, Homer. I thought you'd never ask."

About the Author

Michael Allen Dymmoch was born in Illinois and grew up in a suburb northwest of Kentucky. As a child she she kept a large number of small vertebrates for pets and aspired to become a snake charmer, Indian chief, or veterinarian. She was precluded from realizing the former ambitions by a lack of charm and Indian ancestry, and from the achieving the latter profession by poor grades in calculus and physics. This made her angry enough to kill. Fortunately, before committing mayhem, she stumbled across a book titled *Maybe You Should Write A Book* and was persuaded to sublimate her felonious fantasies. Moving to Chicago gave Michael additional incentives to harm individuals who piss her off. On paper of course.

Death in West Wheeling

When a local schoolteacher disappears from rural West Wheeling, acting sheriff Homer Deters investigates. Before long he's got three more missing persons, two unidentified bodies, a car theft, a twenty-three-vehicle pile-up in the center of town, a missing tiger, and a squad of agitated ATF agents to deal with.

With no help from the Feds, Homer turns to his buddy, Rye Willis, and West Wheeling's eccentric postmistress, Nina Ross, to locate the missing, identify the bodies, and bring a murderer to justice. Packed with regional charm and Deters' wit, Death in West Wheeling shows how wild one case can get.

M.I.A.

This gripping novel of suspense is a tale of violent men and violent passions, of missing friends, of loss and love and discovery.

The accidental death of Rhiann Fahey's second husband leaves her paralyzed by grief and has her son Jimmy cutting school and drinking. The widow's problems are compounded by unwanted advances from her dead husband's friend. She does her best to cope, returning to work, dealing patiently with Jimmy's misbehavior, telling Rory Sinter she isn't interested.

Then a mysterious stranger moves next door. John Devlin offers Rhiann beer and sympathy. He offers Jimmy work.

When Sinter tries to discredit John, then beat him to death, Rhiann comes to John's rescue. But she discovers her perfect neighbor isn't what he'd seemed—which leads her to investigate, and to see John in a different light altogether.

A beautifully written story with characters who come to life from the first page, M.I.A. shows one more side of Michael Allen Dymmoch's powerful storytelling ability.

The Fall

How far would you go to save your life and your world?

After a nasty divorce, single mother Joanne Lessing finally has her life together, and she's made a name for herself as a photographer. Then, while on assignment, she witnesses a hit and run. Property damage only. No big deal, she thinks. So she does the right thing—calls the cops. Joanne is dismayed when FBI agents arrive with the local detective. They admit the hit and run driver was a mob killer fleeing the scene of his latest hit. Joanne is relieved to find she can't really identify the hit man.

But when she sees the killer again while on another assignment, she takes his picture and finds her new life and her son's future threatened. Caught between the Mob and the FBI, she's on her own...

The Cymry Ring

Ian Carreg is a charming, canny detective with a career he loves and grown children he adores. He's come to terms with the death of his beloved wife and he's looking forward to the birth of his first grandchild. Jemma Henderson, on the other hand, is the beautiful daughter of a famous physicist, a skilled surgeon, and a convicted killer.

When Ian pursues Jemma to Cymry Henge, an ancient stone monument, he is sucked into her escape, and awakes in Roman Britain in the year 60 A.D. Ian and Jemma come face to face with both Celts and Romans, and Ian begins to doubt his own sanity—all he wants is to return home. But as they work together, Ian comes to accept the truth and convinces Jemma to help him foil a plot that could radically alter history.

Caleb & Thinnes Mysteries

The Man Who Understood Cats

Two unlikely partners join forces to solve a murder disguised as suicide and catch a killer ready to strike again.

Gold Coast psychiatrist Jack Caleb is wealthy, cultured, and gay. When one of his clients is found dead in a locked apartment— apparently from a self-inflicted wound— burned-out Chicago detective John Thinnes doesn't believe it was suicide. And Caleb is inclined to agree.

But Thinnes regards a shrink who makes house calls suspicious and starts his murder investigation with the doctor himself. An attack on Caleb that's made to look like an accidental drug overdose starts to change the detective's mind.

Soon, the two men find themselves a whirlwind of theft, scandal, and blackmail. Forced into an unlikely partnership, they'll have to confront not only a killer, but hard truths within themselves that will change them forever.

The Death of Blue Mountain Cat

The art world is the backdrop when a controversial artist reaches the end of his fifteen minutes of fame.

Native American artist Blue Mountain Cat has a style described as "Andy Warhol meets Jonathan Swift in Indian country." When he's murdered at an exclusive showing in a conservative art museum, Detective John Thinnes has no shortage of suspects. Targets of the artist's satire included a greedy developer, a beautiful Navajo woman, and black-market antiquities dealers. Even the victim's wife merits investigation.

Thinnes drafts psychiatrist Jack Caleb to guide him through the terra incognita of the art world, and their investigation turns up a desperate museum director, a savage critic, a married mistress, and shady dealings by the artist's partner. Thinnes and Caleb connect several apparently unrelated deaths as they follow leads from Wisconsin to Chicago's South Side and the mystery's explosive conclusion.

Incendiary Designs

Arson, passion, and religious fanaticism set Chicago ablaze in the deadliest summer on record.

While jogging through Chicago's Lincoln Park, Dr. Jack Caleb runs into murder—a mob setting a police car on fire— with the officer still inside. Caleb rescues the man, but later the cop's partner is found stoned to death. Detective John Thinnes is assigned to investigate.

Evidence points toward members of a charismatic church, but too many of them die in arson fires before the cops can round them up. When arson kills the apparent ring leader, it's too much coincidence. The remaining cop killers plead guilty; the case seems to be closed. But as Chicago heats up in the deadliest summer on record, it becomes clear that a serial arsonist is still at large.

A physician friend of Caleb's is implicated when some of the fire victims are found to have been drugged. To exonerate the man, Caleb sets a trap for the killer, and Thinnes and Caleb are nearly incinerated when the doctor's trap brings the case to a fiery finish.

The Feline Friendship

When a vicious rapist crosses the line into murder, Detective John Thinnes and his prickly new partner draft psychiatrist Jack Caleb to help them track the killer down.

When a young woman is brutally raped in the posh Lincoln Park neighborhood, Chicago Police detective John Thinnes catches the case—even though Thinnes hates working rapes. Worse yet, he has to deal with a new female detective who has a chip on her shoulder the size of a 12 gauge shotgun.

A second victim is murdered, and the rapes become "heater cases." What started as a simple investigation, soon twists around earlier, similar crimes. Tempers flare; the detective squad polarizes across the gender line. Dr. Jack Caleb, a psychiatrist and police consultant, is asked to mediate. But Thinnes's sometime-ally finds himself with conflicts of interest occasioned by their friendship and Caleb's own disturbing case load.

The investigation ranges from Chicago's Lincoln Park to the northern Illinois city of Waukegan. And the explosive climax explores not only the karma of evil but the beginning of a beautiful Feline Friendship.

White Tiger

The TV news report of a woman's murder in Uptown flashes psychiatrist Dr. Jack Caleb back to his time in Vietnam.

Assigned to investigate, Chicago detectives John Thinnes and Don Franchi find the victim's son curiously unmoved by his mother's death. Their preliminary canvass of the dead woman's neighborhood reveals that she was well liked and well off, and she had never quarreled with anyone but her "good son."

When Thinnes realizes that he knew the victim when he was stationed in Vietnam—twenty-four years earlier—he is pulled off the case. But Thinnes can't let go. And when a schizophrenic man shows up at Mrs. Lee's wake, connecting the deceased to another Vietnam vet and to an unsolved murder in wartime Saigon, Thinnes starts a retrospective investigation of that crime, soliciting Caleb's help to discover the identity of the White Tiger and set a trap for the elusive killer.

Printed in the USA
CPSIA information can be obtained
at www.ICGtesting.com
JSHW031956150824
68134JS00063B/3575